D1022054

THE EDUCATION OF OSCAR FAIRFAX

ALSO BY LOUIS AUCHINCLOSS

FICTION

The Indifferent Children
The Injustice Collectors
Sybil
A Law for the Lion
The Romantic Egoists
The Great World and Timothy Colt
Venus in Sparta
Pursuit of the Prodigal
The House of Five Talents
Portrait in Brownstone
Powers of Attorney
The Rector of Justin
The Embezzler
Tales of Manhattan
A World of Profit
Second Chance
I Come as a Thief
The Partners
The Winthrop Covenant
The Dark Lady
The Country Cousin
The House of the Prophet
The Cat and the King
Watchfires
Narcissa and Other Fables
Exit Lady Masham

The Book Class
Honorable Men
Diary of a Yuppie
Skinny Island
The Golden Calves
Fellow Passengers
The Lady of Situations
False Gods
Three Lives
Tales of Yesteryear
The Collected Stories of Louis Auchincloss

NONFICTION

Reflections of a Jacobite
Pioneers and Caretakers
Motiveless Malignity
Edith Wharton
Richelieu
A Writer's Capital
Reading Henry James
Life, Law and Letters
Persons of Consequence:
Queen Victoria and Her Circle
False Dawn: Women in the
Age of the Sun King
The Vanderbilt Era
Love Without Wings
The Style's the Man

THE EDUCATION OF OSCAR FAIRFAX

LOUIS AUCHINCLOSS

Houghton Mifflin Company
BOSTON NEW YORK
1995

Library of Congress Cataloging-in-Publication Data

Auchincloss, Louis.
The education of Oscar Fairfax / Louis Auchincloss
p. cm.
ISBN 0-395-73918-7
I. Title.
PS3501.U25E3 1995
813'.54 — dc20 95-9780
CIP

Book design by Anne Chalmers
Text type: Janson Text (Adobe)
Text ornaments: Rococo Two (Monotype)

Printed in the United States of America

QUM 10 9 8 7 6 5 4 3 2 1

FOR

DAVID CLAPP,

MY WORTHIER SUCCESSOR

AT

THE MUSEUM OF THE CITY OF NEW YORK

All universal stories and research into the cause of things bore me. I have exhausted all novels, stories and plays; only letters, lives, and *mémoires* written by those who recount their own history amuse me and arouse my curiosity. Ethics and metaphysics bore me intensely. What can I say? I have lived too long.

Madame du Deffand
(who might have been speaking for Oscar Fairfax)

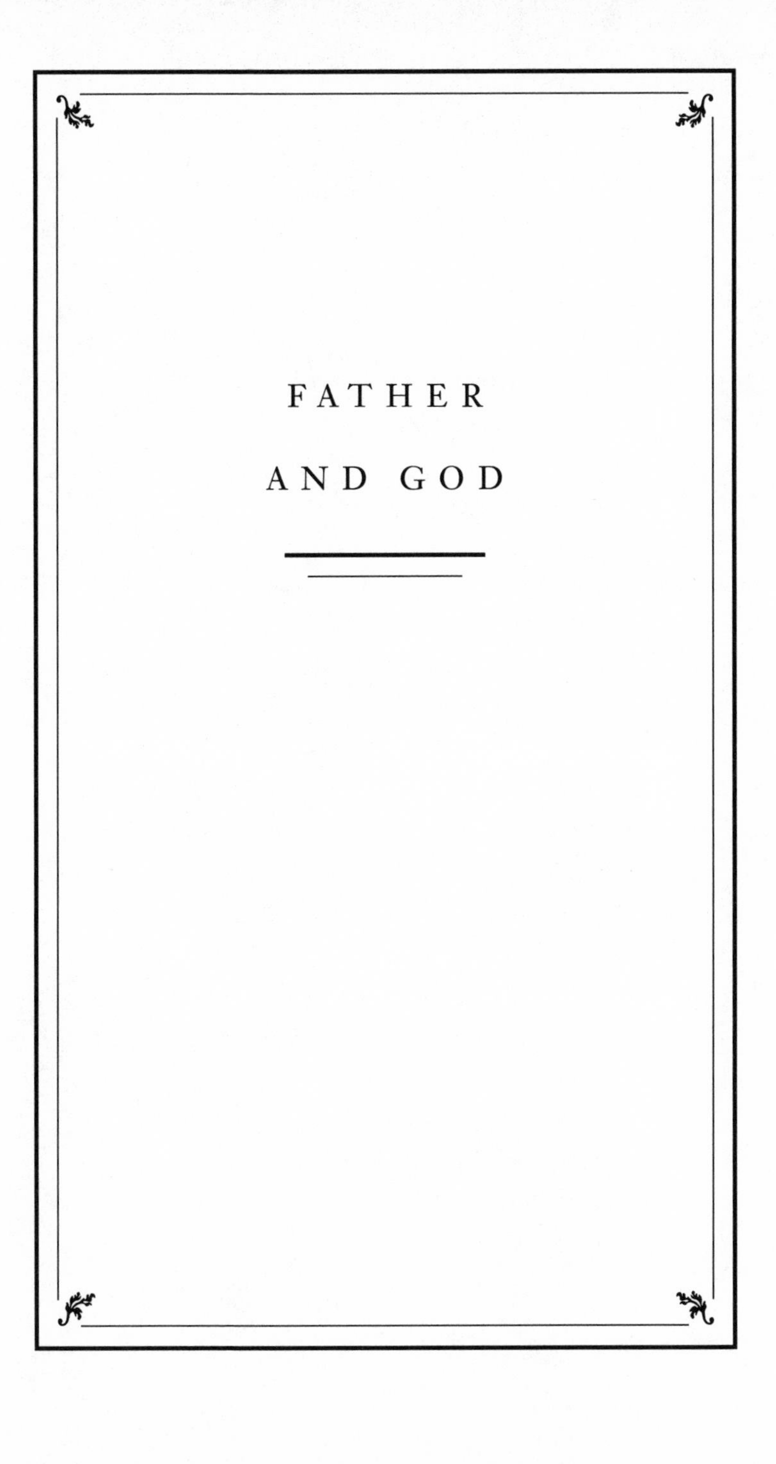

FATHER AND GOD

SARGENT'S PORTRAIT of my father — painted when I was ten, in 1905 — still hanging in the great hall of the Colonial Art Gallery, of which he was for so many years a trustee, might be the image of an American aristocrat of his era — if there had been any. Indeed, that may have been the very question the artist was asking. For if Sargent's famous portrait across the ocean of Lord Ribblesdale, who, though endowed with the stately mien of a cabinet minister, chose still to pose as Master of Buckhounds, represents the absolute assurance of a landed upper class, the master of physiognomies elected to tinge my parent's with a faint hint of self-deprecation.

Lionel Fairfax, long and lean, is shown seated with an air of controlled relaxation in a Louis XV *bergère*, clad in a soft suit of the combined shades of the sitter's prematurely grey hair and the pearly white of his mildly curious eyes. In one hand he is holding a morocco-bound volume, a forefinger between the pages, as if the painter had interrupted, though excusably, a tranquil reading session. The tapering fingers of the other hand, resting on the chair arm, and the graceful manner in which one leg is crossed over the other, might have implied a confidence as serene as the English peer's, had not a certain tenseness in the figure suggested a readiness to spring to action, should action be called for. Evidently it had, on occasion, been called for. And might be again.

Yet if Father was ready to jump up to fight for a cause, he was also prepared to lose it. Victory, defeat or compromise for him were all scenes in a play, either comedy or tragedy, in which he had been given, by forces unknown, a certain role to play. Wasn't that enough? What more was there? There wasn't anything more.

Actually, we *were* one of the very few American families who descended in the male line from a prerevolutionary British peer. A disinherited (we don't know why) nephew of the sixth baron Fairfax of Cameron, who owned much of the Virginia Colony, had migrated to New York to seek a new fortune there, and the family rift was not made up by his descendants' strong Union sympathies in the Civil War. The New York Fairfaxes had done well, though they hardly counted for rich in the new age of robber barons. My paternal grandfather had founded a respected Wall Street law firm, which my father had expanded to a size of considerable importance. Father was also active in civic affairs; he was president of the Patroons Club, chairman of the board of the Colonial Art Museum and chief vestryman of Saint Luke's Cathedral. And as my mother was the daughter of the Episcopal bishop of New York, they were a couple much in view.

Yet there was something in Father's general air that suggested the attitude of Napoleon's mother: "*Pourvue que cela dure.*" It was never that of King Louis's "*Après moi le déluge.*" If there was going to be a deluge, Father was ready and willing to suffer his share in the drowning. I don't say that he really believed that a flood would come, and of course it hasn't yet, and I am writing in 1975. Perhaps it never will. But, like Henry Adams, he believed that his own seemingly impregnable social position was something of a myth, a relic of the eighteenth century — in short, that it had little to do with the contemporary scene. Unlike Adams, however, he never considered himself more of an anachronism than most other people. He was vulnerable, surely, but then who wasn't? Relics had their use; they could even be turned to a profit.

For despite the old-fashioned patrician manner, the soft level voice, which he never raised even in temper, the exquisite attention he gave his interlocutor, signifying dissent only by a rather stately silence, Father had made an accurate assessment of the world in which he worked. He claimed that Henry James, and not Adams, had the real key to it when he wrote, on a return after a long absence to his native shores, that what had happened in the interim was the ultimate triumph of the middle class. James had taken as America's symbol the lobby of the Waldorf-Astoria Hotel. It was all heat and flowers and shouted greetings and noisy chatter and costly shops and huge hatted ladies — the greatest happiness for the greatest number — so long as privacy and peace were shooed away like tramps at your picnic. "Make no mistake," Father would warn us; "the great majority *like* it that way. And watch it spread over the globe!" But he knew that the great majority could still be impressed by a Lionel Fairfax. *Carpe diem!*

Father was often accused of being a snob because he didn't succumb to the burgeoning American habit of socializing with clients. He saw no reason to drink or play golf with persons whose only claim to his acquaintance was that they had sought his professional expertise. "They don't go out with their dentists, do they?" he would ask. But sometimes, particularly when his would-be host was an *arriviste* of the cruder type, his declination would be attributed to a reluctance to stray beyond the black covers of the Social Register. This was absurd. Father cared nothing for the Social Register. It may have been that he had a distaste for the man's way of doing business. Father would represent him, yes, in a case involving no violation of a canon of ethics, but nothing would induce him to be the intimate of a man whom he deemed deficient in moral scruples. A compromise? Of course, it was. Father believed in compromises. He was a lawyer as well as a gentleman.

His shrewd understanding of his times and of *me* was illustrated by the affair of the bicycle. What is a more established maxim than that one should never bribe a child to be good? Father knew just when to throw such rules to the wind.

My marks in the Browning School when I was eleven were below the class average, and there was some question as to whether I would be admitted to Saint Augustine's, the New England boarding school of Father's choice. Without any preliminary talk, he took me to an exhibition of new bicycles and followed me as I roamed longingly about, stopping at last before the most glorious and costly of them all. It was a miracle of shining silver speed and efficiency, with every last gadget, from a bronze box on the handle to a glacé kid leather seat and a horn that sounded Siegfried's motif.

"Do you like it?" he asked with mild irony. "Or isn't it flashy enough for an all-American boy?"

"Do I *like* it? Of course I like it! But I know it's much too expensive for me." My parents were reasonable about presents, but not foolish. I had not been spoiled.

"It's not too expensive for a boy with an eighty average at school. Or even seventy-five. Pull up your marks and it's yours."

I gasped. I had never even dreamed that I could be the owner of so dazzling a machine. Still, I could bargain. Father never minded that. "But suppose I make seventy-five, and someone else has bought it?"

"I'll buy it today and keep it under lock and key until the condition's met."

"Could we make it seventy-three?"

He chuckled. "What an old Scrooge you are! Very well. Call it seventy-three."

At school I went to work as I had never worked before and raised my average to seventy-two. But Father gave me the bicycle anyway. He knew he had achieved his purpose. Before I left Browning for Saint Augustine's I stood third in my class.

Deeply devoted as I was to Father, I never felt as a boy that I was a true part of him or the Fairfaxes. This ambivalence is hard to explain. I know it is not uncommon for children to fancy they have been adopted; perhaps I suffered from some such neurosis. Somehow Father and his clan, and to a lesser extent Mother and her mitred sire, were, as opposed to myself, *real* persons, and I, a lesser being, though kindly treated, existed as a sort of pageboy on the fringe of their more splendid actuality. But even at my level I had the compensation of sensing another division. There was the boy, Oscar Fairfax (I had been named for the bishop), and there was another entity inside of Oscar, an observer who observed Lionel and Julia Fairfax and endowed them with personal characteristics and perhaps — who knew? — even created them, in a kind of mental memoir.

At any rate the semi-solipsist lurking in my psyche has played a permanent and distracting role in my whole life. People have been my constant preoccupation. It has not always been clear, however, whether they existed only in me or I only in them. Existed, that is, in the sense of what I could do *with* them, or *to* them, or perhaps, ultimately, *for* them. Did I want to be a biographer or a novelist or a psychologist or a priest or even a missionary? In the end I took Father's advice and became a lawyer. He said it didn't matter in which I took the greater interest: the clients or the law.

❧ ❧ ❧

Mother suspected early that I needed to be anchored more closely to earth. She was a much less colorful person than Father: small and dry, but with a brisk manner, a sharp wit and a great deal of self-assurance. She was as politically and morally conservative as her mate, not because he dominated her, nor because she loved him (though she did), but because she believed deeply in all the principles in which he at least professed to believe. Had he not, she would have been capable of definite dissent, despite all her lip service to ancient concepts of the submissive wife. But she gave me an occasional glimpse of her uneasy suspicion of a void behind Father's acceptable creed and equally acceptable actions. She was distressed, for example, by the incident of the bicycle.

"I suppose he'll have to buy you a yacht to keep your marks up when you get to college," she sniffed. "Your father seems to hold that anyone's a socialist who even suggests that a man might work for any inducement but a bunch of greenbacks stuffed under his nose!"

It interested me that she and Father, so seemingly as one in their outward demeanor, might be divided in their faiths. Father's, of course, was not really a true faith; it was more a sturdy reliance on the maintenance of forms to hold up the structure of a thinly civilized world. Mother's was a faith *in* faith; she and her numerous siblings believed absolutely in their father. To them, Bishop Fish was God's representative on earth; they believed in God because they believed also in him.

"The Fishes, or Fish, as we might call them, are truly a shoal," Father observed to me once with mild sarcasm. "They follow the leader. Unless it's instinct that holds them together. Or, rather, they're a tribe. Your mother is an admirable woman and the best of wives, but when the chips are down and sides are taken, she's always going to be with the chief."

"The chief?"

"Your sainted grandfather. Who else?"

Father, now that I was nearing fourteen, had been taking me more into his confidence. He had few intimate male friends, and he was never totally at his ease in the company of women. Mother was intelligent but not intellectual, and she shied away from any discussion of abstract topics. My older sister, Henrietta, was hardly at this time companionable; she was moody and irritable and resentful of the least parental interference. There remained only I, who cherished the idea of this new partnership.

"You mean as in this question about the cathedral?" I asked. I had twice caught Mother and Father in active disagreement over a pet project of Grandpa Fish's, and they had dropped the subject when they saw I was listening. The project was Saint Luke's Cathedral, the great Gothic fane then under construction on lower Broadway. It was to be the bishop's masterwork, the shining symbol of the Episcopal Church in America and, in due time, the basilica of the Right Reverend Oscar Fish.

"Precisely," he responded with a promptness that betrayed the strength of his feeling in the matter. "Your mother is much upset that I have any doubts about the project. Has not her father sounded the call and alerted the multitudes? Everyone must fall in line!"

"But aren't you on the committee to raise the money for it?"

"That's just what's bothering me, my boy."

"You mean you don't believe in it anymore?"

"I'm beginning to wonder if I ever did."

"Then why did you get into it?"

"You may well ask. Of course, your grandfather is a very persuasive man. And the cathedral is his passion. And all his children regard it as a sacred duty to do everything they can to see it finished. I doubt it should be. I even doubt that it *can* be. Though the old man, I admit, is a genius at fund-raising. How he can make the rich disgorge! I suppose it's because he loves them so."

"You mean *because* they're rich?"

Father's glance showed that he wondered if he hadn't gone too far. "He doesn't see them that way. He sees them as valued workers in God's garden. If they don't always see themselves in that light, then it's his mission to straighten them out. A mission he thoroughly enjoys." He seemed now to revert to his own thoughts. Suddenly he chuckled. "I sometimes think that when the bishop dies, he'll go to Newport."

"What do you mean?"

"Never mind, dear boy. I guess I've said enough."

It was thus that education really began for me: in the contrast that Grandpa Fish offered to Father. I suppose I could even say: in the contrast he offered to everyone. For if Father had doubts as to the value of his own breeding and inheritance, Grandpa's confidence in himself, his church and his nation was steadfast and serene. He was a small man with a soft, low voice that could rise to golden thunder in the pulpit. He had short, always neatly brushed grey hair, a high brow, a diminutive beak of a nose and eyes of a cool pale blue that seemed to accord you your exact place in the social system, no less but certainly no more. Nothing could ruffle his equanimity; God had taken care of all.

Which did not mean, however, that there could be any slacking in God's work. The bishop's administrative energy and efficiency were famous, not only in the running of his diocese, but in the church as a whole. He was constantly presiding over ecclesiastical conventions and meeting with mayors, governors and even presidents. He had become a public figure, the butt of cartoons in godless journals, a symbol of prim sanctity to the agnostic, though in private he was far from prim, even at times verging on the risqué. I see him now in my mind's eye, blandly wiping his lips with a napkin before rising to answer the tinkle of spoons on glasses and address a respectful multitude of white ties and tiaras in a gilded hotel ballroom.

Grandma Fish had died before I was born, but one of his nine sons or daughters was always "on duty" in his houses in Washington Square or in Lenox, Massachusetts. He did not ask for this; he did not even expect it — it simply happened. And one might have thought that with so many descendants he would have developed only a mild and benevolent relationship with his grandchildren, but such was not the case. He treated each of us as an intelligent adult, worthy of his full attention. I did not hesitate, for example, to bring him my theological problems.

"You tell me, Oscar, that you are having trouble believing in an afterlife? Well, nobody can believe in an afterlife *all* the time."

"Wouldn't it be boring, Grandpa, to be singing hosannas forever in streets of gold?"

"Horrible! But you don't have to believe that foolishness. That sort of thing is for simpler folk who like revivalist hymns. There's no harm in it."

"But no matter what you did in eternity, wouldn't it become boring in time? Think of it! Never ending."

He shook his head as if I had uttered a grave concept. "I'd rather not think any such grisly thought. Of course there wouldn't *be* any time there."

"How could there be no time?"

"Well, that's a mystery, isn't it? We can't know the answer, so there's no point worrying about it."

"And there's something else that bothers me, Grandpa. Father says that people who don't believe in God — even people who don't believe in any god at all — can be just as good as people who do. Do you agree with that?"

The bishop chuckled. "So you're pitting me against your old man now? Well, that's all right. Yes, I believe there are atheists who are quite as good as even the most devout Christians. Ralph Waldo Emerson, for example."

I was shocked. "But we were taught at school that Emerson was a very religious man!"

Grandpa shrugged. "He was a transcendentalist. A deist. He believed that when you die, you become a pulse of eternal nature. But what's the difference between being a pulse — even a happy pulse, if one can conceive of such a thing — and complete extinction? If survival means anything, it must mean the survival of some aspect of our personality. If I'm not to be Oscar Fish in the hereafter — or a reasonable facsimile of him — I don't care to be anything."

Young as I was, this struck me as rather egotistical. Indeed, wasn't it the essence of egotism? But I found myself admiring it. I could see that I was going to have a brisk argument with Father. I looked forward to it!

"Would you be as good a man, Grandpa, if you didn't believe in God and an afterlife?"

"No, my boy, I'm afraid I should be a sad sinner. Oh, I don't say I'd rob and steal and commit heinous crimes. That would be distasteful to me. But I might indulge myself more than I now do. I hope I would go in for pleasure in the high epicurean sense. But one never knows what *that* may lead to."

I had an odd vision of Grandpa in a toga, with vine leaves in his hair, reclining on a couch at a Roman banquet. And then I spied a chance to impress him with my biblical reading.

"Christ himself didn't disapprove of some worldly pleasures, did he? He turned the water into wine at the marriage in Cana."

The bishop chuckled again. "That used to distress one of my old teachers at divinity school. He rather looked down on that miracle and pointed out that it was our Lord's first one. Presumably, Jesus had needed practice to develop a more elevated thaumaturgy! But I liked our Lord's coming to the rescue of the poor host and hostess whose wine had given out and who were faced with thirsty guests. It was a charming accommodation and showed the man in the god. In the same way that his blasting the fig tree betrayed a very human irritation. It brings us closer to him."

I didn't then realize that this piece of biblical sophistry would have cost Grandpa his life in the days of the Inquisition. But it did occur to me that had he been a Medici pope, he would have deemed the sale of indulgences a splendid fund-raising device. His faith was strong enough to embrace any means to his end. He was a realist.

Yet that was just the question that Father was to raise. *Was* he? It came up when Father took me downtown on a Saturday afternoon to check on the progress of the cathedral. The church was still less than half built, but the western façade had been completed except for the two towers. The three doors and their porches, the rose window and the many balconies and pinnacles formed a design of strict symmetry; it was imposing and grave, much like that of Notre Dame de Paris, which had been its fairly obvious inspiration.

There were benches on the little plaza before the church, and we sat on one for what seemed to me a very long time while Father stared moodily up at the edifice before him.

"It's all wrong," he muttered at last.

"What's all wrong?"

"Everything about it. It has no real place in this city or even in this century. It's bogus. It's phony. It's pretending to be something it's not. It's arrogant. It's hypocritical. It won't do!"

He seemed now to be treating me as his intellectual equal. I was thrilled.

"Then what are you going to do about it?"

"I'm going to get off that committee! I'll send in my resignation on Monday."

His tone showed that he was girding himself for a battle that he was not sure he would win. He and Mother rarely showed their differences of opinion to us children, but I knew from Mother's grim look at dinner that night that the struggle must have begun shortly after our return from Broadway.

The next day, Sunday, Grandpa Fish lunched with us. I doubt he had been summoned; his presence at our sabbath meal was a common occasion. But Mother must have had a chance to "get at him" before we sat down, for he opened right up on the subject of the cathedral, rejecting Mother's suggestion that he wait until after lunch.

"No, Julia, I want the children to hear. If their father has lost his faith in our project, there is every reason for them to know why. The church, after all, is for all ages." He now turned a benign aspect on his son-in-law. "You feel, my dear Lionel, that our cathedral does not represent the spirit of the new century? Perhaps you are thinking of the famous letter of Archbishop Hugo on the building of Chartres. He was amazed, he told his correspondent, at the silence and religious gravity of the townspeople as they all joined in the hauling of the carts with the great stones for the cathedral. You fail to observe, I suppose, any such feeling in New Yorkers of our day?"

"Well, yes," Father responded in some surprise. "That does rather express my sentiment."

"Well, I should love to lead such a procession down Broadway, but I fear the mayor might object."

"But how many people would follow you if the mayor gave you a permit? How many of the men working on the site are even Episcopalians?"

"One must doubt that any are. But do you think that the clergy of the twelfth century would not have availed themselves of our modern machinery had they had it to hand?"

"I suppose they would have, yes."

"And if the only skilled workers who could handle the machinery had been newly arrived aliens, do you think they would have looked too closely into the state of their religious beliefs? Indeed, I can well imagine the great Abbé Suger, in the rebuilding of Saint Denis, turning a very deaf ear to any accusation of heresy made of a master glazier." Here the bishop accorded me a friendly wink. "At least until the windows were finished. He was a proud and ambitious cleric, rather like myself. He was the type, I dare assert, without whom the great cathedrals of France would never have been raised."

"But your cathedral, Bishop, will not be the product of the people, as his essentially was. It will be the handiwork of a group of rich men."

"And what makes you think that Chartres and Amiens and Rheims were not the handiwork of rich men? Of course, the poor contributed, but so do they to me. I'm too old a fund-raiser not to know the value of the widow's mite. Nothing opens a fat purse like seeing a lean one do the same. The rich hate to feel they're the only ones being 'done.' That is true today, and I haven't a doubt it was true then. And what is wrong in appealing to the wealthy? Aren't we making them better people? More charitable?"

"No matter what their motives?"

"You mean if their motives are vanity and pride? Or merely to save their souls? Surely some of the good of a good deed must rub off on the donor. Unless his motive is truly evil. No, Lionel, I contend that our cathedral is being built by men of faith for the glory of God, very much as it would have been seven hundred years ago!"

"But even if that's so, Bishop, you must admit its architectural style is totally derivative. It doesn't speak to our time."

"And what would? A grain elevator? A skyscraper? A thousand-room hotel? Why should we be denied the most beautiful form of ecclesiastical architecture devised by man because it's been used before?"

I felt that Grandpa was getting the best of the argument, but largely because Father was loath to use his big guns under Mother's probing eye.

"There is, however, one aspect of the older churches we shall not copy," the bishop continued with a bleak smile around the table. "No heretics will be burned in the plaza before the western porches."

Father seemed to find this a better point than I did. "That *is*, I admit, an argument against the deeper feeling of those days. Great faith seems to go hand in hand with the need to kill those who don't share it. Maybe you *should* burn me before your cathedral, Bishop."

"I may well do so if you give up on me," Grandpa replied with another smile, this one with a touch of grimness.

Grandpa now changed the subject to Saint Augustine's School in Massachusetts, to which I had been admitted and of which he was a trustee. He spoke praisingly of the clerical headmaster and looked forward to seeing me when he came up for board meetings. It was his way of indicating that the issue of the cathedral was now closed and that Father should speak no more of relinquishing his fiduciary duties.

And oddly enough Father didn't. He even declined to discuss the matter anymore with me. I deduced that Mother had discovered to what extent he had contaminated my mind and put her foot down as to further pollutions. Or perhaps he had been reduced at least to neutrality by the bishop's reminder of the brutalities of the ancient church. Mightn't it be better to support a harmless modern sect and avoid its being replaced by something worse? Crazy religions were growing up in America even in 1909.

But that his mind was still not at rest was made clear when he took me that summer on what Edith Wharton would have called a "motor flight" in France. It was our first trip alone together. Mother had gone as usual to spend August with her father in Lenox, and this time she had taken Henrietta with her. We toured very comfortably in a Panhard town car with a chauffeur, stayed at luxurious hotels and ate at many-starred restaurants. Father seemed in a relaxed and benevolent mood, at least until we got to Rouen. There the cathedral upset him.

We had been sitting on a bench in front of it, as we had on that Saturday afternoon on Broadway, gazing up at the flamboyant mass of its façade, when his mood seemed suddenly to change. It was as if he could not face those rows of solid statuary, that florid mix of pointed gables and turrets, that awesome interweaving of delicate traceries with sombre heavy stone. He suddenly turned away from it.

"Do you wonder that Monet painted it in every kind of weather, at every time of day?" he exclaimed. "It hits you in the eye the way a great organ peal hits you in the ear. It doesn't tell you that God is love. It doesn't say 'Enter here and ye shall be saved' or anything moist like that. It thunders at you that God is great. Come to terms with *that*, little man. Do creeds and heresies really matter? Does even saving your puny soul count for anything? No! The only thing that has any meaning is what I, Rouen, am showing you: that there is wonder and majesty in the universe and that to be an infinitesimal part of it for any period, finite or infinite, is good enough for *you!*"

There was enough of Grandpa in me to protest: "But surely, Father, the Christian story is written all over it! Those figures are saints or apostles, aren't they?"

That "infinitesimal finite part" was not going to do for the bishop *or* for me!

"Yes, and kings, good kings and bad," Father continued, ignoring the thrust of my argument. "And gargoyles and angels. And all the damned, too. We never forget the damned, do we? Men are stuck all over the front and the porches like ants on a hill. They're a part of the design, a small part, but there *is* a design; that's the point. Do we have to know anything more? Isn't that enough to make life bearable even for an illiterate, overworked serf with a life expectancy of thirty-five years?"

"You mean the serf was happier than *we* are?"

"I wonder if I do mean that." He appeared to recover himself and patted my knee. "How about a very good lunch? I was told by the porter at the hotel there's a first-class place in the Rue d'Enfer. It's only a step from here, as hell always is!"

He made no further references to the cathedral, nor did we discuss matters of faith for the rest of our short trip. I think he may have been somewhat ashamed of his outburst. But coming home on the *Olympic*, at our last dinner before landing, he told me that he had resigned himself to remaining a member of the bishop's cathedral committee.

"I owe you an explanation, Oscar. You have followed my internal crisis. You have been very tactful. So why do I continue to work for a project in which I have so little heart? Because there is no harm in it. Because so many of our family believe in it. Because some slight good might even come out of it. And because it is no more an anachronism than half the things we see today at home or abroad: a Russian czar, a German kaiser, a House of Lords, an infallible pope, the trusts of Wall Street and Mr. Morgan. *And* myself. An old-school gentleman who has nothing better to offer than a half-finished poorish copy of a Gothic cathedral. Is giving *that* up worth making your mother unhappy?"

The cathedral was never fully finished. Rising costs, fewer parishioners, and liberal successors to Grandpa who preferred missions to bricks and mortar led to a compromise of stubby towers and simpler ornamentation. But it stands today, in 1975, no more a misfit than half of its subsequently built neighbors, and services are still held in it. It is sometimes used for nominally religious pageants with clowns and animals. It has found a kind of function as a public monument and a meeting place for men of good will; it exudes a misty interracial benevolence. It has developed that doomed look of all large structures in a metropolis that builds itself over every generation. They know the wrecking ball awaits them. Perhaps the only man-made thing that expressed what the Rouen façade meant to Father was the rocket we sent to the moon.

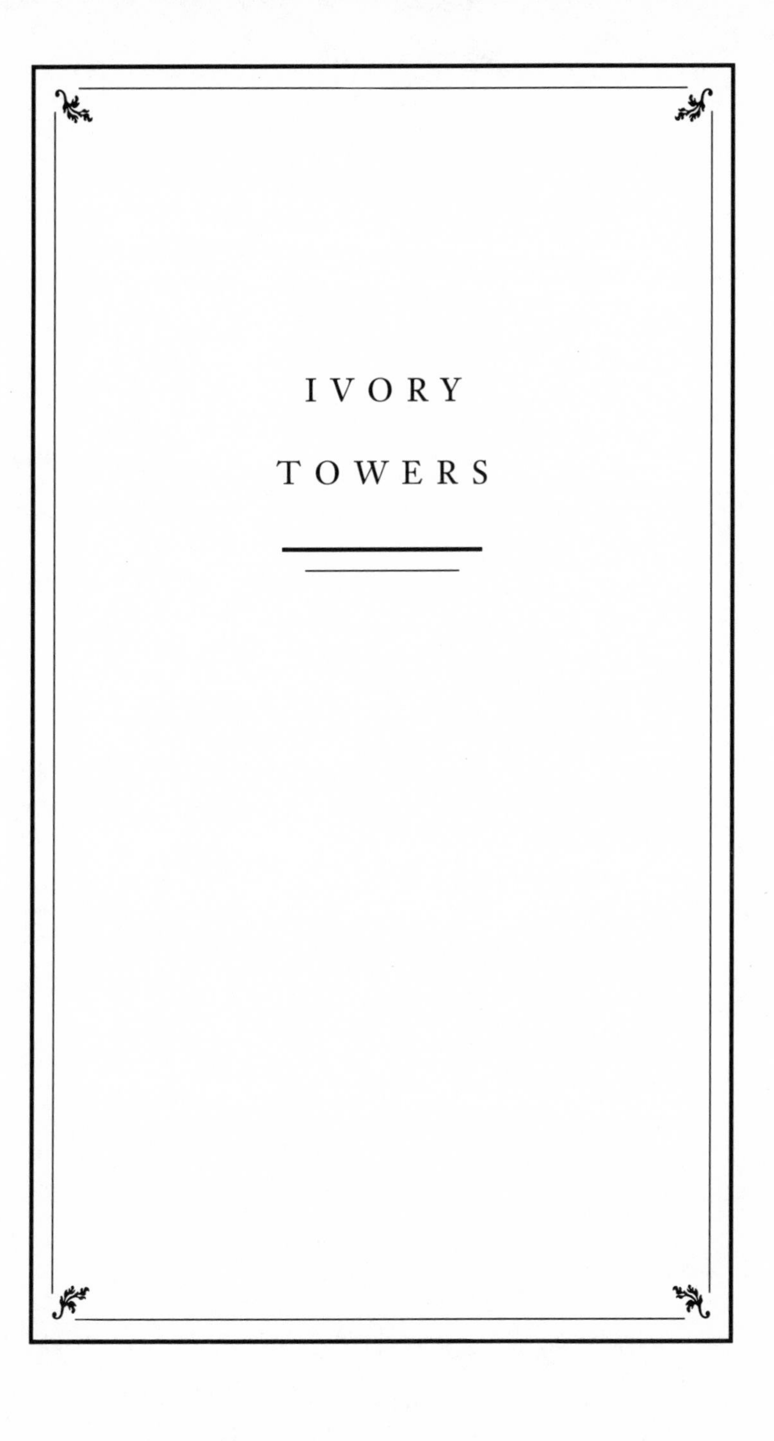

IVORY TOWERS

THE BEAUTY of Saint Augustine's School was made up largely, as is that of so many towns and villages, by water. The serpentine stream, the Alph, which wandered its leisurely way through a campus of variegated architectural styles and green playing fields, somehow managed to reconcile the very different objects along its banks: the simple dark-shingle walls of the original building, the Palladian pretensions of the library, the stern grey stiffness of the Gothic dormitories, the Ionic portico of the Greek Revival schoolhouse. The reconciliation lay, it seemed to me, in the gentle slowness in which the barely moving current bathed the chronology of the academy, so that the Arcadian simplicity of the original setting, designed for only two dozen masters and boys, was able to ease its way into the more structured colony of four hundred young males subject to assemblies and roll calls and marches and highly competitive sports.

It was here that I first learned the charm of belonging to an establishment. I define the term as the nucleus within any identifiable group of people — a school, a college, a town, a state — that sets the tone, the fashion, the rules of conduct and faith for a majority of the others. At Saint Augustine's it was composed of the headmaster, the more assertive members of the faculty and the Council of Prefects, chosen from the most prominent sixth-formers. Liberal-minded folk tend to regard establishments as despotic, exclusive, even sinister. They underestimate their charm because they are usually immune to it. But charm is essential to such ruling groups. Was there not camaraderie of a tempting sort in Hitler's Berchtesgaden, even perhaps in Stalin's dacha on the Black Sea? Surely to be admitted to the salon of Madame de Pompadour at Versailles and chat informally with the suave Louis XV was heaven to French courtiers, and to hunt and dine and exchange witticisms with beautiful peeresses and cabinet ministers must have made weekend invitations to Chatsworth or Blenheim the envy of Mayfair couples. Only Genghis Khan and Tamberlaine could dispense with smiles. And how long did *they* last? People won't settle forever for a mountain of skulls.

I was moderately content in my first four years at the school. I was accepted by my form mates, even mildly popular. I lacked the good looks and muscle and athletic prowess needed to become a form leader, but I was diplomatic and companionable; I got on well enough. In my final year, however, as a sixth-former, I experienced a drastic change. I had the good fortune to be elevated to the chief editorship of the school magazine, *The Voice*, when my unfortunate predecessor had to be sent to New Mexico to cure his sinus troubles, and I found myself at once magically elevated to the Council of Prefects and greeted in the friendliest fashion by the captains of the football and baseball teams, who had merely tolerated me before. It was all very delightful, and I learned that it may be the strong man, not the weak, who has to be bought with gold.

The council worked closely with the headmaster, and I came to know him well. Christianity encased Doctor Alcott Ames like a coat of mail. He was a large, strong man, with big arms and shoulders, a heavy, square balding head, glassy eyes and a prominent nose and chin. But his formidability was greatly lessened by the warmth of his tone and the cheer of his manner. He could be an impressive disciplinarian, and the whole school jumped at his command, but not even the smallest, timidest boy could quite escape the conviction — or at the very least the uneasy suspicion — that Alcott Ames was going to save his soul if Alcott Ames should expire in the process. In his booming sermons, when he spread out his arms and cried: "Christ is calling to you, boys! Christ is calling to you, if you'll only listen!" he gave evidence of a faith so invincible that it seemed almost to create for the unbeliever the very deity it invoked.

I received special attention from him, as he was anxious that *The Voice* play a strong role in furthering his great designs for the school. Censorship? He frankly faced the issue.

"Of course, I do not pretend, Oscar, that *The Voice* is an independent periodical. Nothing at Saint Augustine's is independent, least of all the headmaster. Obviously a church school could not allow you to espouse a heresy. But I have no wish to guide your pen. Write what you will. I never even read proof before a number is out. Of course, if you should take a seriously wrong course, the magazine would have to be placed in other hands. But I'm not concerned with that. That isn't going to happen. I'm after your heart, Oscar, not, as I say, your pen. And I feel that I may already have it. Do you think so, my boy? That you and I are much in tune in matters of the spirit?"

Of course we were! Now. The headmaster's sincerity was overwhelming. When he fixed me with those glassy orbs and told me in that deep resonant tone that the guidance and strength which he received from above were solely responsible for anything he might have achieved in the school, that it was his glory and happiness to be a mere tool in the hands of the Almighty, I had no doubt of the genuineness of his modesty.

"If you can give yourself to God, Oscar, you are sure of a

happy life no matter what disasters befall you. Remember that, my boy. The early martyrs were *happy* men. Even when they stood in the arena facing those hungry lions!"

"But surely not, sir, when they saw their loved ones in the arena with them?"

The fact that I dared so to pull him up showed to what an extent the great man had come down to my level — or raised me to his. Perhaps at that moment he had a vision of the beloved crippled daughter who lived with her parents in the headmaster's house seized by a hungry predator, for his look of bleak surprise was followed by one of puzzled concern.

"No, no, the sufferings of others must always have diminished the joy. That had to be the case, of course. But the basic happiness was always there, my boy. Don't ever doubt it."

I have certainly doubted it since, but never that he did.

The school and its whole history were the undoubted works of Doctor Ames, but he had what he always generously termed a co-founder in the person of the senior master. If Ames was the initial force that stood for rule and order and last judgments, Philemon Sayre provided the balance of a gentler tolerance and sympathy joined to a love of art and beauty almost pagan in its intensity. The relationship of the two men might have been likened to that of God the Father and the Virgin Mary in the Middle Ages. Mr. Sayre, a wealthy bachelor and Harvard classmate of the headmaster, had provided the funds necessary to start the school and had ever since been a cornucopia of beneficences, supplementing the slender salaries of the masters and the scholarships of the poorer boys and beautifying the campus with fountains, gardens, gates and rich landscaping. His greatest single gift was the glorious Baroque chapel, whose windows included some of the finest stained glass of John La Farge.

Certainly no two men could have been less alike; it must have been a case of opposites attracting. Mr. Sayre, who seemed considerably older than his life-long friend, was soft and plump, with a hooked nose and oval chin and long, stringy, thinning grey hair over a high dome and scalp. He was never known to have done a stroke of exercise, unless it was taking the wheel of his beautiful sailing yacht on summers in Nahant. He tended to wear knickerbocker trousers and Norfolk jackets, always of the richest tweed, and scarlet ties bound in huge knots, and he moved slowly, sometimes painfully, being afflicted with arthritis. But his voice was deep and mellifluous, and his sentences, after a hesitant start, emerged as clearly and precisely as if he were reading aloud. And, indeed, when he so read in his poetry classes, he could make Ella Wheeler Wilcox sound like Lord Tennyson.

Mr. Sayre had little to do with the lower school; his particular domain was the last two forms, the fifth and sixth, from ages sixteen to seventeen. Only then were we considered ripe for his courses in Greek drama and the English Romantic poets. This, however, was the headmaster's decision; Mr. Sayre himself was ready and eager to open his mind and heart to all comers. Rumor had it that Doctor Ames wanted to be sure that the boys were firmly anchored in Episcopal theology and faith before they were exposed to Euripides or Shelley.

It was also no secret on the campus that the head and senior masters, however devoted to each other, were increasingly at odds as to the direction in which the school was headed. Mr. Sayre was known to deplore the rigid division of the day into classes, chapel services, hard games and study periods, leaving little time for musing, dreaming, strolling through the countryside, speculating, in short, on what life was all about. It was obvious to all that his gentler preferences had no chance to prevail against the strong will of the headmaster, but he was still a presence to be reckoned with, revered and loved as he was by all. And it was always interestingly true that a campus of little capitalists never altogether lost sight of the fact that if Doctor Ames thundered from his pulpit, it was Mr. Sayre who had built the temple that housed it.

I and a half-dozen other sixth-formers made up the select Upper A Greek class that was privileged to take Mr. Sayre's famous course in Greek drama. This was held in his house, a large grey wooden assemblage of wings and porticoes, designed as much to be an appendage of Saint Augustine's as a bachelor's residence, containing a handsome library that richly supplemented the school's, a small theatre where the boys could put on plays, a huge game room and a squash court available to the upper school. We met in Mr. Sayre's study amid his collection of Greek statues and steles, and our discussions covered a great deal besides the three Athenian tragedians; we roamed from poetry to philosophy, from the exploration of the West to polar expeditions, from the busting of trusts to the rise of German militarism.

I reveled in it. Mr. Sayre seemed to tear a great hole in the wall of school life through which the fascinations of the great world poured in. But however far we roamed, he always brought us back to Greece in the end. It was there, he fervently believed, that true civilization had not only started but reached its zenith. He would quote Anatole France: "It was given to the Greeks to carry art to perfection. It was the privilege of a talented race, living in a good climate, under a clear sky, in a harmonious landscape, on the edge of a blue sea, practicing the principle of democracy."

It intrigued me, whose eye was more and more on the years that lay beyond Saint Augustine's, now that our graduation impended, that Mr. Sayre seemed to believe that what we had at school might be as significant as what was ahead. He would warn us not to waste the present in worrying about the future.

"The boy longs to become a man. And when he does, he dreads to become an old one. The golden years may be right here at Saint Augustine's. The friendships that you form now may be the closest of your lifetime. Young men together in a bright dawn, united by noble thoughts and tender affections. How often you may look back to this time with nostalgia!"

He made much of the Greeks' ideal of friendship, emphasizing that they were not shy of using the word "love" in this respect. But this bothered me, and I asked him whether there might not be a misunderstanding in the concept.

"Jowett, sir, you know, changes some of the *he's* to *she's* in his translation of 'The Symposium.' Might he not have been trying to make it clear that Socrates was thinking of the love of a man for a woman?"

"Jowett was kowtowing to Victorian prudery!" Mr. Sayre exclaimed in a rare burst of indignation. "He was a great scholar and knew better than anyone what Socrates or Plato had in mind. He understood perfectly the high ideals of Greek friendship. But he also knew it was beyond the ken of the Anglican clergy. Love to them meant only dirty things!"

But this did not satisfy me. In French class we had been reading Racine, and I noted that he had altered the plot of *Phèdre*, based on the Hippolytus of Euripides, to give the hero a girlfriend. Surely this had not been to placate an Anglican clergy, or even a Gallic one. I had elected to write my term paper on a comparison of the two tragedies, and I waited after class to consult Mr. Sayre further on the subject.

He gave me as usual his complete attention. He approved my choice of topic, but he roundly expressed his own conviction that Racine had not improved his play by the alteration.

"The very essence of Hippolytus is that he is virgin to women! He is the finest and most heroic youth in all of Greece. And, we may infer, the most beautiful. He proudly tells his father that no woman's flesh has ever touched his own; that he knows nothing of such matters, nor does he want to. The only female element in his life is that of the untouchable goddess Artemis, whom he worships and with whom he drives the dangerous beasts from the land. And when in the end he is destroyed by the jealous love goddess, Aphrodite, the poor dying boy can think only of what his loss may mean to the divine huntress. Who now will hunt with her? Who will hold her quiver? Who will guide her chariot, keep her shrine flowers fresh?"

"Why could not Artemis have saved him?" I asked.

"Because Aphrodite was her equal in power. But she swears revenge on her. It is Aphrodite and sexual lust that have caused the tragedy."

"But that is true in Racine also. Phèdre claims she is simply the victim of the goddess, *Venus, toute entière à sa proie attachée.*"

"Very true. Racine turns his whole play over to his principal female character. A true Gaul. And he does a superb job, we must admit. If you prefer as your protagonist a hysterical woman over a heroic youth, Racine is your man. Oh, he's great, all right." Here he threw back his head to intone the famous couplet:

> "*Ariane, ma soeur, de quel amour blessée*
> *Vous mourûtes aux bords ou vous fûtes laissée!*"

Then he chuckled. "Alfred de Musset is said to have swooned away when he heard Rachel declaim those famous lines. The double *accent circonflexe* was too much for him. But I see, Oscar, that you are made of sturdier stuff. You are still conscious. Perhaps my voice is not as melodic as Rachel's. But anyway, high in Parnassus as we may place the great tragedian of the age of

Louis, we must reserve a still higher one for the successor of Sophocles and his more virile hero. For see what Racine has done with Hippolytus! I ask you!"

Here Mr. Sayre rose to take mincing steps about the chamber to emphasize the degradation of the Greek ideal. "The very name tells you the worst. Eepoleete! Does that sound like a boar hunter? No! It sounds like a *petit monsieur* from the Louvre and the royal levees, a bowing, simpering *kuss-der-hand*, whose heart is given to a little princess of the author's concoction, an Aricie, thank you very much, for whom he *brûlers* with all the *ardeur* of a *jeune premier.* Now tell me, my friend, don't you prefer the Greek version?"

"I don't know," I answered sturdily. "I think *Phèdre* is the more exciting play. *And* the more interesting."

"But it is so interior, my boy! So hothouse. In Euripides we can identify with the chorus, the little people, terrified by the tragic events that happen to great men and yearning to lose their uneasy individualities in a greater being. Gilbert Murray, often maligned, got it right in one chorus at least:

> 'Could I take me to some cavern for my hiding,
> In the hilltops where the sun scarce hath trod,
> Or a cloud make the home of my abiding,
> As a bird among the bird droves of God.'"

I nodded and took my leave. It was time for my next class at the schoolhouse.

❧ ❧ ❧

I now became something of a favorite of Mr. Sayre's, and he began to consult me about a literary project on which he was embarking. He was writing the story of the first decade of the school — what he liked to call the "pastoral years" — when he and Alcott Ames, in their mid-twenties, had set up an academy of some two dozen boys in an old shingle mansion on a site of three hundred acres of lovely meadowland and copses on the banks of the sinuous Alph. Mr. Sayre made no secret of his conviction that the simpler, sparer school of those days had represented a Socratic ideal and a considerably finer thing than the bustling but tightly knit "anthill" of the present time, with its faculty larger than the original number of students. He learned that I could type, a rare accomplishment for a boy in those days, and he wished to make use not only of my editorial assistance but of my dexterous fingers.

"I can easily arrange, dear boy, if you are interested, for your good English instructor, Mr. Carnes, to give you credit for the hour or so each week that you may spend with me here. What do you say?"

Well, of course, I jumped at the idea, and Mr. Carnes indeed assured me that the time spent with such a mind would be well worth missing a few chapters of Dickens or Thackeray. Mr. Sayre and I started our sessions the next week. He wrote so slowly that he had few pages to show me at each meeting, and most of our time was spent over a delicious tea with cookies and his vivid and colorful reminiscences of a past that was unlike anything I had known. Yet, young as I was, I began to suspect that the idealistic Athenian seminary that he evoked could never have existed quite as he described it. But what of that? Wasn't it enough that he was writing a beautiful prose poem? And that I might actually be helping him?

Why could I not have let well enough alone? Because I have a compulsion to be always cutting my cake in slices, for some neurotic fear of losing what I will not share. When I told Mr. Sayre that I felt guilty at having his wonderful tales all to myself, he assured me that I was welcome to bring along a friend or friends to any of our sessions. And so when Grafton Pope, although not a particular friend of mine, expressed an interest in what the senior master and I were up to, I decided at once to invite him.

Grafton was one of those curious victims of cool ambition who are almost redeemed by their curiosity. He was a big, puffy, already balding youth of soft appearance but considerable muscle — he was on our first football team — who assiduously cultivated, often with some charm of manner, the leaders of our form and the more conspicuous masters. He was more successful with the latter than with the former. His sophistication may have impressed his contemporaries, but it also put them off. Grafton had been brought up in France by rich, expatriate, much-married parents, and although his knowledge of languages and sexual matters went far beyond any of ours, he was considered too "different" to be altogether congenial. There was a consensus among us that if it was exciting and manlike to go far, Grafton went too far. I suspected that he at times almost envied us our "innocence" and wanted to be "one of the boys," that he was looking for inclusion in a group, a joy that an only child among epicurean adults had never known.

And then, as I have said, he was curious. Like the rest of us, he cared about success, but he had lived abroad and learned that it came in many different ways. The boys at Saint Augustine's understood the worldly value of sports and money and business know-how, but Grafton had seen streets in Paris named for poets and philosophers, and he had met artists and even actors who were taken seriously by his family. He did not laugh, as some sixth-formers did (though behind their sleeves), at the shuffling figure of Mr. Sayre. He knew that the literary world had great respect for Sayre's translations of Sophocles, and he also knew that the old boy could buy and sell all the other masters put together.

He told me that he might be able to contribute some stories

from his father to Mr. Sayre's book. Mr. Pope had been one of the first students at the school.

"Yes, I know. Mr. Sayre described him as a golden faun."

"I'm afraid those horns have grown quite a bit through the years," Grafton chuckled. "I don't think Mr. Sayre quite appreciates Dad. The other day after chapel he stopped me to ask: 'And how is your dear pater? I hear he has a beautiful yacht in which to roam the Aegean. I don't suppose it's only to renew his acquaintance with the *Odyssey?* No, no, I don't suppose it's only that at all. Yet he was an apt Greek student. Oh, yes, very. A pity so many of the most apt don't keep it up. A pity, yes. Well, well. Life is life, isn't it? Good day, dear boy.'"

Grafton was a born mimic. It might have been Mr. Sayre speaking. But when I took him to our session that afternoon, it was to confront a very different vision of the senior master.

It was a day of freezing cold, and in his study we came upon the venerable scholar warming his backside before a bright fire in the grate. It was very literally what he was doing. His round pink body was exposed to us in its entirety, for he was wearing nothing but a Tyrolean cap with a scarlet feather and ankle-high black polished boots. One hand held a cigarette, the other the volume that he was intently perusing.

"Oh, sir, I beg your pardon!" I gasped, and turned to push Grafton ahead of me back out the door.

"Oh, it's you, dear Oscar. Come in, come in. And I see you've brought a friend. Why, it's the Pope boy. How nice, how very nice. I'll ring for tea."

He seemed utterly unaware of his state as he pressed the button on his desk, and I had a vision of how startled the maid might look.

"But, sir . . ."

"Yes, dear boy?"

"Hadn't you better put on your wrapper?" I had caught sight of this garment, of sumptuous red silk, lying on a chair, and at once the practical Grafton picked it up and came forward to offer it.

"Good gracious me, I thank you! What would Nellie have thought?" He allowed Grafton to slip the robe over his shoulders, even efficiently to tie the belt. "I wanted the full benefit of that lovely flame, and I must have forgot myself. There, there. I'm quite comfortable now. Thank you, my dear . . . Grafton, isn't it? You've taken good care of me."

I must admit that Grafton showed the good effects of his European training. He passed the episode off as easily as if our host had been guilty of an unstraightened collar. In the conversation that followed over tea, which old Nellie now brought in (she would probably have taken her boss's nudity quite in her stride), Grafton spoke charmingly of his father's memories of his school time.

"He says they were the happiest days of his life, sir. I don't know if that's exactly a compliment to his wives, but he loves to talk about the Sunday afternoons he rambled with you along the banks of the Alph, reciting choruses from Euripides."

I could hardly help a twinge of jealousy at the speed with which Grafton became my equal in our host's good will. Mr. Sayre now enthusiastically arose to open a cupboard to trundle out some huge old albums and show us overexposed photographs of masters and boys in that first decade of the school's history.

"As you can see, we were more like a family then. The relation between master and student was much more informal and friendly. Discipline was maintained more by mutual respect than by demerits or black marks. The superiority of the teacher was only the natural one of the man to the boy. The latter knew that his senior was simply helping him to become a man, so no resentment was engendered. Look at this shot of Doctor Ames. Wouldn't any boy have obeyed him instinctively? Look at that serene brow, those strong shoulders, those steadily gazing eyes." The picture revealed Doctor Ames in shorts and a sleeveless jersey, a soccer ball in hand. He was indeed strikingly handsome.

"He is still a fine figure of a man, of course. But then he was a Greek god!"

"An Episcopal god, surely, sir," Grafton ventured with a smile.

"That's right, my boy. That's right. I mustn't let the classics run away with me." Mr. Sayre leaned over to peer more closely at the likeness of his friend. "Yes, I think we can make out the Episcopalian in that strong chin. Perhaps just a wee bit too strong. But a leader must be that. And he was all sunshine in those days."

He turned the page and then turned it suddenly back with a rather foxy smile. "Ah, ah, this is not one to show the ladies." And having established our privilege, he turned the page a second time. "It's the way you caught me when you came in. A shot of our old swimming hole. The masters and boys used to bathe together *in pueris naturalibus.*"

Grafton and I examined the page with a quicker interest. The white figures of the bathers in and out of the creek were very white against the dark background, but few physical details could be made out. It was evident that no bathing suits were worn.

"It's like that famous painting by Thomas Eakins; do you know it?" Mr. Sayre asked. "No false modesty. The innocence and beauty of an Eden, free of Eves and apodal tempters. Man in his youth and strength and fullness of purpose. So Greek. So light and sky clear. How beautifully Walter Pater put it! Here, I have it right here."

From the set of Pater on the shelf behind him he plucked the volume *Greek Studies* and opened it at a page in which there was already a marker. He then read aloud what was evidently a favorite passage. "And here the artists have displayed the Greek warriors, not in the equipment they would really have worn, but naked — flesh fairer than that golden armor, the undraped form of man coming like an embodiment of the Hellenic spirit and as an element of temperance, into the somewhat gaudy spectacle of archaic art."

Here Mr. Sayre plucked contemptuously at the gold buttons of his splendid robe as if to imply that it covered something finer than itself. "Archaic art," he sniffed. "Asiatic. Always preferring the squiggly detail to the simple, the natural. Their images of gods had multiple legs and arms. Disgusting!"

Grafton, walking with me back to school after our tea, was horridly ribald. "Do you suppose the old boy really believes the saggy protruding tummy and bony shanks he exposed us to were embodiments of the Hellenic spirit? Holy cow! I couldn't cover them up fast enough! But seriously, Oscar, I wouldn't go there alone again if I were you. You might find yourself caught in an embarrassing little game of snatch-and-catch."

"What do you *mean?*"

"Well, wasn't he expecting just you? Wasn't that the reason for the bareass reception?"

"No! He *told* me I could bring a guest!"

"Well, maybe he was planning a kind of *jeu de trois.*"

"Grafton Pope, you have a filthy mind. You've spent too much time in Frogland."

Grafton laughed coarsely. "You don't have to have been to Gay Paree to recognize an old queen when you see one."

I was too disgusted to go on with the subject. He made several other vulgar comments, but I declined to respond, and we arrived back at school very much at odds. I knew he would make a good story of our visit, and I suffered keenly at the thought of the sneers and jeers to which poor, innocent Mr. Sayre would be exposed. But what bothered me more was the suspicion that Mr. Sayre might write a book in which people like Grafton would see all kinds of things he never intended. The Graftons of the world — and surely they were legion — might visualize the author of the passages on rural swimming holes as the poor naked creature I had seen that afternoon. Ugh! It was unbearable.

I mulled over my apprehensions for two days and then decided that the only person on the campus with whom I could safely discuss them was Mr. Carnes.

Leslie Carnes, my English teacher, was a dark-complexioned, very serious young man who treated boys as gravely as he did the other masters and harbored a passion for English literature that had set off one in myself. He was also my dormitory master and readily available for consultation. When I brought to his study some pages of Mr. Sayre's book that I had typed, he waited for me to explain before looking at them. When I had done so, he nodded with definite interest and proceeded to read them. After fifteen minutes of absolute silence he looked up with a quizzical stare.

"Did Mr. Sayre give you permission to show me these papers, Oscar?"

Even in my tension I noted that he might have asked me that *before* reading them.

"No, sir, but I'm sure he wouldn't mind. After all, he intends to publish them."

"Yes, he's even told me that. And I know Doctor Ames has expressed interest in his book. But what is it that you wish to consult me about?"

But I wasn't going to be the first to articulate a suspicion.

"Well, sir, if nothing strikes you in those pages, I guess I have nothing to consult you about."

He smiled. But it was a small smile. "As Hamlet said of the gravedigger, we must speak by the card, or equivocation will undo us. I *do* see something that worries me in these pages. I wonder if it's the same thing that you do."

"It's not so much, sir, what *I* see as what others might see."

"And *I* see that I'm not going to catch you. All right, my friend. There's a bit too much about masculine beauty."

I breathed in relief. "That's it, sir."

"But do you think Mr. Sayre sees anything wrong with that?"

"Oh, no, sir!"

Mr. Carnes's stare was searching. Then he nodded. "Neither do I. He is one of God's innocents. A kind of scholarly Saint Francis. I'll be very frank with you, Oscar. You deserve it. You've had a difficult job to do, and you've handled it with kindness and tact. I believe that in his youth it was entirely possible for Mr. Sayre to have loved Doctor Ames with a love that is stronger than what men usually feel for each other. And yet never to have so much as touched him. Never, perhaps, to have even wanted to. Some people call that sublimation. It's a perfectly good thing. Up here you find it among some fine, upstanding single women who choose to live together, often for life. Such unions are called 'Boston marriages.' Mr. Sayre has chosen always to live near the headmaster. Mrs. Ames treats him as a brother, and all the Ames children call him Uncle Philemon. But you are absolutely correct in being concerned with what malicious tongues may say about a man who feels that way about another man. That is why it is imperative to shield Mr. Sayre from his own innocent accounts of his favorite enthusiasms. If he ever knew we were having this conversation, it would break his dear old heart."

"What will you do then, sir?"

"I shall show these pages to Doctor Ames. Don't worry. Your name will not be mentioned. The headmaster, who, for all his deep faith, is highly conscious of the world, will know just what to do. I suspect he will simply go to Mr. Sayre and ask if he may not read the manuscript that everyone knows he's writing. And we can be sure Mr. Sayre will deny him nothing. Once he has read the script, Doctor Ames will act for the best interests of all. Including Mr. Sayre."

"He won't be too sharp with him?"

"Doctor Ames is never the headmaster with his friends. He can be wonderfully gentle."

And I was indeed to see that side of the headmaster only a week later, when he arrived, unannounced and broadly smiling, at my next session with Mr. Sayre.

"I make no apology, my dear Philemon, for breaking in on your work with your young amanuensis. On the contrary, I have come to lodge a complaint. It is the talk of the town that you are writing a book about the founding of the school. And may I ask *why* you have neglected to seek the counsel of your oldest friend and co-founder? Do I know nothing of such matters? Or *am* I to know nothing of such matters?"

"Alcott, my dear fellow, of course, of course! What is my little book all about but you and your wonderful dreams? How could it possibly be otherwise?" Recovering himself from the shock of his friend's sudden intrusion, Mr. Sayre rose unsteadily to his feet and took the few steps forward to embrace him. "My only hesitation in showing you an early draft was that I knew you didn't like my grousing about some of your later programs. But that's a detail. Let us by all means share everything I have written so far. Fairfax here will give you what he has typed. You are excused for today, Oscar, but come back next week and you will see how the headmaster will have improved my humble start!"

But when I came back the following Wednesday, it was to find a rather distracted author. He mumbled about things in a way I could not quite understand. He fidgeted with gadgets on his desk and kept looking away from me. I was, it gradually emerged, being dismissed as his assistant. Doctor Ames, it seemed, had given him some wonderful ideas, which he had to think over, and, for the time being at least, he would need no editorial or typing help. He wanted me, of course, to realize that I had been of great use to him and that he deeply appreciated all I had done. And so forth. I was sure he would not ask for me again.

I shall never know whether he suspected me of having tipped off the headmaster or whether he simply associated me with what may have been the most painful incident in his life and wanted to see me no more. The headmaster, in any event, however kind, must have been effectively blunt, for the printed version of "Saint Augustine's — The Pastoral Years" contained no descriptions of handsome young masters or lovely youths in communal swimming holes. Or anywhere else. It did not even contain any criticisms of the more organized and disciplined academy that had succeeded the "pastoral" one. The headmaster, while he was at it, had killed two birds with his stone.

I took my leave of Mr. Sayre somewhat abruptly, being a bit hurt at my summary dismissal, but in the hall, reflecting on how much more sorely hurt he may have been by Doctor Ames's revelations, I repented and turned back to wish him the best of luck with his little volume. But when I reapproached the door of his study, I saw with horror that he had laid his head down on the blotter of his desk and was shaking with sobs!

Appalled, I tiptoed away.

❧ ❧ ❧

Reading Mr. Sayre's little book today, I can make out how he finally reconciled his ideal of the school with the sterner one of the headmaster. Although conceding the necessity of a tighter organization and stricter discipline for an academy of four hundred boys, he nonetheless maintained that Saint Augustine's had preserved much of its purer quality and that "today" it was "perfectly incomprehensible to those who have never belonged to it and only partly comprehensible to those who have." What he meant by this, or what he tried to mean, was illustrated by his description of what he regarded as a characteristic sixth-former of the 1890s. As the author professed to see him, he was a young man clad typically in a blazer and white flannels, a straw hat cocked at a rakish angle, whose ready wit, never impudently irreverent or actively cruel, nonetheless relentlessly exposed pretension and pomposity; who could quote from Latin classics but only when strictly apposite; who played a hard game of football or soccer without boasting about it afterwards; who conformed to the highest standard of good manners but didn't hesitate to deviate when faced with rudeness; whose attitude to women was gallant but humorously so; who loathed scabrous jokes and made no public show of his quiet faith in a god who was entirely Jesus. In short, an Etonian. But hadn't Philemon Sayre done to the Hippolytus of Euripides essentially what Racine had done? The young hunter was no longer the misogynist follower of Artemis. He was an English gentleman. The headmaster could have had no further complaints.

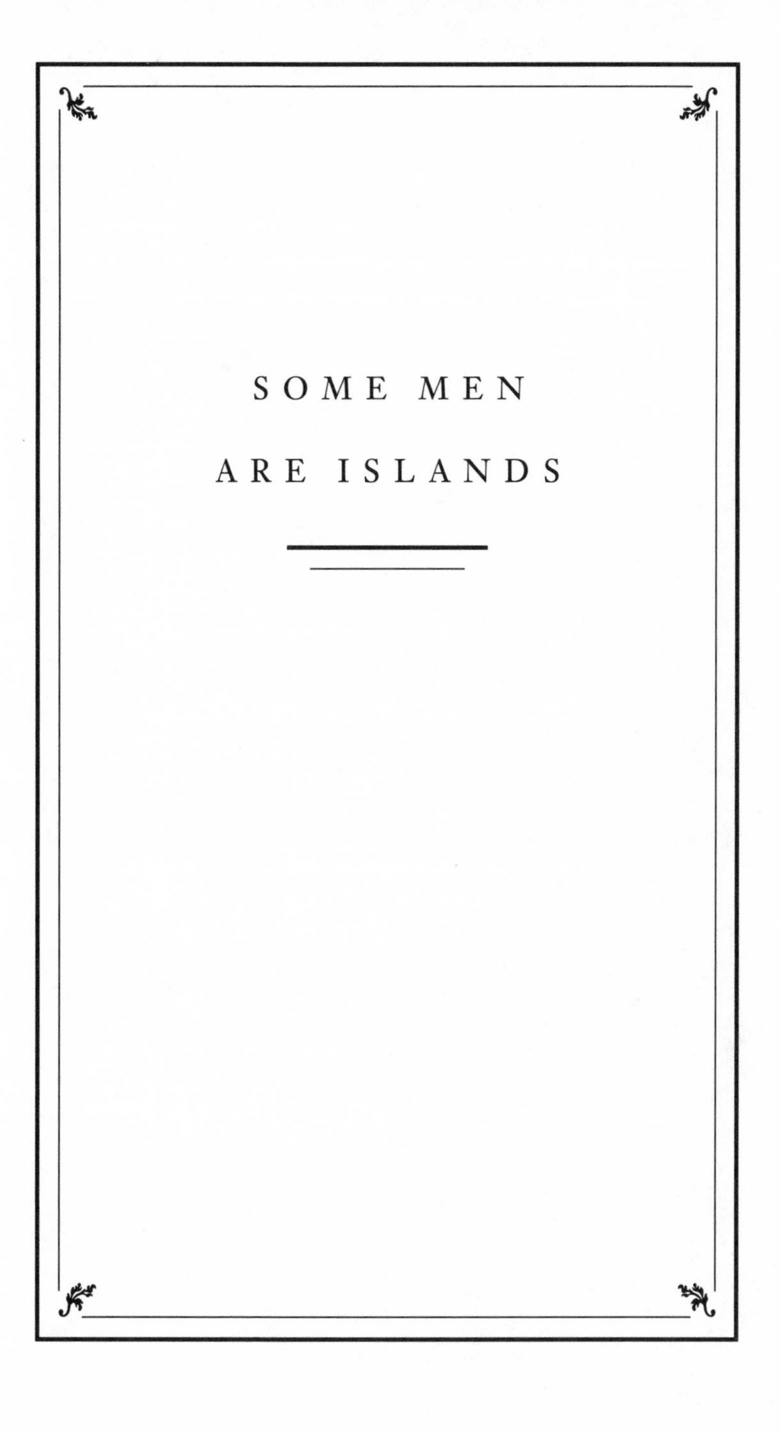

SOME MEN ARE ISLANDS

IN 1915 I was a junior at Yale, majoring in English "lit," an ardent admirer of William Lyon (Billy) Phelps and an avid reader of Robert Browning. I was also an editor of *The Yale Literary Magazine.* I had already almost made up my mind that I would follow in my father's footsteps and study law, but I still had a secret hankering to become a writer or teacher, fantasies that I kept in the back of my mind, never to be brought too roughly forward, for they were fragile and would surely wilt in the bright sunshine of my Eli existence. Writing, insofar as it entailed doing little stories for the magazine, was an acceptable, even an applauded sideline for an undergraduate, something to add to one's "bio" in the class yearbook, or even to look back upon with a pleasant nostalgia from one's ultimate desk in Wall Street. And teaching . . . well, two of my friends returned to Saint Augustine's after graduation for a year as bachelor masters, and that was considered a "good" experience, but only as a hiatus, a breathing space, a time to assess oneself as a thinking man, before the advent of such "realities" as law or business or even medicine. And it would never, of course, have occurred to my mother or even, I daresay, to my more imaginative father that they might have to warn their seemingly conformist son against the sirens combing their golden hair on the treacherous reefs of art. My parents too were "realities," and in what other milieu could a Fairfax expect to exist?

The carnage in Europe helped me to sustain these fantasies, at least until I met Danny Winslow. It lent a not wholly unpleasant atmosphere of epicureanism to my college years. If one was doomed to the trenches, did it matter very much whether one inwardly dreamed of being a poet or a judge? But it was Danny who, more by example than persuasion, finally convinced me that, even if I should survive Armageddon, writing for me would never be more than an avocation. For he taught me, as a co-editor of the *Lit*, what a real writer was. Nothing existed for Danny, neither Yale nor the kaiser nor Wall Street nor fraternities nor even girls, in proportion to his passion for the written word.

Which didn't mean for a minute that he was not of the earth, earthy. A poor, public school boy, he cultivated, largely through me, the prep school crowd. The written word had to be *about* something, and Danny wanted his to be about the revelries of the rich and famous. He delighted in sophistication, in style, in high manners, in careless spending, in a world well lost. And as he had little besides his own good looks to provide him with access to the "great world" that he hoped one day to immortalize, he appealed shamelessly to any who could open its doors for him. He had an uncanny way of making it seem advantageous for you to do things for him. His large sky-blue eyes, his pale, almost beardless countenance and rich, curly auburn hair reinforced his constant unspoken query: "How can I give you the lovely time I want to give you unless you make it feasible for me to do so?"

And he could. He could always pick just the right show if you bought the tickets, and just the right party if you procured the invitations, and even find the right girl for you on a double date if you picked up the nightclub tab.

It probably follows that he had no concern for the dull, the drab, the poor. He frankly shuddered at such things. If I reproached him with this, he would explain, rather melodramatically, that he had no time for the shabby, that both his parents had died young, one of cancer and the other of heart, and that he himself had a "weak ticker." His background was certainly obscure, and his references to it inconsistent. I gathered that his father had been a teacher at MIT and his mother a trained nurse, and he claimed that this "misalliance" had caused the former's disinheritance by a wealthy family. But when I asked him why he didn't look up any of his relatives, who by now might be willing to forgive the innocent scion and take him back in the fold, his answers were very evasive. He lived, it seemed, on the rapidly dwindling proceeds of the small paternal life insurance policy.

As I have said, it was the Yale *Lit* that brought us together. I had been immensely struck by his enthralling stories about wealthy and dissolute idlers in Palm Beach or Newport or other places he had never been to, but which he described in vivid and sparkling prose, putting him in a totally different league from the rest of the editors. I felt a sad chagrin at my instant realization that I was never going to write like him. Yet I was shocked, when I told him this, that he agreed with me.

"But you don't *care*," he pointed out blithely when he took in my dismay.

"What makes you think that?"

"It's like playing the piano. Some do it to amuse themselves and their friends. To enliven a party. To others it's a matter of life or death. The concert stage or the overdose."

"And that grim alternative is yours, I suppose."

He simply shrugged. I was to learn that he could not bear to discuss either the work or the plight of inferior scribblers.

He had other uses for me.

"Why don't you ask me to New York for a weekend? I hear you live in a big house and go to oodles of parties. I don't have a dinner jacket, but maybe I could borrow one of yours."

Now why did I not resent a hand so boldly plunged in my pocket? Why did I actually "lend" him the money he needed for evening clothes? And why did I go to the considerable trouble of getting him asked to the dances he specified? Because Danny not only made you feel you were doing something interesting and perhaps ultimately rewarding in promoting his social life; he gave you a *quid pro quo.* He made it fun for all involved. He was brash, impudent, vivacious and always funny. Mother actually found him "sweet" and worried about his scanty means and orphan status. Even Father was amused.

"In the courts of old there was always place for a jester. Your friend Winslow earns his privilege."

A jester! Little did Father know of the hot flame of ambition that burned behind that smile.

The day came when I introduced him to Constance Warren. I was beginning to wonder whether I wasn't falling in love with Constance, though she showed little enough sign of returning my admiration. She had the kind of steadfastness and calm, grave detachment that attracted my nervous soul. Her brow and chin were squarish, but her skin was like pearl, her grey-green eyes serene, and her figure was well shaped and strong. She could beat me at both tennis and golf, which sports she took very seriously. Indeed, she took everything seriously. She found social life trivial, though at her stepmother's urging she went to a number of parties, and she was majoring in art history at Barnard and worked in a settlement house. She and I differed on almost every important issue, including the war.

"It's only a scrap over empires," she would insist. "A plague on both their houses, I say. We had much better stay out of it."

"It's only a struggle for civilization itself!" I would hotly retort. "But you and your sort won't find *that* out until it's too late."

It was Danny who suggested that I introduce him to Constance, and it was only later that I recalled that it should have been obvious to me that an aspiring novelist would want to meet the daughter of a publisher as famous as Hugo Warren. My recall coincided, no doubt, with my irritation at the discovery that Danny had made what appeared to have been a favorable impression on the usually hard-to-impress Constance. I found out, some time after introducing them, that he had come down from New Haven the following Saturday to take her to a matinee. He had not seen fit to mention this to me.

I took this up, rather aggressively I fear, with Constance the next time I saw her. She was tending her stepmother's pottery booth at a Red Cross benefit sale at Madison Square Garden.

"He's a rather unusual friend for you, isn't he?" she asked. Her tone was cool, but then so had mine been. "I mean, he didn't go to Groton or Saint Mark's or Saint Augustine's."

"You assume *all* my friends are from the same basket?"

"Well, aren't they? Pretty much?"

"And yours, I suppose, are all proletariats."

"Of course not. But I at least know when I'm boxed in. There may be a chance for me to find my way out."

"With curly-haired Danny showing you the way?"

She gave me a searching look. "What brought that on? I find Danny's ideas interesting, that's all. He's so keen on everything. He seems to have no prejudices at all."

"Can you have principles if you have no prejudices?"

"You mean if you care about nothing? I don't know. It's an

interesting question. Perhaps some of us have too many of both."

"Meaning me, I suppose. Because you say I care too much about the war and not enough about your settlement house."

At this point a customer came up, and she had to break off. I strode away, angry at her, angry at Danny and angry at myself for making such a foolish scene. I had to suppose that my feeling for Constance was even stronger than I had suspected. Or had jealousy simply swollen it? Jealousy, the ugly drug that can turn a pleasant attraction into a tedious obsession.

But it was not only with Constance that Danny appeared to have made an impression. It was with her father, his real goal, and even with her stepmother. Hugo Warren, who had come to the fair to support his wife's booth, now spotted me and beckoned me to join him. I had to listen to his abundant praise of a story that Danny had had the nerve to thrust under the great editor's eyes.

"Get him to show it to you, Oscar. It's about an old professor of English at an Ivy League college. It's one of the most remarkable achievements of a twenty-one-year-old I've ever read. Believe me, your friend Winslow is a man to watch!"

So Danny would not be content with my girl, if indeed he even wanted her. He had to have my guide and mentor as well! For that was what Hugo Warren had been to me since I graduated from Saint Augustine's and the tutelage of Mr. Carnes. As a client of my father's and, unlike most of those, also a friend, he came often to the house and had taken a friendly interest in my literary enthusiasms. He had guided my reading, sent me books from his press and had even let me work in his office one summer, telling me that if I ever decided against law, there might be a spot for me in his firm. He was now in his early fifties, a fine, spare, spruce figure of a gentleman, who dressed well, almost too well, in dark good taste, permitting exaggeration only in his silk ties and handkerchieves.

If there was a feminine side to Hugo — insofar as gentleness and sensitivity are deemed that — there was certainly a masculine one to his wife. I bring Vera in at this point because people tended to think of them together. She was a fashionable interior decorator, an important woman understandably aware of her own importance, large in figure, noble in countenance, with the majesty of a female figure on the prow of an old clipper ship. And Danny had apparently charmed her as well!

"Vera says he has a remarkable eye for color," Hugo assured me. "And that if I don't pre-empt all his efforts for literature, she might one day have a place for him in her shop."

As soon as I got back to New Haven on Sunday night, I went straight to Danny's room to ask whether I might read the story. He immediately handed it to me and then sat complacently watching me as I perused it. Neither of us said a word in the twenty minutes or so it took me to read the sketch.

I say "sketch," for that was what it was, a sketch to the life of Professor Allard Sloan, who, next to Phelps, was the grand old man of the English department, a revered figure on the Yale campus, whose tense, high-pitched, beautifully articulated lectures on the British Romantic poets were regarded as a required course by half the undergraduates. But what Danny had done with him was fiendish. He had contrasted Sloan's well-known reputation as a snob who loved to entertain the socially elite of the senior class in his rooms after football games, serving champagne and caviar to members of Skull & Bones and Scroll & Key, the two "smartest" of the secret societies, and their visiting girlfriends, with his reception of students of humbler origin, even if more deeply sensitive to the strains of Keats and Shelley, who, knocking at his door in the hope of enlightenment, were apt to be told through the crack of its opening that he was too busy marking papers to see them now.

The most remarkable aspect of the piece was that the reader was made fully aware that the professor was deeply and genuinely appreciative of the poetry he taught, to the extent even of becoming something of a poet himself, as Danny's wonderfully invented extracts of his lectures revealed. And yet this added not one cubit to the stature of his soul, which remained just as small and mean as if he had never opened a volume of Byron or Coleridge.

Danny's eyes were greedy for praise when I finally looked up. "Well, what do you think? Isn't it great?"

"I suppose, in its way, it really is," I admitted with some reluctance. "But what can you do with it? Not the *Lit*, surely? It's Sloan to the life. As some see him, anyway."

"The *Lit!* Do you think I'd offer anything like that to the *Lit?* Hugo wants to send it to the *Atlantic Monthly*."

I was awed that even he would aim so high. And I certainly noted the use of Warren's first name. Even I had never called him Hugo. "But even if they take it, won't you have to change it? Wouldn't everyone immediately recognize Sloan?"

"And if they do?"

"Well, wouldn't he sue you or something?"

"He'd never do that. It would only make things worse for him. Besides, what would his damages be? That's what he is, isn't it?"

"It's a side of him," I murmured doubtfully. "His admirers insist he has other and better ones. But is that all you have to consider? What about the man's feelings when he reads it? *If* he reads it."

"Oh, he'll read it, all right!" Danny exclaimed cheerfully. "Even if he should miss it, there's always that dear friend who will bring it to his attention. With a comment like 'Sorry to do this to you, old man, but I really feel you *ought* to know what people are saying about this story.'"

"But it might kill him, you know. It might simply kill him."

"Nonsense! Shouldn't he be proud to have produced a student who can write like me?"

I stared. "You assume a scarcely human disinterestedness in him."

"I wouldn't in a layman, of course. But he's a priest at the altar! He should be ready to suffer for the cause. If he can't rise to that, is it my fault? You've heard him sighing and sobbing over the burning corpse of the 'divine' Shelley. Do you think Percy Bysshe would have spared him if he could have used him as a character in *The Cenci?*"

"But couldn't you just disguise the thing a bit? Does it have to be *quite* so plain?"

"Once I've got a thing right, I won't change a single word. It would be like painting a moustache on the *Mona Lisa.* You just don't understand these things, Oscar. You're not an artist."

"But the greatest novelists know how to create characters. They don't have to copy them. Whoever heard of a model for Heathcliff? Or Captain Ahab?"

"It's true that some writers can rely on their imagination alone. But others can't. Every character of *Charlotte* Brontë's is directly traceable to a living model. It got her in hot water, but did she care? She did not, and she shouldn't have. An artist does things the way he has to do them. And if you think I'm going to change or scrap a work of art for some crazy scruple about good manners or being a gentleman, you are just plain crazy!"

I saw it was hopeless and gave it up.

❧ ❧ ❧

The story did appear in the *Atlantic Monthly* and was duly praised. At Yale it enjoyed a brief *succès de scandale.* But Professor Sloan never manifested by so much as a raised eyebrow that the arrow had reached its target, and the matter was soon forgotten.

I raised the question of the author's propriety on a weekend on Long Island, where Hugo and Vera Warren were visiting my parents, but Hugo refused to see anything wrong with what Danny had done.

"The kind of talent that young man has is a prodigious responsibility," he insisted. "I don't go so far as to imply that it would justify his committing a crime. But where minor questions of other people's feelings are concerned, he has to be given a wider rein than the rest of us. What he is developing is a gift that may bring the highest kind of pleasure to many thousands of readers."

"But you would never have done what he did to poor old Sloan," I pointed out. "You don't even like to swat a mosquito."

"Ah, but I haven't his talent. Or anything remotely like it."

"That's hogwash, my love," Vera robustly interrupted. "You *find* the geniuses. You nurture them. And that takes your own kind of genius. You might as well say that *I'm* not an artist because I don't make the curtains and lampshades with which I decorate a room. But it's the *ensemble* that's the real work of art!"

"And the *ensemble* is *your* work, of course, my dear. Oh, I agree! The Vera touch is all in all. But that's not so with editors. We're simply the housemaids who plump up the cushions and empty the ashtrays. Authors need so little."

I knew that nothing could make a crack in the ivy-covered wall of Hugo's beautiful modesty. Yet he was the editor, I also knew, who had rendered publishable at least one great American novelist by persuading him (which no one else could do) to cut his first book in half. His thanks had been a torrent of abuse from the ungrateful author, even after the book's rousing acclaim, and the taking of his second novel to a rival house. And had Hugo been once heard to complain? Never. I was glad, anyway, that he had his wife to boost him.

"Hugo believes that a publisher is like a mother," Vera continued with a rumbling laugh. "Her milk must never dry up. And if she ever permits herself to criticize her golden-haired brat, it must be in the gentlest possible way. The only one of his writers Hugo ever said a sharp word to was that nut who claimed Lord Oxford had written Shakespeare's plays."

"But that was like denying the immaculate conception in the Vatican!" Hugo exclaimed with a chuckle. "*Some* things must be sacred."

What I still could not help seeing as Danny's inhumanity to Professor Sloan cooled my relations with him, and I saw him less frequently in the balance of our last year in New Haven. My relations with Constance did worse. They finally came to a halt. It was not directly because of Danny, whose attraction to her I found I had greatly exaggerated, but, oddly and unpleasantly enough, because she seemed now to equate me with him.

"I don't know why I thought you admired him so," I muttered, on our last dinner together, when she had unexpectedly agreed with me about his selfishness.

"He interested me. That's a very different thing. He interested me as an influence on you."

"Oh? A good one?"

"I hardly think so. He seems to me the logical, ultimate extension of what you yourself are trying to be."

"And what, pray, is *that?*"

"A man who finds more in books than in people. Who worries about the fate of Anna Karenina while not even seeing the beggar in the street."

Really! It was remarkable how disagreeable this girl could make herself to the man who was paying for her meal. But my answer was lame. "I often give to beggars. Even when one isn't supposed to."

"Oh, that's just guilt. We all do *that.* I'm talking about where your *real* interests lie. What your real values are. They're literary, Oscar. Almost wholly literary. What Danny has become — what Danny *is* — should be a warning to you."

"And what about your father?"

"I'd rather not talk about my father."

I smiled grimly. My shot, anyway, had gone home. If any man had lived for books, it was surely Hugo Warren. I shifted the argument. "It seems to me you take a rather high stand for a girl who's majoring in history of art."

"But I never said art and literature weren't things to be *studied.* It's a question of the role they play in your life."

"And you think it's too big a one in mine."

"I do, Oscar. I'm sorry, but I do."

I now see that I should have taken this as a genuine interest in myself. Instead, I struck a maudlin note. "Well, the war, when we get into it, should settle all that. It's taken good care of Rupert Brooke."

My tone disgusted her. "All that rot about his grave! 'Some corner of a foreign land that is forever England.' Is that a serious way to write about a world massacre that's being fought to keep kings and kaisers on their thrones? Ugh! Only a third-rate poet could write a line like 'If I should die think only this of me.'"

I lost my temper. "And I suppose the only difference you see between me and Brooke is that I'd be a fifth-rate one."

"I never said that. I never said you wouldn't be a good writer. I was talking only about your attitude. Towards the world in general."

"And to the war? I suppose it's a crime to believe in the Allied cause?"

"Of course not. I only mind how you *see* it. It's Beau Geste. The Charge of the Light Brigade. The horse guards on parade. 'Tramp, tramp, tramp, the boys are marching!'"

My irritation was so great, I could hardly breathe. "*Parlons d'autre chose.*" I spoke airily and in French to alienate her further. Somehow we got through the meal.

That night, tossing in bed, I resolved that I was finished with Constance Warren. I promised myself that I would not call her or write to her until I had effectively eliminated her image from my sentimental musings. I would not even go to her father's house unless I was assured that she was absent. So there!

And indeed I kept my resolution for two full years. But the war provided the larger portion of my fortitude.

After graduation Danny disappeared, not only from my life but from that of the Warrens. He went down to Mexico to write a novel, and, so far as I could make out, corresponded with no one at all. Then came our entry into the war and my own departure to an officers' training camp in Fort Devens, Massachusetts, and for a time I gave no thought to Danny Winslow or his literary career. But I was to see him again before I sailed for France.

I was on a final weekend leave with my parents in New York when he called at the house in a state of high desperation. It was like him not to ask a single question about my own immediate future. He was concerned solely with the fact that he had come home to face a draft call and to discover that an army doctor could refuse him exemption on the grounds of health. His much-vaunted "weak ticker" had apparently been deemed sturdy enough to withstand the onslaught of the Hun. We met in Father's study, and neither the dark panels nor the signed photographs of eminent jurists nor even the multimedaled portrait of Admiral Fairfax, with its upper-corner glimpse of the confrontation of the *Monitor* and the *Merrimack*, were able in the least to rebuke his bleak dearth of patriotism.

"It's an outrage that one superannuated quack can send a man like me to his death!"

"But isn't it good news that you have a normal heart? It sounds to me as if he were sending you to your life."

"In the trenches? You know I'd never survive them. The noise and stink alone would do me in."

"It may interest you to know, Danny, that I'm doomed to that same noise and stink. And a hell of a lot sooner than you are. It may even be all over before you've finished your basic training."

He stared as if my comments were utterly beside the point. "*You?* But you'll never be killed. You're the one who writes it all up afterwards."

I ignored this. "Let me ask you just one question. Do you feel absolutely *no* sense of duty to your country?"

"Only to keep myself alive. There are plenty of men who are fit just to be soldiers. Why kill off the talented ones?"

I found myself inwardly debating whether or not it was complimentary to me for him to assume that I was so beyond the public hysteria of the war that I could listen dispassionately to arguments that, if uttered in the street, could have led to the tarring and feathering of the speaker — and perhaps the listener. At any rate it was obvious that he would be no use to anyone at the front.

"There is only one person whom I can think of who might agree with you — *and* be able to help you."

"And who is that?" he cried eagerly. "Tell me, tell me."

"Hugo Warren. He's in the State Department now. In some office of war propaganda. I know he uses professional writers. It's just conceivable, I suppose, that if he wanted you, he could get you a draft deferment."

"Have you got his address? Or better yet, his telephone number?"

Of course I had, and of course he used it, then and there, and of course Hugo offered him the job, and *did*, by hook or by crook, somehow secure for him the draft deferment.

❧ ❧ ❧

I went to France as a second lieutenant in the artillery, but because of an unexpected tour of special staff duty in Paris, I did not reach the front until the early summer of 1918 and saw little action. I did, however, receive a minor wound from a shrapnel burst in Belleau Wood and was still hospitalized at the time of the Armistice. It was possibly because of the briefness of my combat duty that I was reappointed to staff work in the first months of peace and did not get home until the spring of 1919. But it had been a "perfect" war for me. At a minimum of danger and discomfort to myself I emerged from the greatest carnage in recorded history, safe and sound, with a mild aura of heroism, at least in the eyes of my loyal family and friends, around my undeserving head.

I needed such small glory as I could lay my hands on, for I found my draft-dodging friend the hero of the hour in a New York that was only too anxious to forget the war. Everyone was reading *The Jade Serpent*, Danny's Mexican novel about a gifted but alcoholic archeologist in the Mayan ruins, and the critics were calling him a second Stephen Crane. Hugo had not only published it; he seemed almost to have adopted his protégé. Danny was now actually living in the Warrens' beautiful Greek Revival house in Gramercy Park, occupying the old bedroom of Constance, who was teaching at the Brearley School and sharing an apartment with a girlfriend.

When I dined there I found Danny in the highest of spirits and delighted to see me. Any old differences between us over his professor story or his war attitude were swept aside; the past didn't exist for him. So why should it have for me? I allowed him to patch up our old friendship; I quite understood that there is nothing more agreeable than demonstrating an indisputable triumph to a formerly skeptical classmate. I had no use now for grudges; I too wanted amusement in the release of a postwar world. And Danny was a great one for providing amusement, even to an industrious law student at Columbia.

"Did you have a model for your archeologist?" I couldn't resist asking him.

"Oh, yes, but his liver gave out. You'll be relieved to learn that he expired before my book was published." Here Danny broke into that frank, cheerful laugh that you couldn't quite believe had followed a remark so seemingly heartless.

"And whom are you writing up now?"

"What would you say to a revered old-time editor and his chic decorating spouse?"

But he winked as he said this, and even I didn't think he would go *that* far. Besides, weren't the Warrens indispensable to his career? He and Hugo and Vera had become almost a trio; people now asked Danny to dinner when they asked the Warrens. Indeed, some of them may have asked the Warrens in order to *get* Danny. The three had developed what seemed their own secret language; they would exchange glances on hearing what they seemed jointly to regard as an absurdity uttered at a party and then all three laugh at once. It could be quite irritating to those not in the know.

But I had succumbed, like everyone else, to *The Jade Serpent.* His style was of a beauty — crisp, limpid, vivid, unforgettable. It was not that one felt sorry for the lost soul of the archeologist — Danny was as detached as his worshipped Flaubert. It was more that the novel created a special world that seemed somehow beyond compassion or judgment. It was simply *there;* one had to accept it. One didn't have to react to it. His prose was like a fresh, clear brook bubbling over a bottom whose muddiness didn't have to concern one.

One night at the Warrens' I found myself sitting next to Constance. She greeted me with her usual look of calm reserve, but I thought her tone was more friendly. She made no reference to the gap of time since our last meeting; she picked me up just where she had left me.

"I'm glad you won your war, Oscar. May I offer my belated congratulations?"

Was she laughing at me? "Did it never become *your* war, Constance?"

"Oh, yes. Once we were in it, I knew it had to be won. I worked in the Brooklyn Navy Yard. In the Bureau of Personnel. For every man in combat there were fifty typists. Victory was assured."

"I'm sure you did a fine job."

She nodded, as if to put an end to the war. "And now you're in law school. Do you like it?"

"Oh, yes. If you're ever in a jam, don't despair. I can always get you out through the small print. And how is your art history?"

"I think in the fall I may go for my master's."

"It looks to me as if we've changed places. You're in the artistic ether now, and I'm grubbing in the cellar."

"We've changed places in more ways than one, Oscar." There was no smile behind her gravity now. "You've become a brave soldier. And it becomes you. I owe you an apology."

"For what, for Pete's sake?" But I loved it!

"For underestimating you. For being a prig and an ass."

"But you were quite right! Honestly, Constance, I did nothing special over there. My parents have touted it up out of all proportion."

"I don't believe that. I think I have a fair picture of what you did."

My immediate concern was how I could alter myself in the future to maintain her undeserved new interest in me. My heart was doing peculiar things. "May I take you out to dinner one night?" How clumsy I sounded! "The way I used to?"

"I don't see why not."

I thought I had better switch now to a less personal topic. I needed time to think out the new Oscar Fairfax before I waxed too sentimental. My eye fell on Danny, shrieking with laughter down the table.

"How do you feel about *his* living here?"

"You mean do I feel he's taken my place? Not really. I've always taken second place to Daddy's writers. I'm used to that. And I've never had a real place with my stepmother. She and I get on well enough, but we're not close. We respect each other. It's fine."

"So you're not concerned that he rules the roost here."

"Well, there *is* one thing that bothers me, now you mention it. His habit, which you once told me about, of putting people in his stories. I mean, putting them in with horrid spectacular details. Do you suppose he's taking notes on Daddy and Vera?"

I told her now what Danny had said to me on the subject, adding that I had not believed it and still did not. She did not share my confidence.

"I wouldn't put it past him. Of course, in one way it might not be a wholly bad thing. If he did Daddy nastily enough, it might cure Daddy of his infatuation with his new genius."

"But he might do it too nastily."

"Why don't you ask him? He'll probably make no bones about it. To you, anyway. And then at least we'll be prepared."

"But surely your father, as his editor, will have a chance to read it first?"

"Unless Danny takes it to another publisher. Those things happen to Dad, you know."

"But he'll have an option on it!"

"Daddy has never enforced an option in his life."

I was delighted, anyway, to have a favor to do for Constance, and the following Saturday night I invited Danny to dine with me at his favorite expensive French restaurant to get him in a mood for candid interchanges. But my money was wasted. We had barely finished our soup before the whole plan for his next novel came out. He was indeed "doing" Hugo and Vera, and he almost rudely cut off my sputtering objections.

"You can't see things as they are, Oscar, because your mind is so clogged with preconceived ideas of how they *ought* to be. You have your own rosy little picture of the Warrens, and you can't allow that mine might be clearer."

"And what is it that I don't see about the Warrens?"

"And it's not just the Warrens, either. It's people. You think they value their privacy. On the contrary, they hate their privacy! They're not always aware of that, of course. But Freud has shown us where we all really live. In the *id!* And in Hugo's *id* he's bareass with an erection on a beach full of people in proper bathing suits, sneering at him. 'Cover it up, Hugo,' they cry."

For all my disgust I was struck by the image. "You mean he *likes* that?"

"In his own way. Like a man who wants to be whipped. There can be a sensuous pleasure in exposure, in humiliation. Even a bit of defiance. Showing an erection to people who think he can't get it up. Look, I *am* a man, even if I'm a gentleman! A gentle man. Too gentle to be a man. But still, look at me!"

I closed my lips tightly. I knew I must not lose my temper. "And Vera, how does she fancy herself?"

"Oh, there's nothing concealed there! She's out in the open! Look at the rooms she designs. Jungle red! All those exploding chintzes and wild lampshades. She's a tigress in fetters. But she sheds the fetters from time to time. Oh, yes, she does!"

"And then what does she do?"

"Well, I haven't got the whole picture yet, but I think her office may be the clue. One of her young aides comes to the house occasionally. I think I'll take him out to lunch."

"You mean you think Vera has *lovers?*"

Danny laughed, almost in surprise. "I won't dignify *that* question with an answer."

"And Hugo? Does he know?"

"Oh, Hugo knows everything. That's his glory. And his cross."

"And how does she feel about that?"

"It tortures her. She feels that he's everything she ought to be: faithful, loving, gentle, kind, understanding. She knows she has the best of men, but she'd prefer the beast."

"I must say, she never shows it."

"Yes, her manners are perfect! But every now and then, when we three are alone at the house, she lets him have it. She'll tell a scabrous story and wink at me — the splendid decorator turned Wife of Bath — and when he simply smiles, she shouts at him, 'Oh, come off it, Hugo, you know you hate it when I talk that way! Why don't you call me a slut and tell me to hold my tongue!' And he simply smiles again and says mildly, 'Very well, you're a slut, my dear, but even God couldn't make you hold your tongue.' You see, she cannot make him lose his temper, though she knows he has one. She knows he's stronger than she is, and it drives her mad! Perhaps she suspects he's holding on to his temper until the day he kills her."

Danny *did* carry one along. I was almost awed. "But he never will."

"He never will. That's *her* punishment."

"Oh, now you *are* being the novelist!"

"Actually, it's all guesswork and intuition. But with a great novelist, guesswork and intuition can become fact."

"And what does your intuition tell you about Hugo? Does he divert himself?"

"With other women? Or with boys? Definitely not. He's too romantic to fall out of love with the Vera his imagination once created. And too loyal to break a vow even made to a god in whom he doesn't believe. And there's another impediment. Vera watches him like a hawk. She'd scratch the eyes out of any woman who so much as looked at him!"

"But that's the double standard in reverse!"

"And with a vengeance! She wants to *possess* Hugo, but if she can't, no other woman is going to."

"I suppose that's a kind of love."

Danny threw up his arms. "Spare me such love!"

As I now began to reflect on what such a novel would do to poor Hugo, I found myself reaching around desperately in my mind to find a remedy.

"Is there anything I can offer you for a subject instead of the Warrens? Suppose you take me? And be just as godawful as you like. I shan't blink."

"*You!*" Danny gave vent to a screech of laughter. "But what in God's name could I do with the likes of you? You're not a man; you're an eye. The greatest voyeur in town!"

"You call me that? *You!*"

"Certainly I do. Because I watch people and re-create them. You watch them because you want to *become* them. You're a kind of monster."

"*Merci du compliment.*"

"But it is one, in a way. You're like the confidant in a French classic tragedy. You don't *do* anything, but without you we'd know nothing about the hero. You're Pylade to my Oreste."

"Then I'll keep my mouth shut and extinguish you."

"Now don't get angry, Oscar. You have your own importance."

"As a footnote in the biography of Daniel Winslow?"

"As its author."

"But I've just told you. I won't write it."

"But you will. It'll be your function. And I won't be your only subject, either. Remember: the confidant always survives the hero. It is Horatio who gets to say 'Good night, sweet prince' as the curtain falls."

Really, his conceit was unendurable. And I knew there was nothing I could do to turn him from his goal.

❧ ❧ ❧

Constance proved as right about Danny as she was to prove about so many things in our shared future. Less than a year after her prediction he took his leave of the Warrens, allowing them to give him a gala farewell party, and sailed for France, the postwar asylum of so many restless and disturbed American artists and writers. Not long after his departure it was revealed that he had left the manuscript of his new novel with a rival publisher. Hugo, of course, declined to enforce his option. When I expressed outrage at Danny's behavior, he shrugged and said: "If you only *knew*, my dear Oscar, how often this happens in our unhappy trade. The juiciest tidbit for many a writer is the hand that fed him. What can he do? It's simply his nature. You know what they say: If you can't stand the heat . . ."

Vera was far less patient. Her cries of indignation were heard all over town. But these were nothing to those which resounded when the book appeared. The picture of Hugo was bad enough

— very much what Danny had described to me — but that of Vera was simply appalling. Not only her hand but her whole arm and shoulder had been gobbled up. Here are the opening lines of one chapter:

"In old Moscow, when Czarina Catherine was ready to choose her night's companion, she would summon the sentries on duty in the corridor, line them up in her bedchamber and compare, when they had dropped their pants, the size of their organs. But hers was the gratification of an absolute power. Elantha's options were more limited. She had to prowl among the youths of the rather epicene staff of her decorating establishment in search of the prettiest boy . . ."

A later chapter shifted the point of view from the omniscient author to that of one Bobby, a twenty-year-old summer employee who aspires to a permanent job with the great Elantha on his graduation from City College. He is a mild young man with a mild girlfriend with whom he hopes one day to be united in a mild marriage; he is so far unknown to women. He can hardly believe what he fears to be the meaning of his boss's "strange oeiliads" (Danny took the word from Goneril in *Lear*), which are soon followed by sly hand pats and then fanny tweaking when they are sorting out materials. Yet there are no words to match these seemingly amatory gestures; all the while Elantha is barking at him for his mistakes, "chewing him out," as if there were no correlation between her fingers and her tongue. But at last comes the inevitable confrontation behind the closed door of her inner sanctum, when she pulls down his trousers and lifts her skirt. What can the poor boy do but close his eyes and concentrate on a kind of masturbation, achieving orgasm in the end with a still limp penis? And then make his escape as fast as he can, like the male mantis fleeing the fate of being devoured by the larger female in a postcoital meal. Needless to add, he does not get the permanent job. He doesn't even finish the summer one.

Hugo had a hard time dissuading his outraged spouse from a libel suit. His argument — that Danny's counsel might find damaging witnesses from the many whom Vera, a hot-tempered employer, had discharged — at last won out. But the affair certainly qualified his general endorsement of his favorite young writer. As he told me: "Of course, the picture of Vera in the book is as odious as it is untrue." He looked at me a bit sharply as he said this, but I offered him no indication of disbelief. "And despite what I have said about writers' greater licenses, I cannot condone it. It is unlikely that Danny will ever find himself in my path again, but if he does I shall quietly turn my back. But had he in the novel confined himself to Hugo Warren, it would have been otherwise. I might even have shaken his hand. I was fair game, and he knew it."

And, indeed, if Hugo has survived to this day in the minds of many who did not know him personally, it is through Danny's novel. For despite the characterization of its hero as the weak and imposed-upon partner of a bizarre marriage, his charm and kindness emerge with a crystalline clarity, and, like his model, he enchants the reader. The stage dramatization of the book provided a starring role for Herbert Marshall; the much later movie, one for Robert Montgomery. So perhaps, in the end, Hugo was right to place his faith in Danny Winslow.

And also in the end Danny fooled me again. For he *did*, after all, have a "weak ticker" and died at the age of thirty-six. By then Constance and I had been married a decade. I wanted to sell the manuscripts of his Yale *Lit* stories, which he had, quite unexpectedly, bequeathed to me, but she suggested that I hold out for a higher market. I still have them, for his values are still rising!

THE NOVOCAINE OF ILLUSION

In 1927 Jason, Fairfax & Dunne sent me to Paris to establish a branch office. I was thirty-two and a recently made member of the firm, and I had persuaded my father (now my partner) that we would not be truly "competitive" until we had a European base. But that was only half my motive. I wanted to spend a couple of years abroad, to perfect my French, to cosmopolitanize myself, in short, to soak my senses in an older and richer culture. I had been only too sharply aware of the growing crudeness of the postwar world: the jazziness, the loose manners, the general loss of "tone," and I wanted to breathe in the air of an earlier and purer era before it should be totally polluted by the fogs of modernity. I realize how smug that sounds, but I am taking great care to reproduce as closely as possible just how I then felt and to curb the temptation to bring myself more attractively up to date. But I will say this much for my then powers of observation. Like my father, I had never adopted the European view that America had vulgarized the world. We had simply been the first victims of the twentieth-century cultural virus that has since swept the globe. It was all very well for Kipling to say of the East and the West that never the twain shall meet, but go to the Orient today and you'll find every city reminiscent of Newark, New Jersey.

Constance was as keen to live in Paris as I. Since her Barnard days she had maintained her interest in art, particularly religious art. She wanted to go in seriously for Romanesque churches and had started mapping out motor trips to Burgundy and Provence as soon as we arrived. I had not told her of my own plan to write a book on artists and writers of the *belle époque*, fearing that she might turn up her nose at another manifestation at what she called my weakness for the "silly clever" art of the nineties. It was always better to be discreet with Constance until one's projects were well formulated.

We rented a big white *hôtel* with large french windows and paneled rooms furnished in Louis XV style in the Parc Monceau and hired four cheerful and tireless servants and a *bonne* for our small son, Gordon. The setting-up of a branch law office was not an arduous task, nor was the work oppressive (one of our principal functions was to take care of visiting partners and clients and get them tickets for the Folies Bergères), and I relished the ample time I had to cultivate the society of those figures who had known the era and the artists I hoped to treat.

It was not long before we met the dean of the American community, the international lawyer, epicure and expatriate bachelor Walter Berry. Constance and I dined with him and had him for dinner, and he gave me some very useful tips about hiring my French legal staff. But I wanted much more. I wanted to share his memories.

I was perfectly aware of Berry's reputation among some of my compatriots as a dry and snobbish old dilettante, and indeed I found him gruff and peremptory, but I did not despair of ultimately penetrating to the man whose discriminating love of art and letters had to be his central passion. For hadn't three great writers, Henry James, Edith Wharton and Proust, accorded him their friendship and admiration? *That* for me would drown out the boos of any mob.

Constance did not share my enthusiasm. "He yawns in my face while I'm talking to him."

"But that's all right if he does it to everyone."

And it seemed that he did. He certainly did it to me. But one day when he accepted, after a long and hardly complimentary pause, my invitation to lunch at the Travellers' Club, I determined to make my direct attack. He kept me waiting a long time, and by the time I at last saw the very tall, lean, white-haired figure, with the drooping moustaches, loom in the doorway of the lounge, I had almost given him up.

At table after a few desultory remarks — my polite questions and his monosyllabic responses — I came straight to the point. Would he help me with a book I wished to write?

"You mean edit it for you?" he demanded roughly. "For grammar perhaps? From what I know of your generation, they've rather skipped that subject. It isn't even taught in your schools anymore, is it? No wonder Americans have such difficulty learning other languages. They can't even speak their own."

But I was ready to swallow any insult. "No, sir, it wouldn't involve that at all. I'd simply like to talk to you about some of the great artists and writers you've known. Some of whom you've even inspired!" Oh, like Disraeli with royalty, I laid it on with a trowel! "Take for example James's famous letter to you in the Lubbock Collection. The one where he acknowledges your gift of a dressing case. You remember it was so gorgeous he had to call it *he* and not *it?* And now I quoted from memory. "'I can't live with him, you see, because I can't live *up* to him. His claims, his pretensions, his dimensions, his assumptions and consumptions, above all the manner in which he causes every surrounding object to tell a dingy or deplorable tale — all this makes him the very scourge of my life, the very blot on my scutcheon!'"

My memory proved a crock of gold. The old boy took my quote as a seal takes a flung fish. "Ah, the great Henry! Who else but he could have written that? Well, well. Tell me about your book, young man."

I cleared my throat. "Well, I start with Henry Adams's thesis that science has brought us chaos along with multiplicity. And that the end of an ordered world, the end of what he calls 'unity,' came with Armageddon in 1914."

"With the Boches, yes. But are you sure your dates are right? Didn't Adams feel that chaos was well on its way when General Grant was elected? As I recall it, he likened him to a caveman."

"That's true. But I'm dealing with the last great sunset of unity, which I put in the decades immediately preceding the war. Wasn't it then that our civilization reached its peak? Then science still ministered to our comfort, not our destruction. As your friend Mrs. Wharton wrote, the motorcar restored romance to travel. It was still a domesticated animal, not one of a thundering herd. And everywhere the arts were triumphant. In America we founded our great museums. We produced writers like James and Mrs. Wharton, architects like McKim and White, painters like Sargent, sculptors like Saint-Gaudens, art collectors like Morgan and Frick and Mrs. Gardner. It was rightly called the American Renaissance! And over here you had the impressionists and Anatole France and Proust and all the brilliance of Paris in the nineties. And in England . . . well, when I think of Edwardian England I seem to see endless lawns and noble mansions and weekend parties with great statesmen and wits. Am I making a point at all? Wasn't it the last great explosion of *style?* And isn't style the essence of civilization? And haven't we lost it?"

"Ah, to whom do you ask that?" Berry raised his hands to his temples in a gesture of despair. "Here I am, doing my feeble best to catch up with the Roaring Twenties, as I believe they are now called, and you tempt me to indulge in shameless memories of a golden past! Fie upon you, young man. But of course you're absolutely right. Talleyrand said that no man who had not lived in the *ancien régime* could have known the *douceur de vivre*, but I wager he would have qualified that statement had he survived to the Gay Nineties. Had he been able for a single fortnight to slip into the shoes of his collateral descendant, my old friend Boni de Castellane, and preside at a costume ball at his pink palace! Or had he spent a weekend at Blenheim when the Marlboroughs were entertaining the Prince of Wales. Or had he journeyed to Poland to visit Elizabeth Potocki and driven a four-in-hand right into the great hall of Lancut! Yes, sir, those were the days!"

I was slightly disconcerted by his emphasis on parties and endeavored to bring his memories back to the artists and writers who would be the primary concern of my book. But it was soon evident that he hated to be tied down to particular descriptions. If I asked about Proust's conversation, he would shrug and say, "Well, you know; he talked like his books"; or if I wanted a sample of the wit of Anatole France, he would tell me he couldn't remember anything specific and that, anyway, men who dominated literary salons, as Anatole France had dominated Madame de Caillavet's, were apt to become terrible bores. When I suggested after our meal that I might call on him at his apartment to glean further reminiscences, he agreed only reluctantly.

"I never took notes, you know. I wasn't a scribbling reporter like Boswell or Saint-Simon. I *lived* in that era, you see. It wasn't my job to write it up."

And indeed when I went to his place I learned more from the inscriptions that some of his famous acquaintances had written in the books they had given him than I did from himself. It struck me at last that what he really disliked in our sessions was the contrast of his friends' accomplishments with his own more meagre ones, that it left him, as James had written of the dressing case, "to tell a dingy and deplorable tale." Berry, I concluded, wanted to be one of the gods himself on Olympus and not merely a recording angel.

This came out more definitely on only my third visit to his flat.

"See here, my friend. I think there are several persons I might send you to who can be a good deal more articulate about the past than I. I was about to say 'glibber,' but perhaps that's not quite fair. Anyway, you will be the judge of that. We might start with Violet Nelidoroff. She's much closer to your age than mine, but she has made a kind of cult of just the figures who interest you, and of course she's no mean writer herself. And where one or two of the gentlemen were concerned, she may have achieved a greater intimacy, shall we say, than was available to me. Not, however, with Marcel." Here his left eyelid descended slowly in what, despite its gravity, I supposed to be a wink. "Though she may have tried, even there. I put nothing past Violet. Anyway, she's an enchanting creature. Not everyone's cup of tea, but I think she may be yours. Go to her at tea time. It'll be worth your while."

I knew, of course, who the Princess Nelidoroff was. Everyone in Paris did. She was a Hungarian who had married a Russian nobleman who had met his death in the revolution from which she had managed to escape. She and her husband had lived in France before the war (they had returned to Moscow when he was called to military duty), and she not only spoke perfect French but wrote it, being the author of several slight but charming society novels. I was aware that there was a tendency in some quarters, particularly among women, to write her off as an airy, even a designing creature, but there was no question that she had been close to many writers and was actually supposed to have been the cause of a serious breach between Maurice Barrès and the Comtesse de Noailles. She was certainly a "must" for me.

She answered my note with a prompt invitation to tea, and I found myself at five o'clock on the given day in an *art nouveau* salon in a little jewel of a house on the Rue Monsieur, facing my hostess over a glittering tray. She was a portrait by Boldini, of an exquisite and delicate femininity, with ivory skin that seemed never to have been exposed to the sun, finely molded long bare arms and a slender graceful figure tapering down to voluptuous buttocks. When she leaned forward to ask me how I took my tea, causing her blouse to slip a bit from her rounded shoulders and a tress of fine chestnut hair to drop over her high pale forehead, she seemed to be attributing her mild disarray to a vivid interest in her visitor.

"Dear Walter Berry tells me, Mr. Fairfax, that you know more about us than we know about ourselves! I mean, of course, we old mummies who lived before the flood. How nice that you should wish to revive us!"

Her "mummies" was too obviously an affectation to warrant a rebuttal. I wondered whether she could have been more than forty. Possibly, for she was very artful. "He assured me that you would be my indispensable guide," I replied. "He quoted Walter Gay as saying that if he were ever tempted to paint a human figure into one of his exquisite unpeopled interiors of châteaux, it would be the Princess Nelidoroff. And he told me that Henry Adams himself had taken you on tours of Chartres. Is it true?"

"It's true that he took me on *one*, the old darling. He even told me that my soul was expressed in the taller of the two spires, the so-called new one. That I was more Diane de Poitiers than Eleanor of Aquitaine. I hoped he meant it as a compliment. But we all know that he considered the 'old' tower the most beautiful man-made thing on earth."

"Well, of course, in architecture he preferred the twelfth century. But I think he wanted his women to be Renaissance."

"*Speriamo!*"

"And what man would not prefer the lovely Diane to the iron Eleanor? Perhaps Mrs. Cameron was his Eleanor."

"She certainly kept an iron hand on him! Nor did I note any velvet glove. She made sure that I wasn't taken on a second tour!"

I called on the princess three times in the following fortnight. She was indeed the opposite of Berry in her reminiscences. If he was reluctant to contrast his doings with the more heralded ones of his friends, she was delighted to bracket herself and her work with that of her peers, and often to her own advantage. She did not hesitate, for example, to suggest that there were aspects of her personality in Proust's Albertine, or that she had given Henri Bernstein some helpful hints for the resolution of his play *Le Secret*, or that it was she who had persuaded Reynaldo Hahn to try his hand at opera. I did not believe it all, but I believed some of it, and I began to wonder whether her lively accounts might not make up several chapters in my book.

Constance did not at all approve of these meetings. I had had by now, of course, to explain the reasons for my unaccompanied visits to Berry and the princess. She insisted that jealousy had nothing to do with her disapproval — she denied that she could have that feeling for such a "phony" as she had found Violet on their single meeting at Berry's — but she warned me that I was being taken in by my own bedazzlement with an age of tinsel that I stubbornly held to be gold. She had a temporary triumph over me at a Sunday lunch party at the Pavillon Colombe in Saint-Brice, where we were the guests of Edith Wharton. We had had letters to the great novelist from mutual friends in New York, but, better yet, I had successfully handled a small legal matter that she had referred to my firm.

Mrs. Wharton was then in her mid-sixties, at the apex of her career, with fine strong features, a straight back and a high clear voice that perfectly articulated her neatly constructed sentences. People who found her "formidable" were simply not used to the more disciplined manner in which she had been raised. She and I were getting on very well in a discussion about her close friend Walter Berry, and the patriotic work he had done during the war, until I chanced to mention the princess. At this her lips formed a line as hard as a mailbox slit.

"Walter and I have many interests in common, Mr. Fairfax, but I'm afraid Princess Nelidoroff is not one of them."

I hastily retreated. "I only mentioned her because she is so devoted a fan of your fiction."

"I cannot return the compliment. Madame Nelidoroff chooses to call herself a Francophile, but I have it on what I regard as unimpeachable authority that when she visited Vienna in 1917, she formed an intimate association with the German military attaché. *Parlons d'autre chose.*"

I abandoned the poor princess with instant disloyalty and partially redeemed myself by returning to the subject of Berry's role in working for the United States' entry into the war. And when my hostess learned that I myself had been in the trenches, my reference to Violet was quite forgiven. Like Berry, she was a real old warhorse.

Halfway through our meal, Constance embarrassed me by announcing to the table the project of my book. The other guests, however, seemed to be amused by the idea, and names of artists and writers deemed worthy of inclusion were suggested. The discussion soon focused on Proust, the last of whose posthumous volumes had just appeared. Someone suggested that he was greater than Balzac and Tolstoy. Mrs. Wharton demurred.

"I don't mean that he wasn't a great writer," she conceded. "But to me there are lapses in his moral sensibility that must deny him the very highest rank." She now cited the passage where the narrator of *À la Recherche* climbs up a ladder to a transom window to spy on Julien, the tailor, and the Baron de Charlus, involved, as she delicately put it, in an "unedifying scene."

I asked her, in the amused silence that followed this, whether she had ever known Proust.

"Well, as I'm sure you know, he was a great friend of Walter's. Proust even dedicated an early book to him. And Walter was always after me to meet him. But when I learned that he was dazzled by all the dukes and duchesses he satirized, I decided he was not my fare. After all, I could delight in his prose without being a witness to his social climbing."

Constance nodded vigorously at this and then jumped rather too noisily into the discussion. "Isn't that true of many writers, Mrs. Wharton? Isn't their criticism of the social ladder invalidated by the way they try to scramble up it?" Here she glanced at me. "Or at least by the glee they take in watching others try?"

"It was certainly true of Thackeray," our hostess replied thoughtfully. "And I'm afraid of Balzac, too. Lord knows it was true of Disraeli! And as for Bourget . . . but hush, he's my good friend."

"It could never be said of *you*, Mrs. Wharton," I put in. "Nobody could think that you were dazzled by the Trenors or the Dorsets in *The House of Mirth*."

"No, I guess not," she responded with a pleasant chuckle. "It has even been said that I fled to France to get away from Fifth Avenue and Newport. But when one has been born and raised in that kind of world, it's hard to be impressed by it, unless, of course, one is stupid or lacking in all imagination. No doubt it can glitter to those who are not in it. Like a dance in a ballroom spied from a dark street. I suppose one should sympathize, yet people rarely do. It's odd, isn't it, that society should despise those who are trying to get into it? You'd think they might take it as a compliment."

"Maybe it's because they see how dangerous the climbers are!" Constance's emphasis mortified me. It was quite out of key with the light tone of the table. "People who want to know other people for the wrong reasons may undermine the very world they're trying to crash!"

The table was silent, and Mrs. Wharton rose. "That's an interesting idea, Mrs. Fairfax, and we might go on with it outside. It's such a lovely day, do you think we should adjourn to the garden, everyone? My roses are really quite fine this year. You must forgive an old gardener her vanity."

❧ ❧ ❧

A great friend of Constance's, David Finch, had now arrived to spend the balance of the spring in Paris. He was a bachelor of some forty years, gentle, short and balding, but of a neat figure, soft voice and charming manner, who taught Latin and Greek at a boys' boarding school in New England, from which he was now enjoying a sabbatical. Well-to-do, intensely intellectual and highly popular with both faculty and students, he seemed to have everything a man could desire, except for a wife and family. But he appeared to be perfectly content without these appendages, nor did he show any ambition for academic honors beyond the privilege of enlightening his pupils. Constance had a younger brother whose troubled youth Finch had been most helpful in straightening out, and her father, in his gratitude, had practically adopted him as a member of the family. Finch's many interests included Romanesque arches and capitals, and Constance, with whom he was reputed to be harmlessly and rather touchingly in love, had insisted that he should join us on all our projected motor trips. I indeed had no objection, as he was the best of travelling companions, punctual, alert, well-informed and good-tempered, and he had always taken care to make himself agreeable to me.

He and Constance now embarked on exhaustive sightseeing in Paris and its *environs*, and one day, when I was told not to expect them back from Fontainebleau before a late dinner, I thought it the perfect time to invite Violet (whom, as I have made sufficiently clear, Constance detested) to come for one of our talks at the house in the Parc Monceau.

It started as one of our better meetings. Violet arrived late, as she always did, and stayed even later, admiring everything in the house before settling down on the divan to sip champagne, but when she embarked at last on her reminiscences, she had never been livelier. She sprinkled her talk with some wonderfully malicious stories about Berry and Edith Wharton, who she insisted had been lovers, and about Henry James and the young Danish sculptor of huge ghastly nude figures whom the Master had so oddly favored. But it was on Proust that she was at her best.

"Yes, indeed, I was a frequent visitor to that cork-lined chamber! He knew by that time, poor darling, that he was not long for this world, and he was working feverishly to finish his book. He was pathetically eager to be supplied with details in matters with which he was not intimately familiar, particularly women's things: hats, dresses, visits to couturières, little points of etiquette. You've read of course *Le Temps Retrouvé*, just out this year. Well, you will remember how the narrator meets the now aged Duchesse de Guermantes at a reception and describes how she has lost her old eminence in the social world. And how, when she invites people to dinner to meet a royalty, and still uses the archaic form that begins: 'Her Majesty, the Queen of Naples' — or whatever — 'has commanded the Duchesse de Guermantes to' . . . or 'has deigned to' . . . the younger people deduce that she must be some sort of *déclassée* duchess! Well, it was *I* who supplied him with that gem! I had actually heard some idiot of a parvenu express that same opinion of the Duchesse de Nîmes when the latter had *stooped* to ask her to meet the King of Spain! What *have* we come to?"

"But, first, where *were* we?"

Violet and I glanced up to see Constance standing, somehow grimly, in the doorway. Violet rose immediately and hurried over with outstretched hand to greet her, but my wife, in removing her hat, managed, without too obvious rudeness, to avoid the contact.

"My dear Madame Fairfax, you catch me boring your patient husband with tales of the dark ages! I was just telling him of my sessions with poor dying Proust. But enough of that. How are *you, ma toute belle?*"

Her *toute belle* did not bother to respond, but took a chair and gave me a long, steady look. When she spoke, it was to address me as if there were no one else present.

"I heard the name of the Duchesse de Nîmes. You know, her brother married an old friend of Father's, Miss Gray. I called on her yesterday and found her most friendly. She wants us to dine with her soon. I told her that you and Princess Nelidoroff had this project about writers of the prewar days, and we then had some talk about Proust. She told me something rather interesting about him and the princess. Perhaps your visitor will be able to verify it."

"And pray what is that, Madame?" Violet's high tone had a

trill of anxiety. "Tell me, by all means. But first I should warn you that old Eliane de Nîmes is known for her *mauvaise langue.*"

Constance still did not avert her eyes from me. "Well, maybe this will be another example of that *langue.* She says that when the princess first met Proust, which was before *Swann* had burst upon the world, she snubbed what she described as a 'little Jewish social climber.' But when he was hailed as a great writer, she immediately pursued him. And their mere acquaintance, according to Madame de Nîmes, has been growing warmer and warmer with each year since his death. She believes it may yet turn out to have been a love affair!"

"*Ah non, ça c'est trop! C'est un outrage!* Really, Madame, how can you repeat such *ordures?*"

"Because I believe them." Constance *still* did not look at my guest.

Violet turned in agitation to me. "I will not further presume on your time, dear Oscar. Madame is obviously tired. We are having a horrid spring, too rainy, too dark, too everything. I think all our nerves are a bit on edge."

And actually blowing me a defiant kiss, she hurried to the door.

❧ ❧ ❧

Constance and I had a terrible row, the worst in our whole married life. Two days later, when we were still hardly on speaking terms, she announced coolly, on my return from the office, that she had decided that a temporary separation might be in order; she was departing in the morning for a motor trip in Burgundy.

"All by yourself? Won't that be rather dreary?"

"But I shan't be by myself. David is coming with me."

"You and David alone together? You can't do that!"

"And just why can't I?"

"How can you ask such a question? How do you think it will look?"

"I suppose it will look like you and the princess."

I gasped. All the French things in the room seemed to jump about. "Are you crazy? Violet is simply helping me with a book I want to write."

"Tell that to the marines!"

"Really, Constance, you don't mean to say that you're actually jealous?"

"I'm not jealous at all. If you choose to make a fool of yourself with that ridiculous creature, that's entirely up to you. But it certainly deprives you of any right to point the finger at me and David."

"Point the finger?" I felt now actually giddy. "Are you implying there's really something to point the finger *at?*"

"I thought *you* were the one implying it. Look, Oscar. Enough of this. David and I are going on a short motor trip to Burgundy. That's your *donnée*, as the French say. What you think of it is your affair. First, I gather, you worry about how it will look to others. Now you begin to wonder how it looks to *you.* But all that concerns *me* is how it looks to *me.* And I think it looks just fine. But no matter what you say or how you fuss about it, I can assure you that it's going to take place, and no later than tomorrow morning."

"You can't mean that you've fallen in love with that little man!" Was it my voice that had uttered that? The unbelievable words seemed to bounce from panel to artificial panel of our fake Louis XV parlor.

"I don't think I'm going to dignify that question with an answer. Except to say that *if* I have, I didn't have to overcome any vulgar prejudice against his size."

"Oh, Constance, what's this all about? Tell me I'm crazy."

"You're crazy."

"Put off your trip for a week. I'll see if I can't postpone my work at the office. We'll all three go."

"But I don't *want* to go with you. The whole point is to get away from you."

"You mean you *prefer* David's company to mine?"

"As a Romanesque expert? Yes, much."

"Let's look at the trip from his point of view. Do you think it's fair to him to take him away like this?"

"Why on earth not?"

"Don't you know that he's supposed to be in love with you?"

"Why should I object to that? It makes him a charming companion."

"Constance! He'll get ideas!"

"Let him! Do you really think I can't take care of myself?"

"Oh, I'm sure you can. But alone with a man in love . . ."

She cut me off. "You must know by now that when I've once made up my mind to do something, I always do it. Very well, then. I'm going on this trip. I've written out my itinerary and where I can be reached every day. You'll find it on your desk in the library. Of course, I'll want to know how Gordon is. And now I suggest that we drop the subject."

"Promise me you won't share a room with Finch!"

"Really, Oscar, you embarrass me. I'm going upstairs to pack. And I don't care to dine with you in the mood you're in. I'll have a salad sent up to my room. And I'll be gone tomorrow at the crack. You needn't get up to see me off."

With which she left me! I had every intention of rising early and making a last effort at least to delay the excursion, but I tossed so restlessly in bed that at last I took two pills, which so knocked me out that I slept not only through her departure but a couple of hours thereafter.

The next week was an appalling one. I found it almost impossible either to work in the office or to sleep at night. I kept telling myself that Constance would never betray me, that hers was the coolest of temperaments, that if she had really wanted to have an affair with Finch she would have taken *some* trouble to conceal it, that I had always known she had scorned convention and held herself accountable to no one, and, finally, that if she *had* wanted a lover she would have chosen a more virile type. But against these arguments the devil's advocate in my soul would point out that there had always been important divisions between us and that Paris had certainly widened them, that Constance had no moral standards where sex was concerned, that she had always maintained that no rational spouse could be seriously hurt by the other's occasional "kicking up" of his or her heels, that monogamy was not a natural state except for Canada geese and that brains and sympathy in a man could have more sex appeal than brawn. I had assumed that her theories were just intellectual games, but why should I have been so sure? Wasn't she perfectly capable of having her fling and returning to me, quite shameless, to pick up her marriage exactly where she had left it? And if I should do the same, would she care? Might she not even, intolerably, just snicker if I had an affair with the princess?

Well, *that*, one evening in a session with Violet, after several gin drinks, was what I precisely decided to have. As I redfacedly recall it, I copied the deliberately planned steps of Julien Sorel in his seduction of Madame de Renal in *Le Rouge et le Noir*. But by the time I had reached over to take Violet's hand, I realized that no such strategy would be needed.

She had been telling me a salacious anecdote about Paul Bourget and Guy de Maupassant in a brothel, which she claimed to have had from the saintly Abbé Mugnier himself. "Maupassant came up suddenly behind Bourget and yanked down his pants, crying, '*C'est tout ce que vous avez à montrer à ces dames?*' And Bourget fled! Don't you adore it?"

It was then that my hand grasped hers.

"I adore this!" I muttered.

Her look of only too genuine surprise took me very much aback.

"Heavens! And I thought you were the prototype of the American *mari fidèle.* But very well! Give me fifteen minutes and then come up to my room. It's at the top of the stairs to the left."

I had two more drinks before I went up. God knows what sort of wretched performance I put on. Violet was as smoothly compliant and easily available as a man could have possibly imagined, but I had nonetheless the humiliating impression that nothing of any importance was happening to her. Looking back on the incident with the burning shame of later days, and proving, if proof were needed, how deeply my sexual emotions were embedded in French fiction, I likened it to the scene in Proust where the elegant Madame Swann gives herself to Bloch, an utter stranger, with the rapid expertise of a professional, in the compartment of a railway car. Violet could have done that — and later coolly cut him dead if she happened to see him in society. At any rate I could rest assured that the episode would have no further consequences for her, except for some legal services that she was later to seek and I to render, without fee of course, when she was sued for plagiarism in one of her novels.

But, alas, it was not so with me. The episode was only too full of consequence. I found myself plunged in a deep depression of remorse. It seemed to me that I had lost for all time what I nostalgically deemed my American innocence, without gaining so much as standing room in the Gallic theatre of sexual sophistication. Not, indeed, that I any longer coveted even a front seat in the latter. Violet's very facility in copulation repelled me, and the clumsy pleasures of our native embracements, at least as I had lawfully known them, appeared to me now as an Eden that I had forever forfeited. The sad and reproachful image of Constance loomed over the ashes of my illusions as the only woman, indeed the only person, I had ever really loved.

The immediate practical effect of my disillusionment was my loss of all interest in the little book I had projected. Constance's arguments against it now struck me as entirely valid. My golden age of writers and artists was auric only in the metallic sense. What they had valued was simply the beauty of *things*.

My mind teemed with relentless analysis. Why were Sargent's portraits of women so much finer than those of his men? Didn't the rich silks and satins of their gowns, the gleam of their pearls, the luster of their diamonds, the glinting colors of their *armoires* and *bergères* and the glaze of their porcelain try to make up for the insipidity of their handsome, aristocratic countenances? What would Henry James's most ably drawn characters of his late style — Strether and Maggie Verver and Milly Theale — be without the glory of Paris in the spring or the smartness of London in the season or the drama of Venice in the fall? And had not Edith Wharton been a pioneer in interior decoration before she illuminated her novels with such wonderful dwellings for her characters?

I began to see everything and everyone in this new light. Saint-Gaudens and Stanford White had been intoxicated with all that was gaudiest in the Italian Renaissance. Proust had reveled in duchesses and titles, seeing human aspirations solely in terms of snobbery. If art at the end was all in all to him, what was art but the depiction of the high life he professed to despise? What was any novel of manners, basically, but that? Even Huysmans, deploring the decadence of elegant tastes, amused his readers only by describing them. I began to wonder whether the only honest artist, of all I had wished to honor, was not Walter Gay, three of whose paintings of châteaux' interiors I had purchased to adorn our parlor. For he never showed any people in them. His beautiful chambers were the true portraits of the souls of their owners.

I turned at last to read again the great passage in Henry Adams's *Education* where he describes how he sat on the steps beneath Richard Morris Hunt's Beaux Arts dome at the Chicago World's Fair, as Gibbon had sat on the steps of the Ara Coeli, and contemplated a world where his old friends might have come in at last as winners in the great American chariot race for fame. Would the people of the Northwest, he wondered, "some day talk about Hunt, and Richardson, La Farge and Saint-Gaudens, Burnham and McKim and Stanford White, when their politicians and millionaires were otherwise forgotten?" But his old friends, he went on ruefully to admit, did not think so; they talked as though art to the Western people was a stage decoration, a diamond shirt stud, a paper collar.

And I concluded that maybe the "Western people" were right.

❧ ❧ ❧

It occurred to me at last that there was one man in Paris who might help me with my inner troubles, who might even have shared them without losing, to put it violently, his soul, and that was Violet's great friend, the Abbé Mugnier. He was the highly cultivated but still saintly old priest, the darling of the *grandes dames* of the Old Faubourg, whose devotion to the great writers of his time had made him as well known in the literary as in the social world. Slow-moving, near-sighted, serene and gentle of manner, a shabby black figure whose usually kindly discourse was tempered with an occasional caustic witticism, his appearance in every gilded salon was greeted with little enthusiastic cries from the hostess gliding to greet him. Violet, who prided herself on being one of his "adopted nieces," had brought me together with him on two occasions, when I had had the joy of hearing him discuss his conversion of Huysmans and his theological arguments with Zola.

When therefore the Duchesse de Nîmes invited me to meet him at lunch in her great *hôtel* in the Rue du Varenne, where I knew I could be sure, because of my hostess's animosity to her, of not seeing Violet, I eagerly accepted. That day the great Abbé was to change my life, but not, as I had anticipated, with a talk about art and literature, but with a talk about *me.*

I had no chance to speak to him during our sumptuous meal in the great paneled Louis XV dining hall, where the ladies on either side of him vied for his attention; but afterwards, when the guests were leaving and I heard him ask the duchess if he might take a little stroll in her garden, I immediately followed him silently towards the back of the house. Before going out he paused in the hallway to examine, his nose almost touching the canvas, a charming little Fragonard of a nude nymph bathing in a fountain, coyly aware of a peering gallant hiding in the bushes. Suddenly a genially mocking voice rang out from behind me.

"*Ah, tu aimes ces nudités, mon cher Abbé? Tu n'as pas honte?*"

It was our host, who had come up to be sure the Abbé found the door to the garden. I had noted that the husbands of the Abbé's friends treated him with less ceremony. They were inclined to be more cynical about his enjoyment of the world.

"*C'est un état d'âme,*" was the Abbé's serene reply as he stepped through the door which the duke now opened for him. Outside I asked him whether I might join him in his stroll, and he nodded benignly. He seemed to have sensed that I wished to consult him about something more serious than his love of gardens, and his mild but educated comments on the flower beds that we passed may have been designed to allow my nerves to settle.

"I wanted to tell you, Monsieur l'Abbé," I blurted out at last, "how deeply I admire the way you reconcile your love of God with your love of beautiful things."

He paused to beam a small, doubting smile at me. "I have learned, my dear young man, that when people say such things to me, they are apt to imply that I'm a sad worldling. You heard our host just now?"

"But I had no such thing in mind!" I protested in dismay. "I meant quite the opposite. I meant that you see God in everything. Or does that sound silly? Of course, he must be in everything, mustn't he?"

"In this beautiful garden and this noble mansion? Even in this *mondain* lunch party? Well, of course, he must be. But where am *I;* that's the point, isn't it? Am I with *him*, or am I with the silver épergnes, the *tartes au crème*, the lovely boiseries, the enchanting ladies? That question I sometimes ask myself when I visit the poor, the sick and the dying."

"But it's only the beauty in all those things that you admire!" I insisted hotly. "As you do the beauty in all the books you care so much about. Oh, I've heard you on the subject of your beloved Chateaubriand. God for you is in art! And that's where I've lost my faith! Can you help me to gain it back?"

"Well, I certainly don't believe that God was with Savanarola when he made his bonfire of the vanities in Florence. Think of all the wonderful things that must have gone up in flames on that terrible day! But that poor misguided monk did have one point. If God is in art, maybe that's why the devil lurks so near the shrine. To catch the votaries when they least expect him!"

"And to send them to hell," I mused, struck with his notion. "Do you believe in hell, Father?"

"My answer to that question is that I must. It's doctrine. But I needn't believe there's anyone in it, need I?"

"I sometimes wonder if my wife, for all her professed free-thinking, doesn't believe there are quite a few people in it."

"Tell me about your wife, Mr. Fairfax. She was not here today. I trust she is not ill?"

"Oh, no, she's quite well. She's making a little tour of Romanesque churches in Burgundy. With a friend. A man friend." I allowed my voice to drop to a sinister note. I must have sounded very silly. But he ignored my implication.

"Ah, yes, how edifying. Those churches are very wonderful. But if I may advert to a less happy topic, I was sorry to hear there had been something of an unpleasantness between your wife and Princess Nelidoroff."

"Oh, Violet told you about that?"

"Violet and I are very close. She has seen fit to adopt me as what she flatteringly calls her guide and mentor. Violet has her little foibles — as which of us has not? — but it occurred to me that Mrs. Fairfax may have been a touch too hard on her. Is that possible?"

"Mrs. Fairfax was brutal to her!"

"Ah, then, my friend, if I may make a suggestion, was there an element of female jealousy in the situation? My niece is very lovely, and you and she had been meeting, as I understand it, alone together?"

I suddenly realized that he knew all. "Has Violet told you what happened between her and me?" The Abbé's silence was that of assent. "I suppose she was bound to, in confession."

"It was *not* in confession, Mr. Fairfax."

"No, she wouldn't have regarded it as a sin, would she?" I

exclaimed in a sudden bleat of bitterness. "It wouldn't be a sin for her, would it, if there was no pleasure in it?"

"That sounds like one of your American puritan doctrines. It seems to me it would still be very much of a sin." The Abbé was now almost stern. "And if I did not mistake your tone a minute ago, you implied that it was one of which your wife and a certain gentleman might also be guilty?"

I was desperate now. "Father, what shall I do?"

"This man she's with. Is he a Frenchman?"

"No, he's a Yank. I think you've even met him. David Finch."

"Ah, yes, a very studious young man. What makes you so sure he is betraying you?"

"You think Americans are capable of adultery only with Frenchwomen?"

"Far from it. But I have seen enough Americans to know that they are not as predictable in these matters as we Gauls. You are great worriers. Which makes me want to ask you something else. May I be frank?"

"Oh, Father, if you only would be!"

He motioned me now to a pink marble bench, and we seated ourselves. "Let us hypothesize that what you now only surmise is the truth, and that your wife and Mr. Finch are actually engaged in a love affair. Isn't it possible that to them — to her, at least — the whole thing could be just as unimportant as what occurred between you and Violet?"

With a single word this now rather terrible old man had transformed my mind into the frame of a ludicrous bedroom picture. "Oh," I murmured.

"And isn't it also possible that what is troubling you is not so much the question of an affair as what the world will think of it?"

I had to brood over this for a moment. "So it's my pride, you think, and not my jealousy?"

"I merely suggest it."

"And what should I do about it?"

"Go after them, my son. Join them in their beautiful quest of the Romanesque. If they're having a serious affair, it's better that you should know. Only with facts can one make sensible decisions. And if, as I suspect, they're not, they will simply hand you a guide book and continue their sightseeing."

❧ ❧ ❧

I caught up with Constance and David in Beaune and tracked them to the Hôtel Dieu, where I found them in the great corridor of the dormitory, with its long line of splendid red-curtained cubicles. When David spotted me and hailed me with unmistakable pleasure, I knew I had been an ass.

"Oscar, what a joy! What good wind blew you to Beaune?"

"A craving for capitals and arches. You don't mind if I crash the party?"

"But it's providential! I'm afraid Constance was on the verge of deciding that two was a crowd."

Constance had said nothing. Her mildly questioning gaze seemed to await an explanation of my curious conduct. She barely responded to my peck of a kiss, and I realized that she must have told David nothing of our tiff. How like her!

"Look now," continued David, glancing at his watch. "It's lunch time, and I've booked a table at the Hôtel de la Poste. You two must have home matters to discuss, let alone little Gordon. I'll have a bite at a brasserie and join you at three."

Constance and I took him at his word, and over our very good meal I apologized humbly for my crude suspicions and crowned my humility with the admission that I had abandoned my book. I explained to her in nervous detail, too much detail, my theory of the worldliness of my chosen craftsmen. She listened, without undue attention but silently, until I finished. Then all she said was: "Well, don't overdo it. Remember Cézanne. And Joyce."

And with that I supposed I was forgiven. I was certainly allowed to join her for the rest of the tour. But when, much later, back in Paris, I summoned up the nerve at last to make a clean breast of what had so briefly and "unimportantly" occurred between me and Violet, imagining that she might see it with her much vaunted independence of mind, might even be amused by the sorry role I had played, she blew up completely and threatened for two ghastly days to leave me, taking Gordon with her. And then she suddenly dropped the subject and never mentioned it again. The priestess of the life of reason was a woman after all.

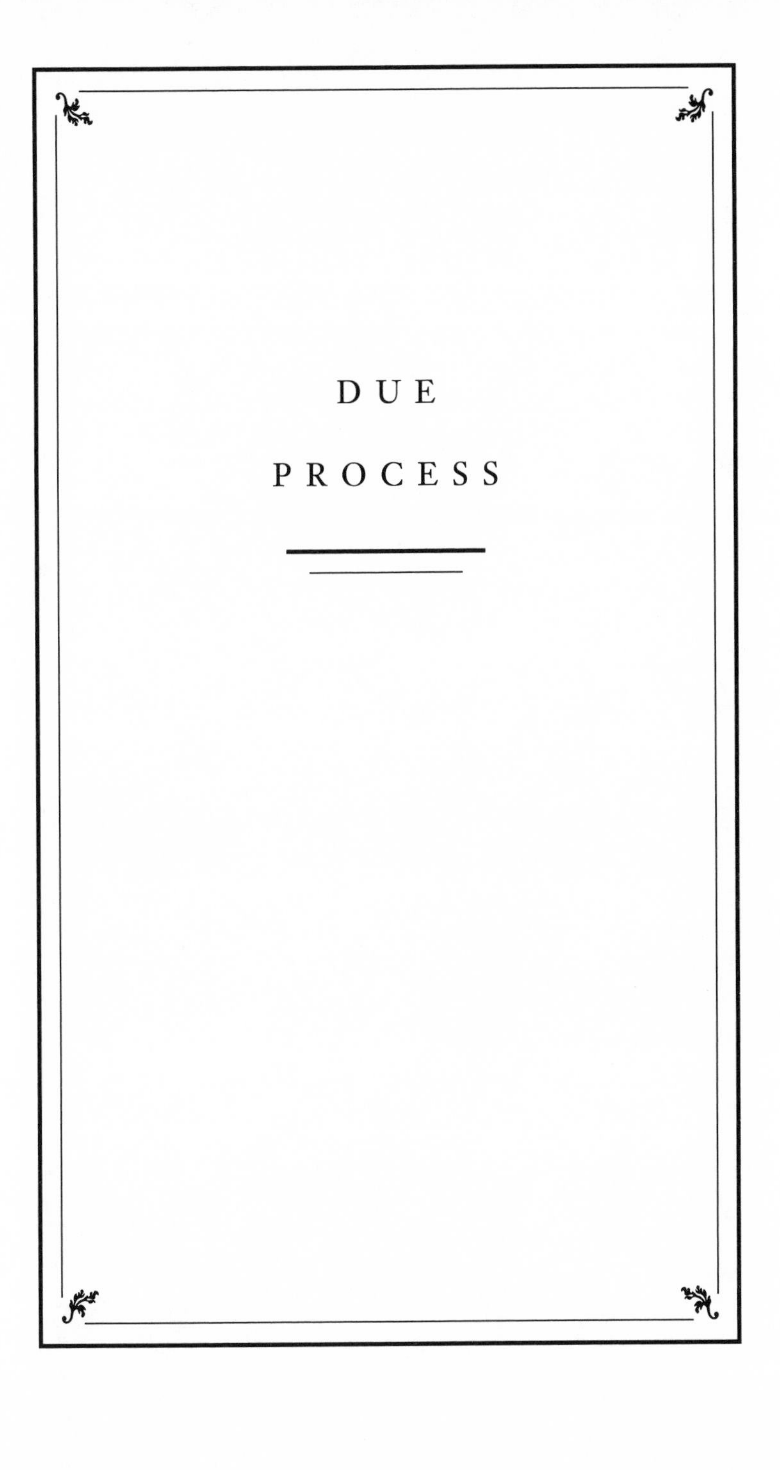

DUE PROCESS

IT WAS a considerable time before I ventured upon another book, and when I did, it was with the approval, or at least with the benign indifference, of my wife. By 1935 we had been back in New York for several years, during which my principal energies had been taken up by office work. My partners, professing admiration for my diplomatic powers with people, or perhaps deeming these superior to my legal ones, had entrusted me with the entire internal administration of the firm, which in many ways was more to my taste than the actual practice of law. I liked being concerned with the personal problems of the clerks and staff, and I made it my policy to unite the firm into a kind of family. Wages, room assignments and working conditions were not alone my business; I made a point of familiarizing myself with the health and home problems of all our employees. And I organized social occasions: dinners for the lawyers, a dance for the staff, a spring outing at a Long Island country club for everyone. A few of the older partners regarded these entertainments as extravagant, but the younger men backed me up, and I think I can pride myself that I was a pioneer in the humanization of an old-fashioned "law factory."

I tried also, but with much less success, to have a hand in the history of the firm that my father, now retired, was writing. When it was at last privately printed, I'm afraid nobody outside the partnership managed to read it all the way through. Father had listened to few suggestions; his style was dry, and the work was lightened by no personal anecdotes other than a few pallid ones about the revered eccentricities of two or three venerable founders. His emphasis on the high-mindedness of his associates, past and present, was such that a reader might have wondered whether they had not been working as much for the public good as for the interests of their clients. It was certain, anyway, that Father equated the two.

But the importance that Father's history assumed in my life was not in what it told about the firm, but in the way his chapter on Gideon Hollister sharpened and intensified my already considerable interest in that great man. Father, who had been his classmate in Harvard Law and who had persuaded him to abandon his native Boston and try his luck in New York with Jason & Fairfax, related details about his friend's early life with which I had been familiar only in outline. Hollister, as a boy, had induced his wealthy parents to let him indulge his passionate desire to harden and test himself by working in summers in western copper mines and ranches. He had taken leave of absence from our firm to join the Rough Riders in the Cuban war and followed his hero, Theodore Roosevelt, in the assault on San Juan Hill. He had again taken leave, this time of the Court of Appeals in Albany, to which bench he had been appointed at the age of forty, to serve on Pershing's staff in the Great War and, in his fifties, had seen action on the Western Front. Even as a justice on the United States Supreme Court, to which President Coolidge had raised him, he had spent summers game-hunting in Kenya. As Father wrote in one of the few vivid sentences of his book: "Mr. Justice Hollister's idea of a perfect vacation is to be alone in the wilderness with only a rifle between himself and a large charging cat or pachyderm."

The justice and I had always got on very well. He was not entirely immune to flattery, but I think he recognized my enthusiasm for the beautifully written opinions on the common law in his New York cases as entirely genuine. There was a part of him that craved recognition as an artist, and I abundantly supplied this. Also, he had been bitterly disappointed in his only son and may have been looking for a substitute. In many ways Justice Hollister was my opposite, but, unlike most men, I have always been attracted to my opposites.

But it was neither the exponent of the common law nor the warrior or big game hunter that gave me my idea for a little book of essays; it was Father's passionate admiration for Hollister as a constitutional interpreter and my recognition of how widely this attitude had been shared by Father's generation. To my parent, his friend's resolute use of the due process clause to strike down any legislation seeking to regulate big business was a case of Saint George slaying the dragon. I had very different views, but the drama of the conflict fascinated me.

Hollister's endorsement of unbridled capitalism had not been so evident when he was expounding the common law in Albany, nor had it even been much noted in Washington in the prosperous twenties, when so many were intent on rapid enrichment, but in the Great Depression, when statute after remedial statute fell before the judicial axe, his name had become as much anathema to liberals as that of his fellow justices Van Devanter, Sutherland and McReynolds.

But there was another side to the rock-ribbed individualist; there was the scholar who claimed that reading with him was a "disease," the collector of Chinese ceramics and Hudson River School landscapes, the student of English poetry and prose, the author of the famous common law opinions on torts and contracts which read like short stories by Henry James. For when Hollister the judge was not dealing with states and great corporations but with individual human beings — the victim of the defectively constructed automobile, the unwary trespasser mangled by the public nuisance, the small businessman trapped in the illusory contract — he could be very humane indeed.

These two very different men who made up Gideon Hollister were discernible in his physical appearance. Like many of the pugnacious, he was on the short side, with a trim torso always nattily attired. His lips were thin, even a bit grim; his chin as square as might have been expected; his complexion clear and unwrinkled; and his cheeks had a mild reddish tinge. But his thick hair was of a soft cottony white and his eyes were of a serene light blue. His tone could be sharp and caustic, particularly when he was addressing fumbling lawyers from the bench, but it could also be wonderfully mellifluous, when he was lecturing at clubs or bar associations on the origins of law. A widower, he lived alone in a pretty little red brick house in Georgetown full of shiningly polished gems of Colonial furniture and his collection of China trade plates and platters.

He readily agreed to assist me with my projected book of essays and offered to put me up for the night any time I cared to come to Washington to "pump" him.

"Of course, you realize I'm not a legal scholar," I warned him.

"I do, and I deem it a point in your favor. What is really needed today, my dear Oscar, is a law commentator with a clear mind, common sense and no crazy prejudices. The public is desperately in want of some straight thinking in our constitutional crisis. You've heard, of course, of the president's nefarious court-packing plan?"

"But he hasn't submitted it to Congress as yet."

"No, he's holding it up, the old fox, to give us septuagenarians the chance to quit. The bill would give him an additional judge for each of us who balks. Making a court of nine jurists and six rubber stamps!"

"But will he get it passed?"

"Who knows, in these crazy times?"

During that winter of 1936 Constance and I spent a total of three weekends with the judge. She would go sightseeing with Gordon (when the latter was with us), and I would sit with my host and listen to him. He loved to talk, and I was careful not to distract him with note-taking, knowing that I could quickly scribble down all I needed when the session was over. He would hold forth, almost as if I had not been there, about the major events of his long and interesting life, emphasizing the glories of an adventurous past, which he contrasted with the "shabby security-seeking" of our present time.

On a memorable afternoon of our second weekend he gave me what I hoped might be the binding thread of my essays. He had started the session with some reminiscences of his youth.

"My father sent me to Michigan two summers in a row to work for his friend Louis Agassiz, who was rehabilitating the abandoned Calumet and Tecla copper mines. *That* was a job that would have daunted the 'quickie' fortune hunters of today! But do you think Agassiz could have done it with labor unions shrieking for higher pay and warmer beds and not letting him fire the shirkers?"

"It would have taken longer, certainly."

"It would have been impossible! I tell you, Oscar, this equating of the weak with the strong — equating, hell; putting them *over* the strong — will be the ruin of us. If the squire of Hyde Park had been president a generation back, this country would never have been developed."

"But you admired the great Theodore. And didn't he bust the trusts?"

"I admired him more as a soldier than as a politician. He made too many compromises. I think it bothered him that so many of our financiers, like Morgan, had never worn a uniform or even taken any outdoor exercise. That may have landed him in the arms of the leftists! But even he would have gagged at the extremes to which his jaunty and irresponsible fifth cousin has gone."

I had to get him off *that.* "Let me ask you something else, sir. Our friends of the English bar claim it is better not to be constantly hampered by a written constitution. Might not you and your colleagues on the bench be better able to define the fundamental liberties of man and the fundamental restraints on government without having to twist and strain phrases dating from the eighteenth century?"

I feared an explosion, but none was forthcoming. Instead, he nodded thoughtfully several times before answering. "It's a good question. You might even argue that we don't really *have* a written constitution. In a practical sense, that is. What we have is a document containing two clauses that preoccupy the bulk of our constitutional litigation: commerce and due process. Some dozen little words that have given rise to millions and millions of others to construe them. If you could build a monolithic national government out of the power to regulate commerce, couldn't you have done it with many other powers given in that same piece of paper? Properly construed? If you can create what you want with one word, can't you do it with another? Or with none at all?"

Well, I could certainly make something out of that! Wasn't I face to face with the fascinating conjunction of the man of action, the man of battles, the man who would bend the wilderness to his will, with the man of close reasoning, of intellectual quibbles, the man to whom words were everything? Or nothing?

❧ ❧ ❧

In the spring of that year I spent a week in Washington without Constance, putting up at the Willard, as my business was not with the judge but with establishing for my firm a small branch office in the capital. I found it a good time to spend an evening with Julian Hollister and get from him some opinions about his father that, I could be sure, however hostile, would be at least provocative. For Julian was quite as brilliant as his sire, and even more mordantly amusing. There was no reason, either, that the judge should learn of any such visit; the two were barely on speaking terms.

I had known Julian, of course, most of my life; we had even been classmates at Saint Augustine's until he was expelled for demonstrating too blatantly the "wrong attitude." Indeed, from Doctor Ames's point of view, as well as from Julian's father's — as well, I might add, from that of the whole society in which he had grown up — Julian's attitude was the wrongest possible one. But he and I had managed to remain friends, largely at my urging. He used to pay me the dubious compliment that, even if I offered lip service to the establishment, I was at heart a dissenter.

"You may *look* like a stuffed shirt, Oscar, but the whole thing is really a joke to you. A rather bad joke at that."

Even in looks Julian was his father's opposite. He was tall and bonily thin, and he moved awkwardly, though as a boy he could cross his long legs behind his neck. He had a thick crop of messy black hair and a long oval face with dark, jeering eyes. His voice was harshly emphatic, and his loud laugh seemed always at his hearer's expense. But, believe it or not, he had charm. And his wife, Elizabeth, who taught economics at Georgetown University, though small and brown and plain, had simply the kindest heart in the world.

Julian, who was my age, at this point forty-one, had taught government at Harvard, written a Pulitzer Prize–winning biography of Woodrow Wilson and was presently a member of the president's "brain trust," drafting New Deal legislation. One can imagine how his father felt about *that.* I found Julian only too glad to hold forth, over many whiskies, on the parental iniquities. Elizabeth put in an occasional mild reproach.

"Really, dear, let's not convince Oscar that your father is a complete ogre. Remember all those New York cases where he stood up for the little guy."

"The *little* guy, exactly! The humble sufferer. The old woman run down on a grade crossing or the booby swindled by a loan shark. Someone who would never dream of spitting at a robber baron! Some miserable soul who could only pull the forelock before the railroad monarch, the strike breaker, the sweat shop proprietor. Oh, yes, such might be in line for a bit of judicial bounty, for a few coppers of damages flung at their feet. Why, the decision might even offer His Honor the chance to display his graceful prose! A veritable Tennyson on the high bench! Opinions as lovely as his landscapes of the beautiful West before it was raped by the tycoons to whom he has sold our Constitution."

I guided him now, as firmly as I could, from this general diatribe to the more particular origins of his eschewal of the paternal *lares* and *penates.* Elizabeth took up her needlepoint as if in preparation for a long evening. Julian needed only his whiskey, which he drank in large quantities without showing any effect but in his greater emphases.

"I didn't really rebel until my last year at Saint Augustine's. You remember *that*, I'm sure, Oscar."

"When you were 'pumped'? How could I forget it?"

Pumping was a disciplinary proceeding left to the boys — the faculty discreetly absenting themselves — and administered to one who had shown the gravest absence of the "right attitude." Julian was a fourth-former (*aetat* fifteen) when he committed the arch heresy of publicly refusing to attend the football game with Saint Paul's, the final match of the season and the principal athletic event of the academic year. The upper school had met in the assembly hall with no masters present — a weird session, like a witches' coven — and the culprit's name was shouted out, followed by a "Step forward!" A group of sixth-formers then rushed poor Julian down to the cellar and ducked him in a laundry tub within an inch of his life.

Julian's expulsion from the school followed on the Sunday after his ordeal, when he had skipped chapel and gone up to an empty sixth-form dormitory to rip in pieces the photographs of the parents of his principal tormentors, found on the bureaux of their cubicles.

"Up until then," Julian now continued, "I may have been inwardly smouldering, but there had been no external outburst. Yet I believe that Father had scented from the beginning that I was at heart a coward. That my awkwardness at all forms of athletics, particularly football, was put on to avoid rough contact with other boys. He was determined to change me, with the fanaticism of a Torquemada, who would burn a man to save his soul. But as time went on and I got worse, and he could see how I hated his Wyoming pack trips and how unnerved I was by big animals and banging guns, I think his resolve to alter me turned into a grim dislike. He wanted to punish me, punish me for being the milksop he had created!"

"But you will admit, won't you," I interrupted, "that you *were* working against him? Just a bit, anyway? After all, you became a perfectly decent athlete when you grew up. Didn't you tell me you broke eighty on the Chevy Chase course last year?"

"Well, naturally, when I saw that a game could actually be *fun*, things were different. That never crossed my mind when I was a kid."

"Where was your mother in all this? Didn't she ever take your side?"

"Well, you remember Mother."

"Of course I do. I admired her immensely. A student of Greek! So tall and pale and serene. I used to think of her as a high priestess. Like Norma in the opera."

"And sexless, too, wasn't that it?" He cackled disgustingly. "That glazed skin which would never raise a male organ. Except, I suppose, on the night when Yours Truly was conceived."

"Oh, Julian." But Elizabeth didn't even look up from her needlepoint.

"It always surprised me that Mother wasn't a more active feminist," he continued. "But, then, men hardly existed for her. So long as she could teach her Greek classes at Barnard, she was content with the status quo. I was a male child and could be given over to Father. It would have been otherwise had she had a daughter."

"Oh, Julian, really!" Elizabeth for a moment put aside her work. "You do exaggerate so. Your mother was devoted to you. And she was always divine to me."

"Doesn't that prove my point? A really loving mother wouldn't have clasped a daughter-in-law to her heart quite so fast, would she?"

Elizabeth glanced at me with a hopeless shrug and resumed her work.

"I used to wish I'd been born a woman," Julian resumed. "It seemed to me they had all the advantages. They could sit at home in comfort and safety while men went to work or war. I looked forward to going to boarding school to get away from Father's air of sustained disapproval. But when I got to Saint Augustine's, it was only to find that he had a deputy on that benighted campus. The great Doctor Ames, a kind of god on earth, or supercoach, who had three hundred imps to torture the athletically reluctant! Like those little devils with spears you see in Renaissance paintings of the Last Judgment."

"So you rebelled at last."

He nodded. "At last. I became a man. You might even say that Father had won! After that day when I was pumped, I found myself glowing with a glorious new emotion. It was hate! And when I found myself ripping to pieces those fatuous photographs of self-important daddies and simpering mummies, I knew happiness for the first time in my life!"

"What happened between you and the headmaster after that? We never heard. But one of the masters quoted him as saying you had to be out of your mind."

"He *had* to believe that!" Julian clapped his hands at the joyous memory. "He announced to me solemnly that I was to be sent home that very night. That I might not be safe in the school from retaliation by my outraged victims. Of course, I should not be returning. There was no place in his school for a boy like me. I looked him squarely in the eye and answered: 'A boy like me, sir? You mean a boy who is damned? But what about the man who caused my damnation? What about you? Do you think Jesus will have any use for the likes of you? He'll pitch you straight into hell. Except of course there is no hell or heaven. There's nothing. And nothingness is good enough for you. I hope when you die, you'll have just a moment of consciousness when you realize this. That all your dreams of bliss hereafter were vain. And that you'll hear me laughing.' And do you know what, Oscar? He paled. The old skunk actually paled!"

"I don't wonder."

"And do you know something else, Oscar?" The question came from Elizabeth, who was holding up her work to the lamp to examine a stitch. "Julian has been brave ever since. Perfect hate casteth out fear."

Julian stared from her to me and then threw up his hands. "I know. You both think I'm hipped on the subject. That I don't make sense. I'm going to take the dog out. I need some fresh air. Don't go, Oscar. I'll be back in a few minutes and make you a nightcap. And we'll talk about this new court bill."

When he was gone, Elizabeth got up to make herself a drink. "Of course, there's a lot of the old man in him," she told me as she resumed her seat. "He's just as combative. It took a lot of guts to get himself exempted from the draft in the war to work with Colonel House's peace planners. It was all secret, you see, so he couldn't tell people that he wasn't just trying to save his neck. He knew he was doing work more important than being in the trenches, and he had to take being called a draft dodger on the chin."

"Still, he had the satisfaction of humiliating his father."

"Oh, he had that! And do you know that Colonel House told him he *could* tell his father what he was doing, and he *didn't?*"

"How like him!"

"How like him indeed. He and the judge have built walls around themselves."

I was glad to return to the judge. "What is Justice Hollister trying to keep out? Or in?"

"The image of himself as a fearless man. He's like Ernest

Hemingway. How a man dies is much more important than how he lives."

"Can he really exist on just that?"

"Oh, yes. To what extent it's living may be another matter."

"But what about all his ideals? All the sacred rights that he believes are enshrined in the Constitution? The right of a man to hire and fire, to do almost anything he damn pleases? Doesn't he believe in those things?"

"Only when his emotions are involved."

"And when they're not?"

"Well, that I don't know. But it might be interesting to find out."

❧ ❧ ❧

Elizabeth's bleak and simple diagnosis of her father-in-law's psychic problem fertilized, in my all-too-receptive mind, first a bold idea and then an even bolder plan of action. Indeed, the latter had me so excited that I am afraid I sadly neglected some of my administrative tasks at the new office. I spent two whole mornings on a back bench in the Supreme Court chamber listening to the arguments in the Washington State minimum wage case. Gideon Hollister was as usual mostly silent, scribbling what may have been notes or even private correspondence (I knew he sometimes did the latter when counsel bored him), but when he did raise his head to ask a question it was almost in the manner of a law professor quizzing an ill-prepared student. Yet I noted with interest that he was just as acrid with the lawyers attacking the validity of the statute as he was with those defending it. This boded well for my project.

On the evening after my second court visit I called on the judge after dinner and found him alone in his library. He had been reading a rather heavy new history of the Renaissance and was evidently glad to be interrupted. I accepted readily the brandy he offered me, and we settled down to talk, at first about Florence and Lorenzo the Magnificent, but soon about more recent topics. At last I brought up the subject of the present case before his court.

"I heard the arguments this morning. They were very interesting. Of course, I shouldn't ask you this, but that's just the reason I'm going to. A serious essayist should have some privileges. So here goes. Is there *any* chance the court might overrule Adkins *versus* The Children's Hospital?"

He glared at me. "Do you mean, is there any chance that *I* might so rule?"

"Well, I didn't dare put it quite like that. But now you ask me, yes, is there?"

"Any chance that I might sustain the right of a state legislature to impose minimum wages in a particular industry?"

"Yes, sir. Just so."

"It must be obvious to you, Oscar, that I should not and will not answer such a question. But what interests me is why you are asking it. What makes you think that I have altered my thinking since publishing my book on liberty of contract, which I know from our previous discussions that you have read? Or do you simply assume that I have become as senile as Mr. Roosevelt deems all jurists over seventy to be?"

"You know I assume no such thing, sir."

"*Do* I know it?"

"I think the president's position on the ages of judges is an outrage."

He grunted. "Well, good."

"And if he submits his bill to the Congress, I will add my voice to the public chorus opposing it. I will even take time off from my firm to work for its defeat."

"What strategy do you propose? Through bar associations? And lobbyists?"

I braced myself for the big moment. "Yes. But particularly by my doing what I'm doing right now."

"And what, pray, are you doing right now?"

"Endeavoring to persuade you to vote to sustain the constitutionality of the Washington minimum wage statute!" I bowed my head in expectation of the storm.

But when the judge had taken this fully in, he was less violent than I had feared. He was simply biting. "You will kindly elucidate me, sir, as to why you believe yourself able to persuade me to throw over the moral and legal principles of a lifetime. And play hopscotch with the rule of *stare decisis!*"

I saw with relief that I was at least to be given a hearing. He was back, so to speak, on the bench.

"Let me explain, sir, to start with, that I take no position on the sociological merits of the statute. I am not here concerned with the welfare of the workers. Nor am I even concerned with the question of whether or not the statute is *really* constitutional."

"And what the hell, then, *are* you concerned with?"

"With saving the court! Even at the price of holding a statute constitutional that isn't!"

"So that's what you're after." He nodded grimly. "If my brethren and I go down on our knees and grovel before the dictator from Hyde Park, if we hand down the decision his solicitor general wants, then perhaps, and only perhaps, he may graciously reconsider his bill to pack the court."

"Mr. Roosevelt isn't going to be president forever, sir."

"What makes you so sure of *that?*"

"Oh, come, sir, he's mortal. And if he gives up his bill or fails to get it passed, you will have gained precious time. Under another administration you may even be able to overrule what you decided against your conscience."

But now I *had* gone too far. "You assume, sir, that I'd play dirty pool with the law of the land?"

"I take it back! The case would stand, of course. But would that be the end of the world? Even you, sir, might have no objection to minimum wages and hours, say, for women and children, if a constitutional amendment allowed it?"

"Those things are not my affair. As a judge, I mean. What you must explain to me is why our court would be worth a plugged nickel if its members put aside their personal convictions to indulge in games of political jockeying."

"But only *one* game, sir! You know the French proverb: *Aux grands maux, les grands remèdes.* Jefferson blinked at the Constitution when he bought Louisiana and doubled the size of the nation. Lincoln suspended *habeas corpus* to win a war and violated property rights to free the slaves!" I hurried on as I saw he was about to protest. "Look, sir. Your vote, it is known, is the swing one. It will make a majority either way."

"Ugh, what a vulgar way of looking at justice!"

"But isn't it true? If the statute is upheld, and the country begins to see that the court is no longer determined to block the New Deal . . ."

"We don't block anything!" he exclaimed indignantly. "Each case is decided on its merits!"

"But that's not how the country sees it. It's not how the lords of the New Deal see it. But if they can be convinced that the court is now taking a more liberal view, the bill may be torn up, or at least defeated in Congress. And Mr. Justice Hollister will have become the most important man in the nation. He will simply have saved our tripartite form of government!"

The judge now sat for some minutes in absolute silence.

Whatever he was thinking, it was surely not an unequivocal repudiation of my argument. I did not dare utter another word for fear of causing a reaction. I had sown the seed. I must wait to see if it would grow.

When he spoke at last it was only to dismiss me. But his tone was not unfriendly. "The trouble with you, Oscar, is that you're not writing my life. You're trying to make it up! Now go home, will you? It's late and I'm tired."

I hurried away, exultant. I was too stirred up to go back to my hotel yet, so I called on Julian and Elizabeth, whom I found alone. Over a double Scotch I expanded exuberantly on my accomplishment — or what I hoped had been that. Julian at first simply sneered at me. Only the giddiest romantic, he insisted, could even conceive that so ancient a leopard could alter his dappled coat. But he admitted at last that Chief Justice Hughes was rumored to have been working behind the scenes with a similar scheme, and he became suddenly thoughtful at the idea of what effect a double attack might have on his pressured sire. I left him brooding; he hardly bade me good night.

Elizabeth saw me to the door. In the foyer she told me that she was sorry I had told him what I had.

"But why? Hasn't he all his life wanted to convert the old man?"

"Never! Don't you see? He wants the old man *punished*, not converted. The very idea that Mr. Justice Hollister might turn out to be a more important liberal than Julian Hollister the brain truster is anathema to him. His wicked sire a greater figure in social history? But it would be unbearable!"

"God! Why couldn't I hold my tongue?"

"Well, don't worry about it. There isn't anything he can do about it. His father would never listen to him, one way or the other. And I'm on your side. I'd love to see the old fellow redeem himself and bask in a new limelight."

❧ ❧ ❧

But there was, alas, something that Julian could do about it. Only two days later I read the following in the column that he wrote for *The Washington Post* under the alias "Prosit":

> Only those from the Styx are unaware that the White House has been delaying its court bill to give the old geezers on the bench the chance to catch up with the century and, by quitting, save their august tribunal the mortification of being packed. It is also no secret that the wily and diplomatic Chief Justice has been trying to convince at least one of the recalcitrants, who believe that our Constitution was drafted by God for the benefit of John D. Rockefeller *et al.*, to "wise up" and save the number nine for muses and judges. And rumor now has it that he has found his man. Gideon Hollister will be shriven by High Priest Hughes after confessing his guilt in placing the due process clause at the service of Wall Street and promising to be a good boy in future. And how will he reconcile his new position with his old? Very easily. He is known for his private view that the Constitution is simply the straitjacket out of which the jurist-magician must be able to make his periodic escape. It will be both amusing and instructive to see how Mr. Justice Houdini Hollister does it!

❧ ❧ ❧

It was Mr. Justice Roberts who listened to his chief and made the majority that sustained the minimum wage law and laid the ground for the defeat of the court bill. I had never the heart to discuss the matter with Justice Hollister, who remained with the right wing of the court until his death, two years later, and will be remembered in judicial history only for his uncompromising opposition to the social legislation of his day. Whether or not he ever seriously considered adopting my proposed course of action I do not know, but I had no heart for my little book of essays after the episode. The vision of what he might have been and the realization of what he was put too much bitterness between me and the empty page on my desk.

He never forgave Julian for the article. The latter told me of their grim last confrontation, only a couple of months before his father's death. Julian was driving home from his office, in a sudden rain squall, when he spied his father trudging along the sidewalk without an umbrella. He at once pulled up, opened the door and called out: "Father, please get in. I'll take you wherever you're going."

The judge gave him a cold look and walked on.

THE UNHAPPY WARRIOR

THE FIRST TIME I saw Grant Richards was in 1925 in the Surrogate's Court on Chambers Street, that vast, ornate, unexpected but welcome Renaissance palazzo amid the duller oblong cubes of lower Manhattan. He was representing the young Hungarian widow of a New York real estate magnate, Sol Dittson, seeking to establish her right to the residuary estate, which he had bequeathed to her at the expense of his middle-aged son and daughter, for whom my firm were counsel. I had just been made the most junior of our partners, thanks in part, I assumed, to Father's gentle but firm push, and as trusts and estates were my bailiwick I was present in court, not to argue or to examine witnesses, but to advise Gus Seton, our senior litigator, on relevant points of the law of wills. Gus had also two of his top clerks with him, for the case involved many millions, but Grant Richards was alone in representing the beautiful defendant, whom we had charged with the grossest undue influence in the matter of her husband's testating. I had wondered, with so much at stake, why she had not chosen an attorney of national repute. Grant, at thirty-five, was beginning to be known as a tough and able lawyer, but his firm was a small one, and he had no fame outside the city. The answer might have been in the rumor that he was the Widow Dittson's lover.

His looks could certainly have justified the rumor. He was broad-shouldered and thickset, with the strong build of a football player, which he had been, almost famously, at Cornell. His dense black hair, closely cut, intensified the rugged aspect of his countenance, and his dark brown eyes probed and seemed to penetrate the witnesses he examined. Yet his deep voice was unexpectedly mild; he would creep up on the person testifying, and when he snared him in a contradiction, instead of challenging him, as one might have anticipated, with a roar, he would simply shrug and smile at the jury as if to say: "Don't worry, my friend, we all have our lapses. Why not? We're all human, aren't we?" His attitude seemed to imply that most people are capable of committing almost any horror, given the right circumstances. The effect on the jury was to disillusion them with the plaintiff's witnesses without antagonizing them by the kind of righteous bluster in which so many trial lawyers indulge. He struck me as a man who, for all his apparent toughness — and I knew he had been decorated in the war — could make a joke of anything, however sacred. But he had charm. Far more, alas, than our Mr. Seton.

The surrogate had decided for him in his fight with Seton over his right to impugn the characters of the decedent's children, on the argument that their many faults might have done more to alienate their father than any undue influence on their stepmother's part, and his cool, smiling, persistent and deadly examination of the alcoholic, four-times-married son and the drug-addicted hysterical daughter drove the former into absurd displays of temper and the latter into fits of tears. This, added to Richards's showing that they had already received millions from their mother's estate, would have been almost enough to convince the jury that no testator in his right mind would have left them any more, had not Seton had an equally lurid success in showing the greed and vile temper of the beautiful Hungarian and the weakness and susceptibility of her aged spouse. But I could see that if it turned into a case of "a plague on both your houses," the simplest thing for a jury to do would be to let the will stand.

We decided at the office that we had better seek a compromise, and I was delegated to sound out Richards. He and I met, at his insistence, not in either of our offices, but in an expensive midtown French restaurant, in a secluded alcove where the waiter, obviously well known to my host and equally well tipped, did not "see" him pour whiskey cocktails from a pocket flask into our empty water glasses. Grant, as he now made me call him, would not discuss the case until he had had two drinks and the chance to size me up. Presumably he wanted to be sure that I was not the vulgar type of lawyer who would try to pry some minimal advantage out of mutual candor. In ten minutes he had me pinpointed. I was a gentleman. But whether or not he admired gentlemen, I didn't know. I am still not sure.

"Let's put it on the table, Oscar. If we weren't representing our clients, we'd be glad to see the whole estate go to the Salvation Army. Have you ever in your life seen such a set of 'pitiful rascals'? Isn't that how Prince Hal described Falstaff's recruits?"

I paused at some length before answering. The Shakespearean reference must have been to flatter me, to show that he and I were no ordinary mouthpieces. "Do you find the beautiful Magda Dittson such a pitiful rascal?"

"Well, she's a rascal, all right. Perhaps she's not exactly pitiful. We all need a Magda in our life from time to time. But you have to keep an eye on them. They can never be fully domesticated. Even when they look sweetest, they can suddenly scratch. You don't turn your back even on a purring panther."

I decided that the rumor about his relations with the widow was true. But Magda this time, I felt sure, had met her match. She might well be dropped when she had paid her fee. And would she even resent it? Looking at those hard yet twinkling eyes, I wondered whether he wasn't that rare male who could leave a mistress and keep a friend.

"Why did she have to get the *whole* estate?" I asked bluntly. "Wouldn't a third or half have been enough? And then the children wouldn't have contested."

"How could I be sure of that? They hated her guts enough to bring a suit even if you told them they couldn't win it. And they could afford it, too. No, my friend, I was sure we'd be in court no matter how small a share she got. So I decided to put her in the driver's seat with the whole kit and caboodle."

"*You* decided?"

"Don't try to trip me up, my friend. By advising the old man, I mean. Who followed me perfectly. Who agreed to make her his sole executor and sole outright residuary legatee. So now if your clients lose, they get nothing. Whereas if Magda loses, she will still be entitled to her intestate share of one third of the estate. The risk your clients take in not settling on my terms is considerably greater than hers."

Well, of course this was true. And our clients, smarting with the punishment they had already taken in court, were dreading further lashes. Whereas Magda's skin was obviously too tough to have been more than grazed by the drubbing Seton had given her. I returned to the office with Grant's offer of one third of the estate for the decedent's children and found it gratefully accepted.

The only thing our firm really got out of the Dittson case was Richards himself. The children, once they had had a chance to discuss the settlement with all their nasty friends, decided they had been badly advised, and we had to sue them through three courts to collect our too-modest fee. But I had had the opportunity to see that Grant might be just what Father needed to replace himself and the other senior partner, who were both approaching retirement age. The middle rank of the partnership were all competent lawyers, but none, as Father had often complained to me, had quite the spark and vigor and administrative talent needed to head up a major firm. I told Father about Grant, and he agreed at once that I should investigate him.

Working out the details of the settlement gave me the excuse to have several lunches with my candidate and even on two occasions to bring him home for dinner. Constance liked him immediately, a very good sign, though she wondered at the ease with which I had secured the company of so attractive and socially popular a bachelor for a simple family evening. Of course, it later became clear that Grant had divined exactly what I was up to and had his own eye already fixed on just the position I wanted him to fill. But that was fine. I wanted him to want it.

I learned that he was the son of an army officer and had been raised largely in military posts abroad, in Hawaii, the Philippines and the Canal Zone. But his father had never attained a higher rank than lieutenant colonel and had ultimately retired bitterly from the service to take up the narrower life of a small New Hampshire dairy farmer. He had, according to his son, been denied promotion because of the jealousy of incompetent superiors who had seen only unruliness in his urgent proposals for newer arms and tactics and training. Disillusioned with a military force run by the obtuse while the country's brains went into business and law, he persuaded Grant, who had wanted desperately to go to West Point, to go instead to college and law school and rise to be a leader in a society too obsessed with money to support its own soldiers. "And *then* perhaps you can do something to make things right" had been almost the senior Richards's dying words.

Grant made no bones about having thoroughly enjoyed the carnage of the war, which had almost made up to him for missing West Point, and only regretted that his father had not lived to see him awarded a medal for valor in an action at Château Thierry. He wanted to hear all about my experiences, but I insisted, with justice, that they had not been comparable with his.

"Of course, I know it's the fashion to play it all down now," he told me. "People are saying it wasn't worthwhile, that we never should have gone into it at all. But that's because the old men who hadn't fought screwed up the peace treaty. The generals would have done better. Napoleon made good treaties. So did Julius Caesar."

"Would Pershing have done any better than Wilson? Or Haig than Lloyd George?"

"But that was just my father's point! That the best brains in England and America didn't go into the armed forces. They only did in Germany, and it took the whole world to beat them!"

"So you approve of a military state."

"Just as much as one run by brokers and bankers. I prefer officers and gentlemen to polished pickpockets."

"You're a pretty polished pickpocket yourself, if you'll allow me to say so. You did quite a job on the Dittsons. And someday you may admit to me that the beautiful Magda really did exert undue influence on her senile spouse!"

He chuckled. "When in Rome we do as the wops. I think I'm going to let the divine Magda pay my fee in Dittson stock. I've a hunch it hasn't peaked yet."

It hadn't, and he made a small fortune, though he lost much of it in the 1929 crash. Nothing, however, caused Grant to more than briefly stumble.

My father took to him even more warmly than I had expected. A child of the Civil War, the great-nephew of a famous admiral and the son of a young aide to General Sherman, Father was delighted with the patriotism that Grant cheerfully and cleverly demonstrated to him. Nor did he even object to Grant's rather torrid reputation as a ladies' man. Father was the kind of Victorian male who believed that a "good" woman would never succumb, even to such a charmer as Grant, and that a "bad" woman deserved anything she got. Early in 1926 he offered Grant a partnership in the firm, and Grant accepted.

A year had not passed before it was evident to all that the new partner was destined for the first position. His cheerful, open friendliness seemed perfectly compatible with his political astuteness, and his expertise in corporate law as well as litigation won the respect of even grudging rivals. And he dazzled the clients. Whenever he brought one to my office for the preparation of a will or trust indenture, fields in which he had little experience, he would entrance them with some fabulous explanation of the law involved, making it up outrageously as he went along, knowing of course that I would draft the documents without reference to his flight of fancy. He seemed to enjoy playing close to the precipice, as if to test his own balance.

And he managed, despite his long hours of toil, to maintain an active social life. No one, seeing him at the opera, splendid in white tie and tails, with a sleek and stylish woman on his arm, would have imagined that he had spent the whole day in court on a grueling case. We all expected that the ultimate Mrs. Richards would be the toast of the town. Nobody dreamed it would be my sister.

Henrietta, two years my senior and hence thirty-three when she and Grant met, was as unlike myself as any sibling could be. Mother used to say she could hardly believe we had emerged from the same womb. Henrietta was not only older, but bigger and much more assured than I; she had been something of a tomboy as a child and was still cheerfully, even rather aggressively, unmarried. She was an able equestrian, though a bit on the heavy side for fences, and had established herself as a competent administrator on the boards of the Sloane Babies Hospital and Miss Chapin's School. Henrietta was round-faced and plain, with dull brown hair that was always either messy or too crisply waved, but her high spirits and hearty manner made her the best of company.

She had been in love, to my knowledge, only once, with a pretty but weak young man, who had retreated on the expectation, ungratified, I'm glad to say, of a much richer match. Henrietta had literally kicked him out of the house when he ruefully returned to renew his now unwelcome advances, and ever since she had appeared to resign herself to the single state. She lived with our parents, but in no condition of subjection. She occupied her own floor in the tall narrow limestone family mansion, on East Seventy-third Street, with a large front chamber in which she could entertain her friends. Henrietta had become in her own right what Mother liked to call a "personage."

Grant's relationship with Henrietta started off on a rather hilarious note. He was a favorite guest of my parents, and I soon noted that Henrietta made a point of being there when he came. He purported whimsically to be dazzled by her accomplishments and awed by tales of her horsemanship and her many committees, and would suggest to Father that she be made a "lay" partner of the firm, in charge of management. Henrietta, to my surprise and slight embarrassment, became positively coy with him. She invited him to the family place in Long Island for a weekend, where she would give him lessons in jumping; he at once accepted, and she asked Father whether he couldn't be her lawyer in the firm in place of the superannuated but faithful clerk who was assigned to her matters. When I learned that she had been twice seen at the opera with Grant, I decided to ask him what he was up to. I knew that my parents, however glad to have him for a son-in-law, wouldn't lift a finger to make him so. Henrietta, after all, was her own boss.

"You mustn't lead her on, you know," I told him at a lunch. "No one falls as hard as an old maid when she does fall."

Grant took this with his usual ease. "I suppose an older sister is always that to a brat of a kid brother."

"Well, isn't she one?"

"You mean, won't she always be? I wouldn't expect a kid brother to see it, but your sister has plenty of sex appeal. She's ready for romance, my friend. Really ready."

"But that's just what I mean. Are *you?*"

"Well, isn't it a great old American custom to marry the boss's daughter?"

"Marry!" I stared at him. It was impossible to tell when Grant was serious. Or when he wasn't. He had a way of being both at the same time. "But you don't have to marry Henrietta to head the firm. You're a shoo-in. And you *know* that."

"Me? A poor army brat? Who didn't prep at a proper New England school? Who's not even listed in the Social Register? Wouldn't I be presumptuous to aspire to a Fairfax?"

I paused to consider this. Of course I knew that any presentable and successful downtown lawyer of decent Protestant antecedents could aspire to pretty much any "old New York" family, and it was hard to believe that someone as shrewd as Grant did not know it also. But people can have strange hang-ups about class distinctions.

"Come off it, Grant. You must know we'd snap you up."

"Do I?"

"Well, be careful about getting too close."

"Are you protecting your sister?"

"From disappointment. Not from wedding bells."

He gave me a long look at this, and I began to wonder whether he *wasn't* serious. Could a man like that be in love with Henrietta? I recalled that a male who is absolutely confident of his own virility has no great need of pulchritude in a woman to stimulate his desires, and that he can sense in a plain woman an appetite for carnal pleasures that may be productive of steamier performances in bed than those of her fairer sisters. And I had to note in the weeks that followed that Henrietta, who was now constantly escorted to opera and ball by her father's brilliant partner, seemed to gain, almost excessively, in high vivacity. That she was exuberantly in love was only too evident.

Most parents would have thought it too good to be true, but Father and Mother were so assured of their own value, which they attributed also to their offspring, that they took it calmly enough. Father did, however, eventually ask me whether I thought Grant would "come up to snuff."

"I think, on the whole, that he's gone too far to back down now," I responded sagely. "I doubt you'll need your shotgun."

"Of course, I realize he could make a better match in the worldly sense. Henrietta and you will have what your mother and I have when we're gone, but it won't be any great fortune. Still, a Fairfax is a Fairfax, I suppose. And Henrietta has plenty of character."

"Too much, if anything."

"And I'm not forgetting that this will have its effect on you, my boy. If Grant gets the first spot in the firm, as it's beginning to look he will, how will you enjoy working for your big sister's spouse?"

"Aren't you forgetting, respected parent, who brought him to the firm in the first place? I'm perfectly happy about it."

Father smiled in that quiet, benevolent way of his, his only means of conveying affection. But it was enough. It implied a trust that almost created trustworthiness in its recipient. "Well, you've always seemed to know what you wanted. And that's a good deal more than half the way to happiness."

Grant at this point went abroad on a bank merger and was gone for two months. He had not proposed to Henrietta before he left, nor did he once write to her while he was away. She made no effort to conceal her chagrin and humiliation, and Constance and I began to find excuses not to attend the weekly Sunday lunch at my parents'. But when he returned he went straight from the boat to Seventy-third Street, pounded on the door of her living room and asked her to marry him the moment she opened it. She fell in his arms. He had simply needed the time in Europe to "think things over."

Their wedding was large and grand. Henrietta, despite her mature age, had a dozen bridesmaids; Grant had only myself, as best man. The bitch goddess Success seemed in the years that followed to have only smiles for this favored pair of her worshippers. Even the Great Depression provided higher rungs for their Jacob's ladder. Grant's early losses in the market were more than made up for by the large fees for the massive corporate reorganizations that he manipulated to help reshape a declining economy and that carried him at last, by a unanimous vote, to the senior partnership of the firm. Henrietta bore him, in rapid succession, five healthy little girls. Even this was right; Grant might have had trouble with dissenting sons. The Richardses had a penthouse overlooking the newly fashionable East River and a Tudor manor house in Long Island; he served a term as president of the City Bar Association; she, of the Colony Club. It amused me, at cocktail parties, to hear people who barely knew them refer to "Grant and Hetty," as if they were close friends.

My only concern was that, as Henrietta grew older and stouter and ever more domineering, she might fail to satisfy the sexual appetites of which her husband had given such public evidence in his long bachelor years. This concern turned out to have been actually optimistic. There was no question of "might fail"; Henrietta, we learned, never had fully satisfied Grant, even at the start. Probably no woman could have. She did not discover his carefully hidden adulteries for a good nine years; but when she did, she exploded in screams and recriminations that shook the welkin, locked Grant out of the apartment and appealed to Father to get her a divorce.

Father was totally unsympathetic. He certainly did not approve of Grant's conduct, but he adhered strongly to the Victorian principle of keeping such matters within the family. A good wife did not yawl and clamor about so trivial a thing as a husband's occasionally spilt lust; so long as he didn't throw his girlfriends in the public eye, she should look the other way and mind her own business. If there was to be any question, Father's manner implied, of his having to choose between a hysterical middle-aged daughter, who hadn't the sense not to rock a boat crammed with her own advantages, and a son-in-law who had raised his firm to heights he hadn't himself dared to hope for . . . well, Henrietta could figure that one out for herself. And Mother agreed totally with Father, not because she was easily swayed by him, but because they shared exactly the same principles. And also, I'm afraid, because she liked Grant a bit more than she liked her daughter.

Henrietta, in her outrage, turned to the kid brother. I also was on Grant's side, as a practical matter, but I knew better than to let her see it.

"Father and Mother have no morals!" she exclaimed wrathfully. "They care about nothing but appearances."

"Well, what would any of us be without them? So long as

your marriage *looks* like a happy one, can't you copy it? Put the image and the fact together?"

"And let honor and duty and fidelity go by the board?"

"How are honor and duty involved? I understand about fidelity."

"Could an honorable and dutiful man behave as Grant has behaved?"

"I think so. Hasn't he been a good and dutiful husband in every respect but one?"

"But that *one*, Oscar!"

"Please answer my question."

"Well . . . yes, I suppose so."

"And if you hadn't happened to discover what you did discover, you'd be perfectly happy?"

"But my happiness would have been a fool's paradise!"

"Isn't that what paradises usually are?"

"No cheap cynicism, please."

"But don't you see that if you can bring yourself to wink at this one thing, you'll be perfectly happy again? And the girls, too?"

"And Grant, too! Oh, too too!" she cried in derision. "With his harem intact!"

"I didn't want to leave him out of the general euphoria. Seriously, Hetty, is he depriving you of anything? Doesn't he still sleep with you?"

"Aren't you being just a bit crude?"

"You mean the only sexual relationship we *can't* talk about is yours and his?"

She paused to consider this. "All right. Yes, we still do. I guess an old bull like that can do it with anyone. I'm hardly flattered."

"Well, who married the old bull? Your only mistake, my dear, was in thinking you could change the old bull's nature. Accept him, and your troubles are over. You and Grant will get back on the bandwagon and drive to the top of the hill. Isn't that what you really want?"

"Really want? To put up with his bedding every tart he lays his eyes on?"

"No! To drive to the top." I jumped up to emphasize how serious I was. "Are you really going to be such a fool as to smash your life in pieces for a few stray orgasms on Grant's part? Would you care if he masturbated?"

"Don't be disgusting, Oscar."

"I'm serious. What's the difference? The only difference will be, if you're determined to go on with this, between the woman you were and the woman you will be."

"And what is that?"

"The difference between a proud, happy and important woman and a forlorn and self-pitying divorcée! Choose!"

She didn't make the choice immediately, but she did in two more weeks, and Grant was readmitted to the penthouse. Father gave me all the credit for the reconciliation, but I have always believed that Henrietta would have ultimately reached the same solution on her own.

The great thing about my sister was that when she did decide on a course of action, she adopted it wholly and in good spirit. I was never again aware of a serious quarrel between her and Grant. They presented to the world a united, even a rather boisterous front, which may have fairly represented the inner state of their wedded life. I even remember a time at the Warrens' when Hugo was showing us a Renoir water color of a pink, big-bottomed nude that he had just acquired, and Henrietta, turning away from it with a chuckle, called over to her husband, for all the room to hear, "Come and look at this, dear. It's more *your* affair than mine." Grant kept his other life, on the whole, out of sight, though he did have a couple of detected liaisons with ladies of Henrietta's world, one of which, with the wife of a prominent banker, led to a rather messy divorce. Grant was not named co-respondent — the matter was handled formally in Reno — but everyone knew the facts, and the lady, returning to New York, told all her friends that she expected him to leave Henrietta and do the right thing by her. She was soon disillusioned, and had the further humiliation of being roundly snubbed by Henrietta and a group of her friends in the members' dining room of the Colony Club.

The war in 1941 brought Grant into national prominence. He had rejoined the army, well before Pearl Harbor, in the confident hope, despite his fifty years, of combat duty when the time came, but of course he was far too valuable for that. Secretary of War Stimson needed his expertise in negotiating army contracts with industries that ran into the billions; he also wanted him, as the fighting spread over the globe, to visit the combat areas and report on the effectiveness of the materials purchased. To give him the necessary clout in the bases visited, General Marshall raised him to the rank of major general; Grant, in short, became one of the noted figures of the war in Washington.

Henrietta rented a large and beautiful yellow Palladian mansion in Georgetown, with a dome and white Corinthian columns, where she entertained the high brass, congressional leaders, diplomats and visiting royalty. She got ample supplies from the War Department; her parties were considered a part of the war effort. My sister had always been a genius in the art of having and eating her cake.

There was, however, one flaw in her good fortune, which she confided to me on a weekend visit that Constance and I made to her and Grant in the capital. Grant, she told me, had been exposing himself, quite unnecessarily, to extreme danger on his visits to combat areas. He had boarded a PT boat for a raid at Guadalcanal; he had flown in a bombing mission over Germany; he had landed with a first wave on a beach in Sicily. Mr. Stimson himself had suggested to Henrietta that she speak to him about this. She thought I might do better. I told her doubtfully that I could only try.

I rose early the next morning, which was Sunday, to accompany Grant on his daily brisk walk with his Scottish Highlanders before he went to his office at eight. It was a mild, clear winter day, and the bright colors of the neatly painted little Georgetown houses in the neighboring streets, with their black iron grills and cozy garden plots, seemed impossibly far from the war that must have occupied the thoughts of my rapidly striding, uniformed companion. He had been only half-listening to what I was telling him, but when he suddenly took in what it was really about, he pulled up with a frown.

"But those things are part of my job!"

"Your boss doesn't seem to think so."

"Then he can tell me so. Directly. Until then, I do as I see fit."

"Why, Grant? Why is it worth it? Are you getting some sort of a jag at putting your life at risk?"

He was not in the least put out by this, or even by my attempted interference with his life. He was, as always, extraordinarily dispassionate. But I knew that I would get nowhere. There was a kind of glow on his countenance, as with a man — or fanatic — or prophet — with whom all argument is in vain. "I don't expect you to see it, Oscar, but there's a consistency in what I do. You're too essentially a civilian. There's nothing wrong with being a civilian, but it's not what I am. I've always been an army brat. A real soldier can't just sit at a desk. He's got to be part of the whole thing. He's got to see and feel and understand just what the fighting men are up against."

"You think *everybody* should be at the front? Eisenhower and Marshall? The whole lot?"

"Oh, there have to be exceptions, of course. But I'm not that indispensable. And think what this war is, Oscar! The most glorious conflict in all history! With all that's vile in humanity on one side, and all that's fine and brave and true on the other! It's a joy to be in this war. And it would be a joy to die in it!"

I stared into those flickering eyes. "You're having the time of your life, aren't you?"

"Well, why not? After all the mean little deals of our law practice, the mean little victories, the pockets picked, the money counted!"

I nodded ruefully, seeing it all at last. "The day of the warrior has returned. The noble warrior. The *happy* warrior. You always wanted it." I took the leashes from him and walked ahead with the dogs, leaving him for a minute to muse. I would argue no further. But he soon caught up with me and put an arm over my shoulder.

"You *do* see it, don't you, Oscar?"

"I do. But I'm praying for an early peace."

❧ ❧ ❧

My brother-in-law was in many ways a very moral man, but his code of ethics varied considerably from my own. He would sternly reprimand his daughters if they were rude to a servant or waiter, or failed to answer an invitation to a party, or kept a library book overdue ("We're not that kind of people"), yet he believed that every man and woman, when of age, should feel free to engage in any sexual behavior that they chose and that even adultery was not a sin. As a lawyer I had seen him engage in practices that verged on the "sharp," yet he had served a term as president of Legal Aid and had given considerable time to *pro bono* work. He believed that the Germans responsible for the Holocaust should be shot, yet he had supported the internment of the Japanese Americans in California. Therefore, when, in the winter of 1945, I noticed a distinct lowering of his spirits despite the ebullient atmosphere of approaching victory in the air up and down the Potomac, I couldn't but wonder if he were brooding about the danger of the war's being over before the enemy had been sufficiently punished. Or perhaps simply the danger of the war's being over!

Constance and I had moved to Washington, where I was to spend a year as head of our branch there, and I used to have an occasional sandwich lunch with Grant at his desk in the Pentagon. When he finally, however, dropped a hint of what seemed to be depressing him, it was the reverse of what I had apprehended. He muttered something about a weapon too powerful to be believed.

"You mean that the Japs have?" I asked in dismay.

"Oh, no, quite the reverse."

And then he was silent. But obviously he was thinking of a weapon to be used *against* the Japanese. And why should *he*, of all people, care how many of *them* it blew up? Unless it was so damaging that it might blow us all up. I was to find out soon enough that he was neither worried about how many people were killed at Hiroshima or Nagasaki, nor how many people in the world might be killed by bigger and bigger bombs. He was concerned solely by what the bomb had done to the warrior.

This I learned when we dined, the four of us, Fairfaxes and Richardses, over two bottles of champagne, the night of the news of the Japanese decision to surrender. Henrietta, Constance and I were exuberantly gay; Grant was actually sombre.

"If we'd only waited a bit before dropping those showy firecrackers," he growled, "we'd have won fair. They were just about ready to give up."

"But how could we be sure?" I demanded. "An invasion might

have cost many more lives than were lost in those two cities. Even more Jap lives." But I was thinking of my son, Gordon, an army lieutenant, who might have been in the landing forces.

Constance, as always, was less personally motivated than I. "Well, I agree with Grant," she affirmed. "We could have waited. Or at least dropped the bomb on a less populated spot. I think it was terrible, the way we did it! And we talk about war crimes."

"Would you try Truman and Stimson?" Grant asked grimly. "That should startle our allies."

In making my next comment I kept my eyes fixed on our host. "I wonder if what concerns Grant tonight is the human devastation of the bomb."

"You're right; it's not." He met my stare defiantly. "The Japs asked for this war, and they got more than they bargained for. When I think of their barbarities in China and the Philippines, I can't worry about atomic victims. What concerns me is what the bomb has done to *us*. We're all civilians now. There won't be any place in the future for soldiers or warriors or heroes. Oh, there'll be a military, all right, full of technicians who'll build bigger and bigger bombs to lob into crowded cities. If you can blow your enemy to bits, you win. If you can't, you cower. There's no place for valor or even strategy. There'll be no Churchillian phrases about fighting on the beaches and in the streets. If the foe can extinguish you with one blow, you give in; that's all."

For a moment we were all silent, contemplating his grim forecast. Then Henrietta struck a cheerful note.

"But maybe it will be the end of wars. If nobody dares risk one. Can't we hope for that, Grant?"

"You can hope, my dear, for anything. And be comforted by the fact that what everyone predicts rarely happens. But say goodbye to the Caesars and Napoleons, the Montgomerys and the MacArthurs. The day of the bully with the big stick has dawned!"

❧ ❧ ❧

In the postwar years Grant, much to my disappointment, declined the important federal offices he was offered and devoted all his energy — very profitably to me and my family, I admit — to the practice of law. He professed no interest in the occupation and reconstruction of Germany and Japan or in what he tersely called the "futility" of the Cold War. "Both sides know it has to be kept cold," he explained to me, "so every diplomatic interchange is only a game of bluff. Not for this chicken, thank you very much."

Henrietta resumed her role as a social leader in New York and gave many large and brilliant parties. The side tables and grand piano of her parlor were adorned by five large silver-framed portrait photographs of her five daughters, triumphant in sumptuous wedding gowns. She was a thoroughly happy woman.

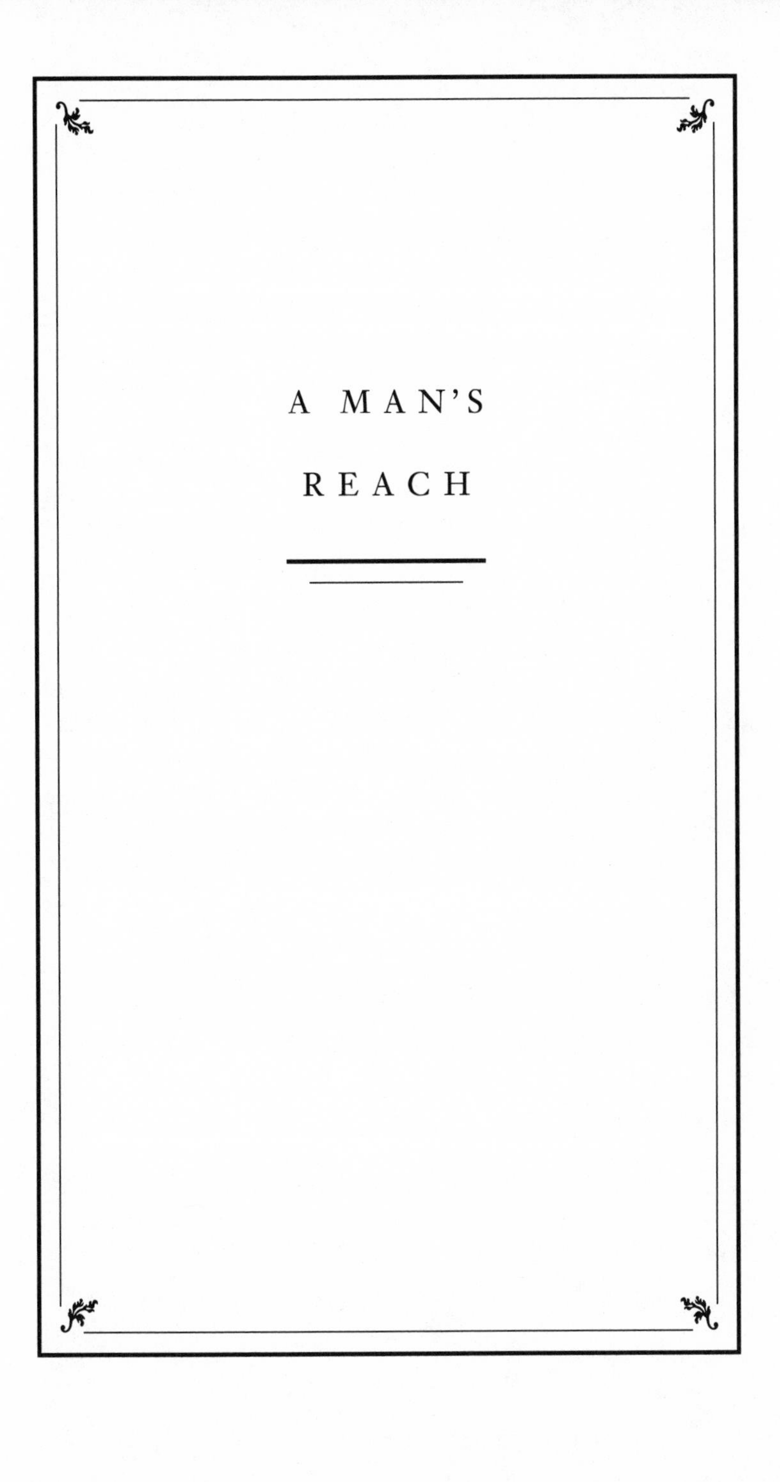

A MAN'S REACH

As a boy I always spent my summers in Bar Harbor; my parents were among the early summer colonists on the island. Like many such resorts it had originally been a vacation spot for artists and academics, who had found both tranquillity and inspiration in its hills and woods and rocky coastline, but such intellectuals serve only as pioneers for the next comers: the urban rich who take speedy advantage of their good taste and move in to drive up the local prices to their exclusion, replacing their simple camps with seaside mansions. My father had built one of these in the eighteen-nineties, with a rusticated stone first story topped by two of dark shingle and a peaked roof with huge dormers, on the Shore Path to the village, with a fine view of the usually sparkling ocean and the two small tufted isles known as the Porcupines. I had inherited and kept it, for the big island has never lost its spell for me, and Constance, however disdainful of the Swimming Club and its devotees, always loved to climb the mountains, as the hills are more nobly dubbed, and would "do" a different one each day when the rain and fog (never alluded to by loyal Bar Harborites) allowed the sun to endow the land and sea with the peculiar magic of the Maine coast.

The explorer Champlain, first viewing the island from his vessel and struck by the bareness of its hilltops, christened it L'Île de Mont Désert, but later enthusiasts insisted that what he had really meant was L'Île de Mont Désir, and such it has always remained for me, the island of my desire. The rich grey-green of its rocks and pounding waves, of its long range of lovely hills and thick forests, bathes them in an enchanted atmosphere that isolates the summer visitor from the petty cares and meannesses of the mainland even more surely than the glittering sapphire of the Atlantic. Nothing seems quite real in Mount Desert. The air, the sun, the sea endow it with an amiable gentility that smoothes over the pricklier things we bring with us from our mercantile places of origin. Compare, for example, the dressy crowd at the Beach Club in Southampton or at Bailey's in Newport on a Saturday at noon, waiting for the sun to come over the yardarm to order the first cocktail of the day, with the ladies at the umbrella tables at the Bar Harbor Swimming and Tennis Club. In the first two you can hardly be unaware of the pride of position and the pomp of wealth, but in the third your awareness of these same qualities is tinged with sympathy and amusement, as if you were watching a group of delightfully painted marionettes. My own awareness that I am seeing people in a golden haze has never disturbed me in Bar Harbor. There should be a time in every year when illusions are allowed to prevail.

In 1930, however, the first full year of the Great Depression, illusions were difficult to retain, even there, even on the brightest day of midsummer. Several of the big "cottages" were still in their winter shutters as their owners economized at home or took rooms in a hotel, and the appearance of a steam yacht in the harbor was a cherished rarity. But it was to the "natives," as those villagers who endured the rigors of a Maine winter were known, deprived of much of their livelihood by the closing purses of the summer folk, that my real sympathy went, and in particular to the widow and small son of Tom Griswold. He had been the affable, highly efficient manager of the Swimming and Tennis Club, who had known the needs and desires, as well as the good and bad habits, of all the members. His talents were manifold, from the tactful instruction of a new hostess on how best to organize a club function to the quiet but firm policing of young topers or indiscreet débutantes. He could even collect unpaid dues without causing offense. But lung cancer closed his useful career in his mid-forties, and Helen, his widow, found herself near destitution. Tom had wisely advised her to turn to me in need, and she did so, in the way that most appealed, with a very definite plan. She wanted a small capital to establish a beauty parlor, and I canvassed the summer colony with enough success to enable her, in only a few months' time, to set up Helen's Beauty Nook on Champlain Street.

It was an almost immediate success. I made a point of speaking personally to every lady who owned or rented a cottage, and it became a point of honor with them to make at least one appointment with Helen each summer. Many soon went to her exclusively. That I thus ruined an older establishment was to be regretted, but that is frequently the price of a free market. I have long learned that doing a good turn for one person may involve a bad one for another, but I cannot concede this to be a reason for eschewing good turns. That way darkness lies.

My backing of Helen's salon, however, would have been nothing without Helen herself. None of our ladies would have paid more than a single token visit to the Beauty Nook had the product proved in the least inadequate. But Helen had made herself an expert in hair styles, permanent waves, facials and even manicures. I had at first feared that her looks might be against her. She was large and plain, with no idle fat on her body; her obvious strength was that of a pioneer woman, and I even wondered whether her carefully set greying hair was not a bit ludicrously out of character with her stark air of seeming to suspect any too-elegant customer of being "fancy pants." But the ladies rightly saw her front as a guaranty of honesty and capability, and when they found that her mind, which might have been as simple and elevated as that of a rustic character in a Sarah Orne Jewett tale, was actually a mine of summer colony gossip, accumulated over a lifetime and made all the more amusing by her slow Maine drawl, they began to regret having to lose her services after Labor Day. To discuss whether Billy Dumphey had cheated at the bridge tournament or whether the club bandleader was really having an affair with the new soap heiress from Baltimore, while having a permanent that would make one shine at the umbrella tables, became a definite summer pleasure. Helen soon had to take on two assistants and a manicurist, but she always found time for a few words with the occupant of every chair.

The gossip, however, like the memory stored with every name and incident of summer history, was only one part of Helen's nature; she showed me a very different one. As her principal benefactor I was always treated with gratifying candor. Helen made no secret of how artfully she manipulated her fashionable clientele. She was a very serious and honorable person, and she did me the favor of attributing these qualities to myself. Her husband, who had been a very handsome as well as an able man — the "natives" must have been surprised when she "landed" him — had been her only passion, and he had now been replaced by their son. I had not seen Max since he was a sturdy twelve-year-old; she never allowed him to stick so much as his nose into the Beauty Nook, and on the few times when I called at her small clean clapboard house, at the end of a village alley with a happy view of the sea, he was out fishing or clamming or some other summer pursuit. At length I suspected that she was keeping him from me.

"What about it, Helen?" It was now July of 1933. "Aren't I good enough to meet your Prince of Wales?"

"Oh, *you're* good enough, Mr. Fairfax." She could never be persuaded to use my Christian name. "The question is, is *he?* But I think he's getting there. I'll be bringing him around one of these days."

"Why must he be so perfect to meet the likes of me?"

"Because I want him to impress you. I want him to make you want to help him."

"How?"

"Well, I don't mean financially. Thanks to you I have a nest egg that should see him through college and maybe even law school."

"He's already decided to be a lawyer?"

"Oh, yes, very definitely. And I approve. The law is the best way up. It's like the clergy in the Middle Ages."

"Happily it doesn't bar marriage. But the way up to where?"

"You know, Mr. Fairfax. Up from being the son of a village beautician."

"If he's a good boy, he'll be proud of that."

"Proud of *me*, you mean. He is a good boy, and he is. But he doesn't have to be proud of my job. Or of my social position. Nor do I want him to be. Far from it. And that's where I look to you. You've been so good to us, I dare to hope you'll be even gooder!"

"I'll do anything you ask, Helen."

"If you'd just take the boy under your wing a bit. Give him some guidance."

"What makes you think he'd listen to me?"

"Oh, he'll listen to you. I'll vouch for that."

I kept a small motor launch with a captain for deep sea fishing and trips around the island, and I suggested to her that I should take her son for an outing the following week. Max was waiting for me on the pier at the appointed hour, arrayed respectfully in what I guessed was a new red sweater and spotless white ducks. But I liked the way he greeted me, with a firm handshake and a polite but in no way deferential salutation. I inferred that his mother had dressed him but that his manners were his own.

His looks, at seventeen, which were to vary very little with the years, enhanced his air of self-confidence. He was a bit on the short side, stocky and well-built; his hair, thick and very black, was crew cut, and his eyes, large and brown, qualified his frank curiosity with a certain reserve. His features were regular and strong; he was handsome in a way that I recognized as peculiarly attractive to women.

It was a beautiful morning, and the sea was very calm. Sitting in the fantail, we talked about summer activities and wildlife on the island. He told me that he had seen a moose on Sergeant Mountain, a rare sight in those days. At last, when I had induced him to have a beer, I broached, as he had obviously been expecting, the subject of his legal career.

"Are you at all attracted by the idea of a big city practice, say in Boston or New York?"

"No, sir. I intend to practice right here in Bar Harbor."

"You surprise me. I should have thought the field was too limited. Wills and real estate; isn't that about the size of it? The summer people won't do you much good; they all have their own counsel at home. Who might retain you for a lease or a purchase, but that's all. The chances are they wouldn't even let you see the client."

He startled me by springing at once to a vigorous defensive.

"I wouldn't need the summer people. Or their lawyers. I wouldn't even want them. I don't mean to put *you* in that category, sir; I know all you've done for my mother. But I think the citizens of Mount Desert, the real citizens, I mean, have plenty of problems of their own that I could help them with. And my practice wouldn't have to be confined to this island, either. It could reach to Bangor, or even Augusta. For I'd like to go into politics, too. I'd like to do something for my state. Maine should be developing more businesses. I hate to see us contenting ourselves with being called 'Vacationland' and selling sentimental postcards and cushions stuffed with pine needles and antique stores full of fakes."

He might have been a fiery young Saint-Just, eager to bring down the blade of the guillotine on the necks of the members of the Swimming Club.

"Your mother doesn't seem to share your low opinion of the poor summer visitors."

"It's not really so much my low opinion of the summer visitors as it is my high one of the real Bar Harborites. We're an occupied nation; that's the gist of it. India might stop hating the British if they ever pulled out."

I was intrigued by his comparison. "But, my dear boy, think of all the business the summer people bring. Think of what they mean to your mother."

"I think of the price she pays for it."

"The price?"

"Do you really want to know?" He paused. "Mother said I could be frank with you."

I chuckled. "Your mother knows me like a book. Frankness is a subtle ploy. It always works with me."

But he was remorselessly serious. "I'm not trying to work anything, sir. Whatever I say I mean. What Mother may not have calculated is that I'd be honest about *her.* And that's what I mean about the price she paid. The price was keeping the 'natives,' as your friends call us, out of her hair salon — I'm sorry, I gag at the term 'Beauty Nook' — during the season."

"Why did she have to do that?"

"Because the summer ladies like to see the spot as an adjunct to their club, a place where they can meet and gossip freely without being subject to contact with the lower orders."

"But I thought your mother was popular with everyone in Bar Harbor, the 'real' Mount Deserters, as you call them, as well as us warm-weather swallows. How does she manage that if she has to be so invidiously discriminating?"

"Oh, she makes it up to the locals in the other nine months of the year, when she charges less. And she tells them frankly what she's up to. That it's the only way she can make a go of the salon. They understand. After all, most of them are in the same racket."

I was beginning to think that he was taking his mother rather lightly. "You know, of course, that she does it all for you."

"How could I not know it!" he exclaimed with sudden pain. "I know that she's sweated and slaved for me! And I'm going to pay her back, too. Not in dollars and cents, of course, but in becoming the man she wants me to be. Or ought to want me to be."

I admired his qualification. In fact, I was beginning to develop a considerable admiration for this young man. "You mean you won't stoop to her compromises?"

"Well, I don't like the word *stoop.* But it's certainly true that my mother has made compromises. That she's made them for me means that I mustn't despise them. And I don't. But neither do I have to repeat them. If I did, what would have been the good of them?"

"I like that. You owe it to her to be better. Yes, I like that very much. But do you tell her so?"

"I tell her everything."

"And how does she take that?"

"Not always so well. She tells me I must learn to be more practical."

"Don't."

At last he grinned. "I shan't."

I asked him now to tell me more of his life story. Some of it I already knew from Helen. He had gone to high school in Bar Harbor and graduated first in his class and was to matriculate at the University of Maine that fall. He had excelled in hockey and baseball. In the summers he had had various jobs: taking summer people on fishing trips, working for the Bar Harbor Motor Company, but he loved to read, mostly history and biography, and he got his books from the local library, where his girlfriend worked. It was the blueprint of the boyhood of an American success story.

The very next day I took his mother to lunch at an oyster bar down the street from her salon. I had no time to lose if I was to implement the plan I had already conceived.

"Hold on to your hat, Helen. I want to send Max to Yale."

Had I expected astonishment I should have been disappointed. Helen had foreseen the impression her golden boy would make. "I know you're a great man, Mr. Fairfax. But isn't it a bit late in the year to fix that up? Even for you?"

"I handled a fund drive for them. They owe me something. And if not this fall, I can surely arrange a transfer from Maine University next year. But let's strike for now. I gather his College Boards were tops. Do you think you could persuade him to let me try? He's awfully patriotic about his home state."

"Don't I know it! The trick will be to make him see that he can do more for Maine as an Ivy Leaguer. Greater professors, wider contacts and all that."

"And tell him, too, that it will guarantee his admission to Yale Law School."

"I'll go at it tonight."

"Telephone me. I'll be in all evening."

"He's a great kid, isn't he? I knew you'd like him."

"What's the girl like?"

"The girl?"

"The one in the library."

"He told you about her? Really? Maybe I've underestimated her." Helen shrugged impatiently. "But she's nothing, really. One of those neurotic mice that appeal to a man's pity. And collapse, once they're married, to be a drag on their husband for life."

"Dear me, how can you be so sure?"

"They're common enough in small towns. You, dear man, wouldn't know. But don't worry, I can handle *her*. And now I must get back to the shop, because I'll be leaving early to catch Max before he goes out for the evening."

"Helen, you haven't even ordered!"

"All the better for my waistline. Bless you, Mr. F!"

❧ ❧ ❧

Helen did a good job on her son, though she admitted to me that it was more difficult than she had expected. Max had at first insisted that to accept my offer would be another sellout to the voracious summer community, and she had used in vain the usual arguments about the benefits to be reaped from a seat of learning with more resources and more distinguished professors. Where she had finally prevailed was with the warning that his blind devotion to his village and state smacked of a small town provincialism that would hardly grace a future congressman or governor. It was his duty, was it not, to become as big a man as he could? When she informed me of her success, I put in a call to President Angell, and the transfer was approved in a week's time.

I was careful not to see too much of Max when he came to Yale. I had no wish to let him pigeonhole me in the role of condescending patron. I assured him there would always be a weekend bed for him in my New York brownstone, and he availed himself of this twice in his freshman year on occasions when I sent him theatre or opera tickets. His manner was reserved, even constrained, but he gradually warmed up as he perceived that I neither asked nor seemed to expect anything of him. When in the fall of his sophomore year he invited me to come up to a football game, and I took him to a good dinner at Mory's afterwards, we grew closer. Oh, but I had to be careful! He was still suspicious of the "summer colonist" in his benefactor.

For benefactor I had now indisputably become. I had finally persuaded him to let me relieve his hard-working mother of all costs of his tuition and allowance, though only on his stipulated condition that I take his legally binding note to repay me. To have refused would have been to insult him. He now began to like me well enough, but I was perfectly aware that he made it his duty to like me. How else could such a puritan justify taking my money? Our arrangement had to be businesslike, and Max would do business only with men of whom he approved.

It was perfectly clear, anyway, long before any of my small sums were refunded (as of course they all ultimately were), that my investment was paying off. In this freshman year Max's work habits had been almost compulsive, but as a sophomore he had begun to look around and make friends and even, to Helen's amused satisfaction, to spend some of his allowance, at first hoarded as "tainted" money, on smarter clothes. He was elected to the Zeta Psi fraternity and "heeled" successfully for *The Yale Daily News.* When his mother told me that he was looking for a summer job as a tutor, I offered him one in Bar Harbor with my son Gordon. Poor young man, he could hardly refuse me.

I say "poor man" because the job would commit him to live in one of his hated summer cottages in Bar Harbor, not because Gordon would prove in the least a difficult charge. At fifteen, having just completed his fourth-form year at Saint Paul's School in New Hampshire, my son was a tall, pale, dark-eyed, silent boy of a gentle disposition and a curiously strong will, a near genius in calculus, who treated me with a guarded courtesy that might have been the cover of an amiable condescension. Obviously I was not engaging Max to cultivate the boy's intellect; I simply hoped that he might induce him to take some slight interest in tennis or sailing or any outdoor activity. So far Gordon's sole idea of summer sport had been a stroll down the Shore Path to the village library. My other goal, of course, was to get a closer view of my protégé.

Constance, as usual, saw what I was up to. "If he gets Gordon up a single mountain, I miss my bet," she observed dryly, though she liked Max. "What he'll do is fall in love with Varina. You'd better discourage her visits."

Varina Pierce lived with her parents, Judge and Mrs. Allen Pierce, right next door to us on the Shore Path in a less pretentious but still commodious shingle pile. They were Philadelphians, sympathetic and charming, of an old and distinguished but by no means wealthy family. With their two handsome sons and two beautiful daughters they dominated the social life of the summer colony; almost everyone had a child more or less in love with a Pierce. Varina, the eldest and my goddaughter, now twenty-two (older than Max), had from childhood flatteringly chosen me as her guide and mentor. My role, it appeared, was not so much to bring her in due course "to the bishop" as the prayer book directs, as it was to indoctrinate her in all the ways in which she might consume the great rosy apple of life, skin, core and all. I was delighted to play my part as long as she wished, confident that it would end as soon as she attained the age of boys and dances. But no, she seemed to need me even more then, for she did not marry immediately on "coming out," as everyone expected, and had taken all her courses at Bryn Mawr with the utmost seriousness.

"I wonder if her ambition isn't to get you away from me," Constance commented once when Varina had left the house after spending two hours with me on the verandah.

"She might if she thought you'd put up a struggle," I retorted. "She has no taste for easy victories."

I guess I have made it sufficiently clear that Varina was a charmer, almost too much so, like the blond heroine of an illustrated magazine story, with a radiant complexion, mocking blue eyes and a high habit of laughter. Constance, who never liked her, no doubt because I did so much, observed once that her face was too flat and her features too small for permanent good looks, that she lacked bone structure and would be as plain as the day at forty. Instead, Varina has retained her beauty and youthful appearance, almost spookily, to this very day. It is a common joke that she must keep a portrait of herself, like Dorian Gray, to wither in her attic. Indeed, the gods had given her too much.

"Too smart for her own good" was the way Constance put it. Varina wanted the world, the whole world, the "great world"; she had visions of power and influence, as the consort of some great man, or even on her own, as an early woman member of Congress, or in the cabinet, like Madame Perkins. Lady Astor was one of her ideals: rich, beautiful, noble, politically eminent. Could any woman want more than that? Varina could. She craved the intellectual world as well; she dreamed of the admiring company of famous writers and artists. The stage, too; even the movies were not to be scorned. Varina would have glimpsed a convent with a curious eye had she suspected that there were greater joys to be had in isolation and chastity.

At Bryn Mawr she had been converted by a teacher to the programs of the New Deal, and she was ready at one point to go even further and to toy with socialism. Should she, she asked me once, go so far as to drop her listing in the Social Register?

"I have a little rule in these matters," I cautioned her. "You might find it useful. Before giving up anything I suspect may have become anachronistic, I always look behind me. If there's a line waiting for the place, I keep it."

"No matter what that entails?" she exclaimed, her eyes widening in reproach. "No matter how immoral? Oh, Uncle Oscar, I never thought you were such an opportunist!"

"Then get to know me better, my dear. Once you've decided your end is a good one, be very careful about scrapping your means. Use every tool that fate has endowed you with. You happen to have been born with a very good shed of them: looks, brains, charm and social position. Hang on to them all! Don't be the kind of ass who bleats 'I want to make it on my own' or 'I want to be loved for myself.' None of us knows just why we get ahead or for just what we are loved. We might be humiliated to learn! The point is to get ahead. *And* to be loved."

"And you think some man — some man, I mean, who *appeared* to be worth my interest — might actually love me because I was in the Social Register?"

"Who knows? There's a character in Proust called Mademoiselle Legrandin, intelligent and cultivated, who marries Monsieur de Cambremer for the secret pleasure of being able to refer to one of his noble relatives as '*ma tante de Ch'nouville,*' using his family's stylish habit of dropping the *e* in that name."

"But really, Uncle Oscar, you can't think I'd be attracted to anyone who was that much of an ass!"

"But you'd never know; that's just the point! The example is extreme, I admit. But even the highest-minded people are subject to motivations they'd rather die than admit. Look to the product, not the cause. Frances Perkins would still be secretary of labor even if Roosevelt had appointed her for a secret admiration of her hats!"

"Then he would be the crazy one!" she exclaimed with a hoot of laughter. "And speaking of Miss Perkins, isn't hers the way a smart girl should be heading? Marriage isn't the only ladder anymore. Who's her husband? Mr. Wilson? Who's ever heard of Mr. Wilson?"

"Nobody, I grant you. And of course careers are opening up for women. But it's slow going. Marriage is still the way for what you want now. You should marry a great man. One who has the kind of career that he has to share with a wife. A statesman or diplomat. Or even the owner of a newspaper. Where you and he can be essentially partners. Where he will need your help, not only as his housekeeper and hostess, but as the person who shares his aspirations and ideals, who *works* with him."

"What about love? Or shouldn't that count?"

"But of course you must have love as well. It's just as easy to love a great man as it is a small one. Just keep yourself from falling for the sexy little tricks of sexy little men. I wouldn't give this advice to every girl, my dear. But you are not going to be happy unless you have something big. And that's a *good* thing, too."

"Yes, Socrates."

❧ ❧ ❧

Gordon and Max, I was happy to note, got on splendidly from the start. I had told my son that I had no intention of forcing a tutor on him, that Max was hired only to be his companion if he wanted one, and that if he didn't, Max could be *mine*, his duties to consist of taking me fishing or around the golf course. But Gordon, after only a brief stand-off, appeared to have decided that such a switch would not be necessary. Max, with remarkable ease, even, I surmised, with a subtle adroitness, had made his way into the boy's affections in less than a week's time. Gordon had never had a real friend before; he was too diffident, too hard to convince that anyone worthy of his esteem could ever return it. And now Max was suddenly his hero.

When I congratulated Max privately on his success, he insisted there had been no art to it. "He's a remarkable kid, Mr. Fairfax. You really ought to be paying him for what he's teaching *me*. He's giving me a course in calculus, and on our walks he makes me practice my bad French."

"But it's you who've brought him out. Which is something his mother and I have never succeeded in doing. And there's nothing like asking for more from someone who's already given you the moon. Do you think you might help him a little with his social life? You and he haven't been once to the Swimming Club."

Max's face darkened. "Gordon hates the place."

"That's just the point. It's silly to hate it. It's not worth hating. If he really hates it, that's something he ought to get over."

"But he doesn't really know any of his age group there. And I certainly wouldn't know any of mine."

"And don't want to, either. I see that plain enough. But it wouldn't do you any harm to give that chip on your shoulder a bit of vacation. My goddaughter, Varina Pierce, is coming for dinner tonight. She pretty much rules the roost up here in the younger set. She'll be delighted to introduce you around."

But Max's expression showed that this was not going to be easy. "May I be frank, sir?"

"Aren't you always?"

"Yes, when I talk to you. But I don't have to be always talking."

"Go ahead."

He scratched his head. "Well, I certainly don't want you to think I'm ungrateful for all you've done for me."

"Max," I put in firmly, "I don't want you *ever* to be grateful. I have a hobby of believing in people. It's how I get my kicks. I happen to believe in you. You and I don't owe each other anything."

"I see that, sir. And it's not just gratitude. I *like* you. You're the nearest thing to a father I've ever had. But what troubles me is that I feel you want to make something of me. And maybe that something is something I don't want to be."

"I see it. You think I want you to be smart and social, like some of the young asses at the Swimming Club."

"Well, something like that. Why, for example, did you give me that credit at Jay Press in New Haven? Was it because you knew I'd *have* to spend it, if I did, on stylish suits?"

"I wanted to be sure you were well dressed."

"But why? So I could impress the preppies? The Grotties and Hotchkissites?"

"So that you could feel at ease with them. I didn't want suits and ties to be a barrier."

"But would they be? To any decent sort of guy?"

"No. But the world's not made up of just decent guys. It's important to know how to get on with all types."

"Is that what you really want? For me to get on with *all* types? But snappy clothes might be a barrier between me and the scholarship men. Look, Mr. Fairfax. Let me put it this way. I have an idea that you want me to be tapped for Scroll and Key. As you were."

I paused to consider my reply. It would be important because he had now given me the chance to explain my real goal. Scroll

& Key and Skull & Bones were the two most esteemed of the six Yale senior societies; Bones made its selections on the grounds of merit, in studies, athletics or extracurricular activities; it included the leaders of the class. Keys, on the other hand, was more urbane, more social, more like a gentlemen's club in New York or Boston.

"I've never specified a goal for you, Max. And Keys, in any event, would not have been it. I try to divine what it is that *you* want for yourself. And I suspect that I'm correct in thinking that it's the real top. If you want anything, you want Bones. Well, I believe you have a good chance for it. And with my Yale connections, that is not altogether a wild guess."

Max now came as close to blushing as I was ever to see him. And it occurred to me that it was even possible that he did not quite like my hitting the nail so neatly on the head. If I was Mammon to this young idealist, and if Mammon had read him so correctly, nay, if Mammon was advising him to follow the very course he himself had in mind, what did it tell him of the direction in which he was headed?

"You've got me pegged too high, sir!" he exclaimed in a kind of disgust. Was it self-disgust? "What have I done to make you think I'm Bones material?"

"It's just a hunch. But I've learned to have faith in my hunches."

"You're going to be disappointed."

"Oh, that won't bother me in the least. There's a life after Bones. And no bad pun intended."

Varina, at dinner that night with just the family present, talked with great animation about a wonderful treasure hunt whose fantastical clues had taken the "bright young people" in their motors on mad dashes over the whole island. One of the objects to be brought to the judges was a "redheaded man with false teeth," and Varina's partner had incurred the wrath of a famous steel magnate in Seal Harbor, who was rumored to possess both qualifications, by calling on him at his mansion and asking if they could "bring him in." She did not direct her remarks particularly at Max, but I could see that she noted him, and when after dinner she took him into the library to play backgammon, it was obvious that her interest had definitely been aroused.

I also observed that Max stared at her somberly during much of our meal, and I now recalled what Constance had said. It was odd that I should have forgotten it. Did Varina want to add another scalp to the row hung up in her tepee? Or was it the jealousy of an earlier "favorite" for a later one? She had always regarded me as her particular property. Did she want to share me with even a handsome young man? I loved my goddaughter, but I knew her.

Gordon's account, a day later, of his and Max's meeting with Varina and her group at the Swimming Club did little to allay my apprehension that my enlistment of her social services on behalf of these two young men might not have been one of my happier ideas. Gordon, who regarded females with considerable distrust (an attitude he was not to shed for several more years), was indignant at the way Varina had "toyed" with his tutor. I suspected that he was rather more annoyed at the tutor's evident susceptibility to such toying. He was in no mood to release any part of his new friend.

"When we came out to the pool in our bathing trunks, I suggested to Max that we sit by the shallow end, away from all the *jeunesses dorées* clustered around the high dive." Gordon's cool, affected tone sufficiently expressed his opinion of those he sought to avoid. "But your charming goddaughter wouldn't have it. As soon as she spotted us, she left off adorning her lovely limbs with sun oil and tripped sexily down the length of the pool to speak to us. Oh, you should have seen her, Pater, demurely holding up the front of her suit to protect her chaste bosom! She had unloosened the shoulder straps, of course, to receive a more perfect tan. 'Wouldn't we please join her and her rabble?' I replied that we were fine where we were, but Max, frowning at my churlishness, leaped to his feet, and off we went."

"Well, really, Gordon, how could you not have?"

"I? Only too easily. But not my besotted tutor. We joined the idiot group and were introduced around, receiving their condescending stares. None of the fair sex, of course, deigned to more than touch their knuckles to my extended paw, but I could see their shrouded interest in Max's muscles. He, poor lad, was at a loss for words; I'm afraid he showed himself rather a hick. 'Is it true you're the son of the great Helen?' one of these freshwater mermaids inquired. 'If so, we're all very much in your debt. We couldn't appear in public without her aid.' Max was riled by her tone. 'My mother's name is Mrs. Griswold,' he snarled, and a constrained silence fell over the group. But trust the adored Varina to break the spell. 'But my dear Max,' she cooed, 'Lydia wasn't trying to put you down. She was quite sincere. Who are any of us to sneer at an honest trade? Lydia's own money comes from soup. And Neddy's grandfather started with a pushcart, didn't he, Neddy? And what about your family, Peggy? Wasn't it carpets? And retail, too? Ugh! What was Mr. Fairfax's motto for you? From rugs to riches? Oh, it's too lovely!'"

I was thoroughly irked with Gordon now. "I wish Varina weren't quite so free with my gags."

"Oh, she quotes you everywhere. You're the source of half her wit. But at least she doesn't claim it's hers. I'll hand her that."

"But not much else, I gather. And how did Max take all this pretty persiflage? Was he placated?"

"Well, he was still rather *farouche* for a bit, but when the divine Varina took him away from the group and sat with him at the edge of the pool and chatted with him while she dangled her beautiful legs in the water, he softened up. Indeed, she soon had him eating out of her hand. Oh my, yes, he would have eaten a toad out of her hand. I'm not sure he didn't."

I didn't bother to comment on this, but I couldn't be unaware that Max and Gordon went every day now to the Swimming Club. Gordon made no attempt to conceal his dislike of this, and he and Max had daily disputes at breakfast in which the tutor endeavored to convince his ward that it was a perfect day for swimming or that he needed a tennis lesson or that his father wished him to mix more with the younger people at the club.

"We all know who *you* want to mix with," Gordon would respond crudely, but he always ended up by going.

Now, I had every reason to know that Varina had been seeing a great deal in the previous winter of one Theodore Lewis, Jr., the thirty-five-year-old son and sole heir of the owner of a Pennsylvania newspaper chain. Teddy Lewis was a "catch"; he was amiable, handsome (despite a slightly too rotund countenance), cultivated and supposedly high-minded, and it was generally believed that, when Lewis Senior should release at last his conservative grip on the journals, his son would lead them into a more liberal future. That I should have seen Varina as a potential partner in this estimable enterprise was only consistent with my stated views as to her goal in life. Here love could be united with a career tailor-made for her aspirations. But what was she up to?

One morning after breakfast I walked over to the Pierces' lawn, on which I had spied my goddaughter alone, stretched out on a deck chair, reading a book. I patted the two friendly black Labradors that ran to greet me and seated myself at the end of her chair.

"I've come to ask you something."

Her instantly closed book showed how ready she was. "Something about your precious protégé?"

"Is that what you call Max?"

"Well, isn't he? Aren't you sending him through college? And won't you send him through law school? And launch him on a great public career?"

Her large pale blue eyes mocked me. She and I, since her seventh year, had been on terms of absolute equality. Unless, indeed, it could be said that she was the superior.

"So you know all that?"

"Everyone knows all that. There are no secrets in Bar Harbor. You, of all people, should know that. Besides, Max told me."

"*He* told you?"

"Why not? Isn't that like him? He doesn't want anyone to be under any illusions about him. Don't worry. He's devoted to you."

I felt unreasonably pleased at this simple and surely not surprising statement. But Max was always a bit of an enigma. "Very well, then. Now you know what *I'm* doing for him. What are *you?*"

"Oh, I'm studying him. I'm trying to find out if he's as good as you think. I start with the presumption that he must be. After all, you've always taken a flattering interest in me, and I've got to believe you have grounds for *that.*"

"And suppose you come to the conclusion that I've put my money, so to speak, on the right horse. In both cases. Then what?"

Her smile was more than mischievous; it was almost sly. "Well, haven't you told me I should marry a great man? How could I do better than take the one you're creating?"

The subject was getting out of hand. It was time to be serious. "I thought you may have already found your hero."

"Ted? Oh, nothing's settled there. Besides, I'm beginning to wonder if his old man may not live forever. He seems tougher every time I see him."

If I was serious, she was still not. She was having too good a time with me. Might she be jealous of my interest in Max? "Griswold is still a boy, really. We don't know how he'll turn out yet. He's got a long way to go. And he's a good four years younger than you."

"Three."

"Don't play with me, Varina. It's not like you."

"On the contrary, it's very much like me. I've had my share of Maxes in this life. And I've never hurt a hair on one of their little heads!"

I was beginning to get angry, and I paused to be sure of my control. "But this time you don't know what you're dealing with. He's a very intense young man."

"But that's just what makes him attractive! Really, Uncle Oscar, I don't know what's got into you. If your protégé is going to be damaged by a flirtation with a pretty girl at a summer resort, he hasn't the stuff in him for your noble dreams! Now please, beloved godfather, go home and let me finish my book. You're getting all worked up, and that's hardly becoming to Socrates."

I nodded, with sealed lips, and turned to go back to my house. She had reached the point where opposition would only make her worse.

The next day I made a point of going to the Swimming Club at noon, the hour when my contemporaries, at least the ladies, gathered around the umbrella tables for cocktails and gossip, and the younger fry, finished with tennis, assembled in bathing suits by the deep end of the long pool. I spotted Max, seated by Varina in the center of her group, his eyes ridiculously fixed on hers. Really, could I have dreamed he'd be such an ass?

Gordon came over and watched me watching.

"Some tutor you have," I observed sarcastically. "Is *that* what I'm paying him for?"

"Isn't it? I thought you wanted to expose him to the *haut monde*. To give him polish. And lessons in *galanterie*. Now, I suppose, you're wondering if you haven't overdone it."

I reserved for another time my lecture to Gordon on filial impertinence. "I'm wondering if I hadn't better send you both to Gant for a couple of weeks." Gant was my fishing club in Canada. "Mrs. Pierce told me this morning that Varina was going up to Murray Bay at the end of the month to visit the Lewises, so she should still be there when you get back. And after that it will be time for Max to be thinking of Yale."

"Mrs. Pierce just *happened* to tell you that?" Gordon's lips were pursed for a silent whistle. "Then she knows what's going on. Obviously, she doesn't want to lose the heir of the tabloids for an uncouth 'native' lad. But *verbum sapienti*, Pater. Don't send us off just yet. I suspect the divine Varina may be on the point of giving her rustic swain his quietus. It would be better, would it not, for it to come from her than from you?"

I had to agree with this, so I chose a course of inaction, which, anyway, a good half of the time, solves our most pressing problems. And, indeed, the passage of only three more days seemed to have brought me my god from the machine. Ted Lewis himself arrived in Bar Harbor — whether or not secretly alerted by Varina's mother I have never known — and put up at the Mallvern Hotel. He was soon seen everywhere in the company of Varina. They seemed to be on the friendliest terms.

Then came the night when Max failed to appear at our dinner table. Gordon told me that his tutor had left the Swimming Club after what appeared to have been a row with Varina, not at their usual site by the pool but down by the sea, away from the club house, where the ever-watching Gordon could just make them out. Max had been gesticulating violently and then had abruptly broken off and rushed up the steps, brushing past Gordon without a word. Gordon had followed him through and out of the club house to see him disappear down the main street. He had left the car, of course, for his ward. We assumed he had gone to his mother's.

But when I called Helen after dinner he was not there, nor had she heard from him. He was still not home when we went to bed, but I resisted Constance's suggestion that we call the police. We should wait at least until morning.

I did not, however, sleep well, and when, at four A.M., I heard footsteps on the gravel drive below, I went downstairs to let him in. I found him sitting on the porch, waiting presumably for dawn. In the light of my flashlight he appeared a figure of stone. He neither turned nor spoke to me.

"Are you all right, Max?" No answer. "Are you sober?"

"I am now. I went swimming in the ocean."

"Do you mind if I join you?"

"I don't mind anything."

We sat for a while in silence, he perfectly indifferent to my presence.

"I think it might be a good idea," I ventured at last, "if you and Gordon went up to Gant for a couple of weeks. My cabin is off in the woods, quite a way from the main camp. You'd have the wilderness to yourselves."

"You wouldn't rather I quit the job and went home?" He still did not look at me. "I haven't been much good to Gordon in the past three weeks. You ought to kick my butt out of here."

"But I have no wish to do that. Nor would Gordon want me to. Don't you really know by now that we're your friends, Max?"

He turned to look at me at last, and I could see his face clearly from the light in the hall. It was impassive except for a hint of grim resignation.

"I know you are, sir. But your friendship is wasted on me."

"Let me be the judge of that. But tell me why you think so."

"Because I'm crazy! I completely lost my head over your bitch of a goddaughter." His eyes were suddenly defiant. "*Now* would you like to boot me out? Because I won't take that back!"

"I wouldn't ask you to. I think her conduct has sufficiently justified the term. All I can say in her defense is that she's not always like that."

He shrugged and turned his eyes back to the now paling sea. "I made no sense. I didn't care who she was or who I was. I wanted to marry her! Did you ever hear anything more idiotic? I wanted her to run off with me. I thought I might get some money out of Gordon. Or if he wouldn't give it to me, I even planned to steal his wallet. Do you know he keeps hundred dollar bills in it?"

It hardly surprised me. Nothing about Gordon really surprised me. "And what was Varina's reaction to all this?"

"She was scared shitless. She'd been playing with matches, and suddenly the whole place blew up. She did her best to contain me. Finally she confessed that all along she'd been engaged to that asshole Lewis."

"Did she?" *Had* she been?

"I came back here and swiped one of your whiskey bottles. I walked in the woods and drank it. I would have drunk it all, but it slipped out of my hand and hit a rock. I was potted. I wanted to kill myself. Then I plunged into the ocean and swam out to sea. But all the time I knew I was never going to drown. All the time I saw myself doing exactly what I was doing. I swam back and put on my clothes and sat on the beach till I was more or less sober again. I was a madman playing at being a madman." His snicker was sharp and harsh. "Like Hamlet."

"But fortunately you don't have to kill a king. You might even in time find yourself sufficiently recovered to attend Ophelia's wedding with indifference."

"Do you think she'd ever invite the likes of me?" he sneered. "Anyway, you see what a phony I am."

"My dear boy, we're all of us phonies. In the sense that we're never the romantics we like to dream of. And it's a good thing, too. Don't knock it. Otherwise you might be at the bottom of the Atlantic."

"At least I'd be a genuine corpse. And not the audience of my own bad acting. Oh, I see now well enough what Varina was to me. She was this island. The siren. The enchantress. She was everything I'd never really had. I wanted to fuck Bar Harbor!"

"I think I suspected something of that sort. Let us now hope that the naughty girl has been exorcised. And you had better go to bed with the sleeping pill I shall bring you. I'll see you're not disturbed all day. And nobody is going to ask you any questions!"

❧ ❧ ❧

But Varina was far from exorcised. Her image, I was later to learn, had simply been prodded deep down out of sight in Max's *id.* In the meantime he prospered. He was tapped by Skull & Bones and elected to the board of *The Yale Daily News* and to Phi Beta Kappa. He made many good friends among the leaders of the class. His manner was much easier, his charm more outgoing. Hardly a trace of the suspicious, truculent village boy survived. When he visited me now in New York, he was an interesting and delightful companion.

And yet. Trust me to look a gift horse in its maw. There was something about him that offered the tiniest hint of the unspontaneous, of the young man who did everything perfectly — just a mite too perfectly. Little Bilham, in James's *Ambassadors,* says of his friend Chad Newsome, whom everyone finds transformed into a model gentleman by the influence of Madame de Vionnet, that he had liked him as well in his former state. And that was exactly what I sometimes felt about Max.

I hinted at this to his mother, but she found only improvement in his alteration.

"What you took for a sign of integrity was only bad manners. Max's principles are just as high as they ever were. He's learned polish, that's all, and he'd be a dunce if he hadn't, with the wonderful opportunities you've given him."

When I asked her about the girl in the library, she snorted. "How could he settle down on *that* farm after he'd seen Paree? At least the Pierce girl did that for him. She might not have had any love to give him, but she surely showed him what it *might* be. There was no going back to Miss Mouse after that."

"And how did Miss Mouse take it? Was her little heart broken?"

"Oh, quite. And she was ass enough to show it, calling him up tearily: 'Aren't I *ever* going to see you, Maxy?' Fools like that deserve what they get. They give our sex a bad name. She could have landed Max twice over had she played her cards right. But mothers don't teach their daughters anything these days. In this case, thank heavens!"

I decided that I didn't want to ask Helen what she would have taught a daughter had she had one.

Max's success continued unabated right through Yale Law School, of whose *Journal* he became editor-in-chief. I had all along, of course, hoped that he would enter my firm on his graduation, but I wasn't sure that he had given up his early resolution to practice in his native state. He never told me, and I never asked. But when, in the fall of his last year, it became essential to discuss the matter, it appeared that he was no longer averse to a "big city" start. This came out when I went back to his rooms for a drink after a football game in New Haven. But he struck his old ironical note.

"I realize, of course, Mr. F, that I owe it to my munificent benefactor to do my 'time' in his sweat shop. But not forever, surely? It's not quite *Doctor Faustus*, is it?"

His smile was cheerful enough, but I didn't quite like it.

"What do you mean by that?" I asked gruffly.

"Well, aren't you the Mephistopheles of Jason, Fairfax and Richards? Haven't you supplied me with every earthly delight for the last six years to purchase my soul for your blazing inferno?"

I grunted. "I could have had a dozen just as good for nothing. They line up every spring, begging to be incinerated."

"Yes, but you wanted *me*, didn't you? I wonder why."

"Don't ask fiends their reasons. They might just tell you. But it's perfectly true that I think an apprenticeship in my firm would be the best possible preparation for anything you might wish to do later: politics, finance, the judiciary, even teaching."

"But what you're counting on is that once I'm in there, I'll stick. That I'll be too engrossed to leave. That I'll be caught up in the rat race for partnership. And after that in the even rattier race for senior partnership."

I cupped my hands before my eyes as if I were following a horse race through binoculars. "Come on, Griswold! Giddy up! Hurrah, Griswold! He made it!" I dropped my hands to my lap. "Is that how you see me?"

Max's laugh, still cheerful, had yet a rueful note. "Oh, yes, I see you leading me from the paddock through the cheering crowd. Of course, you warned me, years ago. That was how you got your kicks, wasn't it? You've always played perfectly fair. All you're facing now is the natural meanness of a protégé who wants to attribute his failures to his patron and his successes to himself. I know perfectly well that my seeking an interview at Jason Fairfax has been my own decision."

"Then you *have* sought one?"

"I've already made an appointment. Without even mentioning your name."

"Good! Then I needn't mention yours. Mephisto can return to Hades with his contract unsigned. How about another shot of that bourbon?"

Varina's life, on the other hand, had taken a most unpleasant turn. As Mrs. Lewis she had not found herself anything like the power in the family she had hoped to be. Her father-in-law had shown no inclination to release the smallest part of his tight hold on his chain; indeed, the professed ambitions of his liberal daughter-in-law might even have played a role in the abandonment of any idea of his early retirement. And worst of all, as Varina indignantly complained to me, was that her husband, far from showing the independence of his sire of which he had boasted in their courtship, was now revealing himself as the most submissive member of a submissive family.

"It was all an *act*, Uncle Oscar. He saw all the things I wanted and took for granted they were just the pipe dreams of a silly post-débutante that would go away with the first baby. Well, that first baby's going to be a long time coming if *that's* the way he feels. I'm beginning to suspect the only thing he really believes in is keeping the family fortune intact. He talks about it now as if it were a sacred trust. All that yack about making a better world and a more equal America was just fashionable window dressing to impress me. The kind of bright-colored blazer a man wears only when he is young. After that it's understood, isn't it, that he should be as much a sobersides as his hateful old man?"

The worst part of all this, I reflected sadly, was that there was no hint of love in her tone. What seemed most to upset her was not that Ted had ceased to be the man she loved as that he had ceased to be the man she needed for the furtherance of her own career. Had the business with Max precipitated her into a premature marriage? Mightn't she have fathomed the true nature of her neither deep nor subtle spouse in a few more months of courtship?

❧ ❧ ❧

After Pearl Harbor the navy took both Max from my firm (where he had been employed for a year) and Ted Lewis from his newspapers. Max became the executive officer of a destroyer escort in the Atlantic, and Varina's husband an intelligence officer on an aircraft carrier in the Pacific. Varina worked as a hostess in the Officers' Service Committee in New York, of which I was chairman, where she was just as ravishingly successful as might have been expected. My pleasure in this, however, was dampened by the rumor that she was having an affair with a Royal Navy commander on Atlantic convoy duty. She didn't tell me about it, nor did I ask. We had already fallen somewhat apart because of my lack of sympathy for her openly avowed discontent with her husband, and now the breach was widened. Her cheating on a spouse overseas was utterly disgusting to me.

But the next trial that she caused me was considerably more acute. The British officer proved only an interlude, a brief first chapter in the exercise of her newly found independence. Max used to put up at my house on the rare occasions when his ship docked in New York. On one of these he ran into Varina, reporting to me in my capacity as head of her committee. After the first tense shock of seeing his old flame and finding her openly and shamelessly glad to see him, he stammered out an invitation to go out on the town with him that night, an expedition in which I was obviously not included. He did not return until four in the morning, with only two hours before he was due back on his ship. He was mute about what had occurred or not occurred, and I could only hope that they might not meet again for a considerable period, if at all. I was wrong. I found out, only two months later, when Varina took a week's leave of absence from her work, that she had gone to Charleston, where Max's ship was in dry dock for repairs. Once the hunted, she had changed her role.

Oh, it was all plain enough, even banal. The small town kid, surly and incoherent with first love, had been transformed into the cool and dapper naval officer, already decorated for his adroit ship-handling in the nighttime ramming of a surfaced submarine. When Varina came back to town and invited me to lunch at the most expensive of French restaurants, I prepared myself for the worst.

The first sip of her cocktail brought her straight to the point. Putting down her glass and leaning forward with an air of charming but rehearsed candor, lit up by her most beguiling smile, she confessed, or appeared to confess, that she was helplessly in love. "If, on Max's part, it was puppy love back in that Bar Harbor summer, it's puppy love on my part now. And do you know something, godfather dearest? Puppy love is best."

"Aren't you a rather mature puppy?"

"Ouch! But I guess I had that coming to me. What I really mean is that for me it's first love."

"Poor Teddy. What was it with him?"

"Illusion. Pure and simple. But I don't take all the blame for that. It was partly his fault. He pretended to be something he wasn't. It was as if he'd been hiding under the table and taking notes while you and I were talking about the kind of man I should marry. As if we had given him the hot dope on how to pose as a proper candidate for my hand!"

"And what did he expect you'd do when his mask fell off? He must have known it was bound to in time."

"Oh, by then he thought he'd be safe. I'd be a subdued little housewife, dazzled by his sexual performance, with a baby to distract me."

I sighed. "Well, it's obvious you haven't been either subdued or dazzled."

I turned my attention to the menu, but only to give me time to think. When we had ordered, I resumed. "So what are your plans? I take it there'll be a divorce. Will Teddy oppose it?"

"Not if I claim no alimony. There's no problem there."

"Didn't he make you a premarital settlement?"

She just hesitated. "Yes."

"A substantial one?"

"Well, hardly, in relation to his old man's fortune."

"Shouldn't you give that back?"

"Uncle Oscar, are you crazy? Why on earth should I do that?"

"Because you've been a bad wife to him. That's all nonsense, you know, about his deceiving you. He was very much in love and trying to be what you wanted him to be. It wasn't his fault that he couldn't get around his father. And when you found you couldn't get everything out of him you wanted, you threw up the game. Isn't that the long and short of it?"

Varina had too much at stake to lose her temper with me. Besides, she never lost her temper unless it was to her advantage to do so. The basic coolness of her nature, which she was too intelligent to reveal to sentimentalists, had been manipulated to become a part of her charm. She was fully aware that I was still a factor in Max's life — how important a one she was not sure — and she was not going to risk upsetting his possibly exaggerated feelings of loyalty and gratitude.

"There's something in what you say, Uncle Oscar, though

you put it so harshly. But let me ask you this. Didn't you play a major role in making me what I am? Didn't you point the way to my marrying a great man? And didn't you raise and educate just such a man and place him right under my nose? Be fair now! Didn't you advise me that until women attained their proper place in a man's world, they would have to use the only weapons they had? And what were those but sex and marriage?"

"I may have used some such argument," I retorted hotly. "But I never suggested that sex should be used without feeling or marriage entered into without love! I was advising you how to make the most out of your life. In *every* sense."

"You were advising me how to have my cake and eat it too. *That* was what you were doing. Well, now I'm doing it. Just because I made one mistake shouldn't mean I have to wallow in it for the rest of my life. I love Max, and he loves me, and we're going to be a great couple together. And *you* will have done it, Uncle Oscar. It will be your triumph!"

"A triumph built on adultery and a wrecked home!"

But Varina simply shook her head slowly, with a small fixed smile that seemed to relegate me to a retirement home. "Those are not terms that have much meaning in a world at war. We have to live by the scraps we can pick up."

"I shall have to look about to see if there are any left for me." I stared bleakly down at the prosciutto the waiter had just placed before me. "Don't expect me to dance at your wedding."

She took this firmly as a proposal of truce and now proceeded to relate to me, with calm lucidity, their plans to marry on Max's next leave and to get an apartment in Washington as soon as he should be transferred, as was expected after two years at sea, to shore duty in the Navy Department.

Things turned out as they had wished, and Max and Varina were married in New York in a civil ceremony in a judge's chambers to which I was not invited. Varina had not taken seriously my request to be excluded, but Max had, after receiving the note that, in my bitterness, I had not been able to resist sending him: "I offer such congratulations as may be in order to the man who has at last achieved his ambition to fuck Bar Harbor!"

❧ ❧ ❧

My hateful note had the effect of permanently changing my relationship with Max.

Of course, I was wrong to have sent it. Who was I to believe that I could keep Max Griswold in a glass jar? If Varina had behaved unconscionably with respect to her husband, had *he?* Had not that marriage been well on the rocks before his affair with Varina? What I think I really minded was my suspicion that Max did not face what he was doing, that he was disguising to himself a fundamental change of allegiance from the idealistic standards of his youth, that he was yanking a curtain over his earlier awareness of what Varina had symbolized to him. Now it was all love, love, love, and he didn't care to be reminded that the siren to whom he was so willingly, even so deliberately, succumbing was the siren of the old world he had once despised.

Max, I am sure, never altogether forgave me. But neither did he ever break with me. How could he? He owed me too much, and he was never a man to turn from an obligation. Only three years after the war he became my law partner, as he was later to become that of my son, Gordon, who never wavered in his devotion to his former tutor. And he was always, of course, the husband of my goddaughter, who so persistently refused to recognize my disapproval of her marriage that she ended by making it seem to all the world that she had never been out of my heart and by inducing me, with an ultimately rather amused resignation, to accept her scenario as true. I was a trump card in her hand at bridge, to be used for making the contract she had bid or setting that of her opponents. No, the Max Griswolds were never going to let *me* slip out of their lives. I could only a bit grudgingly hope that I had been as much use to them as they seemed to think.

For I had loved Max — loved him as a child of my own. And I had loved Varina. Nor had those loves ever quite died; at moments they would flare up again, almost to brightness. I have had constantly to remind myself that it was not really altogether foolish or even very arrogant of me to have dreamed that I could make a white knight out of a man whose true destiny was to be only a clever public servant and a superlatively successful lawyer. As Browning said, a man's reach should exceed his grasp, or what's a heaven for?

So what am I getting at? What am I griping about? Has either Max or Varina ever committed so much as a misdemeanor? Are not both widely admired? Is Varina not even beloved? What more had I any right to expect, unreasonable old fool that I am?

Well, let me simply set down the few facts that stick in my craw. In the Kennedy administration, at Varina's strong urging, Max took a leave of absence from the firm to take a responsible job in the CIA. They rented a charming little Greek Revival house in Georgetown, where Varina's "salon" became a shining center for all the bright and beautiful people who made up the court of Camelot. If one went to the Griswolds', the White House was an easy next step. I myself never quite appreciated the spell of the Kennedy family; they struck me as a phenomenon comparable to the Bonapartes in nineteenth-century France, holding the public in awe, not by their political convictions or ideals, which were always subject to opportunism, but by their brilliant appeal to people's sense of imagination and romance. Napoleon had said that in ruling a nation it was everything to be *à la mode;* a government must never be dull. This perfectly suited Varina; whether in public office (she would one day be a congresswoman) or presiding in her drawing room, she was always of the latest fashion, in dress and talk and thought.

And Max? Nobody knew what he did in the CIA, but I had reason to suspect that he went heartily along with whatever was "in." When I offered him my opinion that it was nothing less than murder if, as was widely rumored, his colleagues had plotted the assassination of a foreign dictator, he simply winked and murmured, "Oh, Oscar, don't be so wet."

Max did not survive the purge that followed the disaster of the Bay of Pigs, but this in no way daunted his spirits or clouded his reputation. Everyone recognized that the president had to throw a few heads to an angry public; Kennedy himself had cheerfully admitted that under a British form of government his own would have been the first to fall. Max returned exuberantly to our firm, of which, in the course of time and when still under fifty, he succeeded my brother-in-law as senior partner. He saw in the dawn of the era of corporate raids and take-overs, a form of cutthroat practice at first disdained by the great downtown law firms, his opportunity to make ours the most lucrative in the land. At what I thought was a mad price he lured away two experts from a pioneer firm in the field and set up a merger-and-acquisitions department, which soon numbered fifty attorneys and was eventually to rise to a hundred.

I protested bitterly, but to no avail. I pointed out that a necessary technique in this new "art" was the use of the lawsuit simply to harass an opponent and not, as limited by the old ethical rules, to prevent a wrong or to collect a debt or damages.

"What are we now but shysters?" I demanded.

Max, like Varina, never seemed to lose his temper. He always acted as well as looked the perfect diplomat. The years had not widened his figure or cost him a hair. Straight, muscular, superbly tailored, with an attractively silver-tinted head and a smile whose geniality covered any condescension, he assured me that he appreciated my concern with the standards of yesterday while urging me to face those of today.

"My dear Oscar, what you say about the old rules is absolutely true, and indeed we would be shysters under their definition. But in a few years — if that long — every firm of more than a hundred lawyers is going to be up to its neck in this business. You can't stop social change. You and I, after all, didn't make the world. Remember how you groaned about lawyers' advertising, when that was first permitted? But the only reason we didn't engage in it was that our major clients found it vulgar. Morals were not involved. Nor need they be here. Because morals change. My son Oscar, your namesake, is living up at Yale with a lovely girl. Does anyone accuse them of fornication? Do even *you?* You'll be the first to thank me when you read that Jason, Fairfax and Griswold has the highest income per partner in the country!"

His prophecy came true. The settlement that Varina had received from her first husband was a drop in the bucket to what Max now brought her. But I didn't thank him. I was glad that, as a retired partner, I had so small a share in the bonanza.

But the greatest irony revealed itself in Varina's career. If Max became a hero of the new right, of a free, nay, an almost licentious stock market, with the highest marks for vigor and shrewdness, his image was still hardly a lovable one. He was admired, but primarily in a world where financial success was everything. Varina, however, was admired in other worlds. Her beauty and charm seemed to be only enhanced by the years, and as a hostess, in her great Park Avenue penthouse ablaze with abstract expressionist paintings, she was written up and photographed by exuberant columnists. But even more important, she glowed as a liberal. She reached out to the poor, the homeless. She was a Marie Antoinette who distributed all her cake. She enjoyed two terms as a Democratic congresswoman from Manhattan and was chosen to make a supporting nominating speech at a presidential convention. It was she who in the end mounted the steps of her husband's success to achieve the higher rank of public idol.

And where did *that* leave me?

Constance, who, though always disliking Varina, had never lost her affection for Max, showed an unusual (for her) sympathy for me in what, despite my reluctance to discuss it, she clearly saw as one of the great disappointments of my life. It was in a firm limousine, coming home from a great bar association dinner honoring Max for "his services to the law," that this came out.

"Really, dear, must you look quite so down? Everyone doesn't have to see Max as you do."

"But he bought that medal!"

"Bought it? What on earth do you mean?"

"Well, not with cash. With contributions to Legal Aid. Our firm's given more than any other in the city."

"And what's wrong with that?"

"Nothing's wrong with that. Nothing's wrong with anything! It's only with me that everything's all wrong. And always has been. I'm an ass, Constance. You've always known that."

She reached over to put her hand on mine. "You're only an optimist, my dear."

"What's the difference?"

"All the difference between heaven and hell. You've always

blamed yourself for putting Max off the track to a noble public career in Maine. But you really had very little to do with that. It was his mean old ma who had her hands on his heartstrings before you ever knew him. All she had to do when he grew too old to be handled by her was to let Varina take over. She finished the job."

I mused for several long minutes as we glided up Park Avenue through the glistening rainy night.

"So you claim it all for your sex?"

"Would you rather have it, my dear, for the greater glory of your own?"

"For the greater truth, perhaps. Isn't it possible that Max from the beginning knew pretty much where he was headed? And wanted his mother and wife to be his scapegoats?"

"Ah, your precious Max! *That*, my dear, was what I wanted to spare you."

MY SON,
MY SON

THE GREAT BOMB that had so disillusioned my brother-in-law in 1945 had brought concealed elation to my own heart, despite its cruel destructiveness, for it effectively ended the war, and I had no longer to live with the prospect of my only son and heir disembarking from a landing ship on a coast of desperate Japanese, ready and willing to resist to the last man. Gordon, a second lieutenant at the time of the surrender, was stationed in Guam; by a coincidence in military assignments he had never been engaged in combat. Whether he felt relief or disappointment at his exemption I never learned; all I knew was that he exhibited his usual dispassion at events beyond his control and quietly returned to Harvard to finish the law courses interrupted by his enlistment in 1942. Graduating near the top of his class, and an editor of the *Review*, he had his pick of the great firms, but to my surprise and even greater pleasure he elected to accept the offer of Jason, Fairfax & Richards.

"I had hoped he would strike out on his own" was his mother's comment to this. "Or even try a different city, like Denver or San Francisco. It seems so flat to settle back in the family nest."

I let this pass. I did not even show Constance how pleased I was, though of course she knew. But it was important that she should not suspect me of having tried to influence Gordon's decision, which indeed I hadn't.

Our son had still the trim, rather slight figure of his boyhood, but maturity had brought him, at least to his father's loving eye, a certain charm. His demeanor was still grave, his eyes still faintly distrusting and his manners as formally polite as ever, but his high pale forehead and wavy tawny hair offered at least a hint of the romantic, which was not wholly contradicted by his precise articulation and the close reasoning of his talk. Gordon specialized in tax law, and it was soon evident that he was something of a genius in the field. After he had spent only three years in our office, everyone knew he would become a partner; he achieved astonishing tax savings for some of our major clients, and the oil magnate Hubert Stairs would make no major business decision without his approval. Yet his complete detachment from office gossip and rivalries, combined with his equitable disposition and friendly if slightly distant good will to all, shielded him from much of the jealousy and resentment that infest the competitive atmosphere of firms such as ours.

It may seem hard to believe, but Gordon and I never discussed his future in the firm. He lived on his own floor in our brownstone, as my sister had lived with our parents before her marriage, and, like her, he was as independent in his habits as if he were a boarder. Somehow Constance and I always scrupulously respected his privacy, though he never asked us to or even seemed to feel there was any need. It was the same way with any expression of family feeling. I never had to tell him how deeply I cared about him. I was always sure that he knew, just as I was sure that he cared about me, in his own undemonstrative way. Oddly enough, I suspected him of feeling he had to protect me, though against what I couldn't imagine. When his mother scolded me, he always took my side, and it wasn't that he underestimated our love for each other. It might have been simply that he deemed her the stronger. As indeed she was.

Gordon had many acquaintances among men but only two or three intimates. Even fewer among women. He tended to take to concerts and the revivals of classical plays rather frumpy girls (now women of course) whom he had known since childhood and who seemed willing enough to make do with the simple companionship he offered. Perhaps it was all they had to look forward to.

Until Elvira de León. Of course, I have been getting all along to Elvira.

She was certainly plain enough, but she was somehow not a frump. And this was not attributable to her aristocratic Spanish birth either, for there was something ridiculous about her dark little prancing count of a father and the pale, vapid American mother whose money he had blown in silly Carlist causes. It was more in the calm and serenity with which she seemed resigned to play her little hand of bad cards. Elvira, small and almost bonily thin, with sticklike arms and legs, had beautiful large, dark, gazing eyes that seemed too charitable, or perhaps simply too remote, to reflect the smallness of the world around her.

The Conde de León had been too fervently monarchist, and too Carlist at that, for the still unconstitutionally decided Franco, and the late nineteen-forties had found him, *persona non grata* in Madrid, living in America on the charity of his rich sister-in-law, Miss Rose Mallvern, an old and respected member of the Bar Harbor summer colony, whose grey stone fortress of a cottage was just down the Shore Path from my own abode. There the unfortunate and alien Elvira, hardly the type to attract the frivolous *jeunesses dorées* of the island, led a presumably muted existence in the rigidly ordered life of her aunt's elderly household. It was true that Miss Mallvern, from time to time, from a sense of social duty, would give a stately dinner party for those of her contemporaries of whose moral and political principles she still approved, but these must have only the more deeply enshrouded the poor girl's life.

But she was soon to make a friend. In the summer of 1948 Gordon was spending his vacation with Constance and me in Bar Harbor, and, ever eager to widen his social circle, we had given a dinner for him and his age group at the Swimming Club before the Saturday night dance. At ten o'clock we observed a small cluster of attention over some new arrivals, and Elvira de León, in a sombre black evening gown, enhanced by a glittering diamond necklace, presumably an as yet unpawned heirloom, walked onto the dance floor on the arm of a handsome but vain-looking blond youth wearing the broad blue ribbon of some foreign order across his shirt front.

Gordon, who had risen to lean over my shoulder to ask about ordering more wine for our guests, was suddenly struck.

"Oh, look, Dad, there's poor little Elvira with Prince Louis Carl of Bourbon-Parme! He must be staying at Miss Mallvern's as a guest of her father's."

"But at the cost of her aunt. Who is he? Some Spanish pretender?"

"Oh, they all are. But what's great is that little Elvira at last has something to show all the idiots at the club. Something she's got and they haven't. A real royal prince!"

I was not impressed at her luck. Watching the couple as they started to dance, I could see that His Serene Highness's eye was already wandering. And Elvira's dancing was bumpy.

"Cinderella had better not wait till her coach turns back into a pumpkin," I remarked.

Which was, in a way, what happened. The Mount Desert maidens were, for a night anyway, intrigued by the prospect of royalty, so long as it was young and good-looking, and Elvira did not hold her prince for long. Only minutes after their arrival a merry group surrounded them on the dance floor and led them, with jovial force, to the bar, where, after a noisy round of drinks, Louis Carl found himself back on the dance floor, whirling around with the beautiful and agile Kitty Pierce, younger sister of my goddaughter, Varina.

Gordon saw the whole episode — indeed, some of our guests had joined in the genial kidnapping — and he went at once to Elvira when he spied her sitting disconsolately alone on a ballroom chair by the wall. He danced with her for the rest of the evening and even had to take her home. The oblivious prince had gone on with Kitty to another party.

That was the beginning of their friendship. Gordon had always known her, for even as a little girl she had come over on occasion to visit her aunt on the Shore Path, but the lugubrious atmosphere of the Mallvern household had been a bit too much even for his serious soul. Now, during the balance of his short vacation, he called there daily, and on his last weekend he invited her to lunch at our house. I found her not as shy as I had supposed, but definitely reserved. She was obviously intelligent, her English perfect and her articulation precise.

I asked her whether her aunt's recent house guest was a serious pretender to the Spanish throne.

"Not he, but his uncle, Prince Xavier."

"And is Xavier your father's man?"

"Father favors Prince Xavier's claim, yes." Her repetition of the title might have been a mild reproach, but one couldn't be sure. "The issue has not been without difficulty for my parent, but now I believe that he sees his way clear."

"Why does he have to look so far afield when the late King Alfonso left so many descendants?"

"Because there is still the old issue of illegitimacy in the so-called senior branch of our Spanish Bourbons. It goes back to the eighteenth century."

"But can't that be claimed about any branch of any royal family? About any family, for that matter?"

"It would seem so."

"And aren't the Carlists equally vulnerable, by genealogical standards?" I had done my homework in the library that morning. "Didn't their male line run out in 1936? With the death of Don Alfonso Carlos? Wasn't it necessary to go back generations to track down Xavier?"

"It seems they're willing to do that."

"They? It doesn't include you?"

"Well, it's not a question in which I have a valid interest. The Salic law bars women from succession."

"But not from discussion, surely. You're of age?"

"Oh, yes. I'm twenty-three."

"And don't you want to take a part in these issues?"

"No, Mr. Fairfax, I do not."

"Do you approve then of Franco?"

It mortifies me to recall how I pushed her. But there was something about her coolness and what I inferred, perhaps unjustly, to be her air of superiority that irked me.

"I take no position about the Caudillo. We had a terrible civil war, and he won it. Now it's over. All my family and their friends were for him. I venture to believe that you would have been, too, had you been a Spaniard."

"How can you say such a thing?" I demanded hotly. But I glanced immediately down the table in fear that my tone had been noted. Happily, they were all, including Gordon, listening to a funny story that Constance was telling. "In New York," I explained, "the feeling was very much against him."

"But had all your property been at stake, you might have felt otherwise. I have noted that there is strong anticommunist sentiment in this country."

I had to pause before answering. My temper was frayed. "That is true. But when freedom is at stake, men may be willing to die for it. Or don't you believe that?" Her silence goaded me now into making a total ass of myself. "Perhaps you don't believe anything is worth dying for."

"I hope there are things worth dying for. I think I should like to find what they are. But I am not sure there are things worth killing for."

Her last sentence was overheard, and Gordon called down the table, "What's Dad grilling you about, Elvira?"

"I'm afraid he thinks I'm a nihilist. But nobody need worry. I don't throw bombs."

"Is he bringing up your civil war? Ask him to explain the real difference, if any, between our Republicans and Democrats."

I turned from dangerous subjects and tried, I'm afraid unsuccessfully, to make up to this self-possessed young woman for my rudeness. Of course it was all explained by my fear that Gordon was becoming too interested in her. She was certainly not my idea of a bride for my only son.

My anxiety was hardly allayed by the fact that he chose to come all the way back up to the island, after he had returned to work, on two successive August weekends. It was not absolutely clear that he had come for Elvira's sake, but he did see her on each occasion.

Constance did not share my concern. "She's just another of his girl pals," she commented, when I came up to our bedroom, on the Saturday morning of Gordon's second weekend, where she was packing for a visit to a friend on the mainland, to "alleviate," as she liked to put it, "the rigors of the Bar Harbor season." It was agreed between us that I was exempted from these brief flights. "He's always gone in for Plain Janes. Gordon won't marry till he's forty, and then he'll bring us home some very young and surprisingly pretty girl."

"I wouldn't bet on it."

"Who's betting? Anyway, I rather like Elvira. She's better than all those lovely sillies at the Swimming Club. And what a life, poor girl, she must lead with those idiotic parents and that grim old aunt! You ought to be glad Gordon's giving her some diversion."

"He's taking risks. You can't really want that dour little relic of the feudal ages for a daughter-in-law!"

"I want what Gordon wants," Constance said briskly, closing the bag on her bed. "And if he really wants her, which I rather doubt, she must be better than your description. The boy's no fool. And Rose Mallvern will probably leave her a pot of gold. That should satisfy you."

"You've never been fair to me about those things! Can you really believe I'd sacrifice our son's happiness for . . ."

"Oh, I'm only joking," she interrupted me abruptly. "I'm off now. I'll call you from Islesboro. Take care of yourself for two days, if you can."

I dined alone that night, rather moodily, for Gordon was taking Elvira to the movies. But early the next morning, on Sunday, I had a significant encounter with her aunt.

Miss Mallvern was universally cited as the last great upholder of the high though vanishing standards of yesteryear. But if her slim white-topped and white-clad figure, spotted every Sunday in her front pew in the Episcopal church and afterwards at her umbrella table at the club for her single glass of white wine, symbolized the order and ritual of an earlier day, it was also the image of the efficient board chief of a summer camp for delinquent children whose misdemeanors she faced without flinching and whose psychiatric rehabilitation she paid for from her own pocket. Miss Mallvern may have believed that the world had gone to the dogs, but she had girded her loins for the possibly lost struggle to redeem it.

On the Sunday I have mentioned, taking my usual pre-breakfast stroll along the waterfront and passing Buon Riposo, as the Mallvern castle was inappropriately named, I saw the white figure of its proprietor crossing the lawn with the evident purpose of intercepting me, for she raised a white-gloved hand in gentle salute. I paused to await her.

"May I join you on your promenade, Mr. Fairfax?" It was no indication of unfriendliness that she never used my Christian name. She did so only with her close contemporaries and the very young. Of course, when the latter grew up, she had to continue the familiarity, but this had not happened with me. My father used to say that this was probably caused by her memory of a real estate dispute she had had with him. She was too just to hold it against a son, but, still, a distinction had to be made.

"I'm afraid I have a rather serious matter to take up with you," she continued, as we now proceeded together towards the village. "And I always think that walking is the proper ambience for that. We need not be peering into each other's face for expressions that might qualify what is said."

I smiled. "I shall look at the sea, Miss Mallvern."

"Good. Naturally you have divined that I wish to talk about your son, whose visits to my house you can hardly be unaware of. Let me say at once what a fine young man I deem him to be. Of course you know that. But in view of what I am about to say, it is important that you should know that *I* know it. One doesn't see many of his calibre today."

"I fear that is true. For his sake as well as for ours."

"You mean that he may be lonely? I feel that. And it is even truer of my niece. Indeed, it is hard to imagine a lonelier child."

I demurred. I wasn't going to be sucked into a mire of sympathy for Elvira. "She has her parents. She has you."

"Ah, but what are we to youth? Her mother and I are certainly devoted to her, but we are two old women."

"She admires her father, I'm sure."

"What makes you so sure of that?"

"I have heard her discuss his political views."

"Her father, Mr. Fairfax, is an ass."

The shock of this drew my eyes from the sea. Now I *did* look at her. We had both stopped, and she offered me a small, grim smile.

"I told you I was going to be serious. When I'm serious I must be utterly truthful. Of course, I depend on your discretion. But like all neighbors I know a bit about you. I know, for example, what you did for Helen Griswold. You're a man I can rely on."

"Thank you." But I didn't want to owe her anything. What might she ask in return?

"Let us walk on now. I give you back the sea. My brother-in-law is a well-meaning gentleman. He is straight and true. But he is still what I have just called him. He has seen his country devastated by one civil war, and he wouldn't hesitate to devastate it with another over the question of which of two stupid Bourbons to restore to the throne. Elvira sees all this with a clarity as great as her loyalty. She is inured to absurdity, having been raised in a world that made no sense. Her family, of course, were followers of Franco, but her father had been consul in Bremen and she saw Jews beaten in the streets. Yet the communists, at least to her, were just as bad. Even worse. At one point in the war she was left for safety in a convent of which her father's sister was mother superior. It was raided by the reds, and the poor child had to watch while her aunt and other nuns were flung in a pit and buried alive."

"What horrors!"

"Indeed, what horrors. And when she came over here it was to encounter what struck her as a frivolous society that had no true interest in such things. She had lost her faith in a Catholic god who could not save her aunt, and she has discovered no other in a materialist America. She has found her only comfort and support working in my camp. She believes, you see, in nothing. In *nothing*, Mr. Fairfax!"

Once again we stopped, but I offered no comment.

"And now you want to know why I am telling you all this. It is because I believe she is falling in love with your son. And if that happens, she may lose her very soul in the experience. For hers is too deep and constant a nature. So, if your son has no matrimonial intentions — and it is difficult for me to believe that he has, considering the poor girl's lack of the kind of attraction American men expect — I wish you would warn him to discontinue his visits." Here she held up again that white-gloved hand to keep me from answering too quickly. "Mind you, I accuse him of no false moves or indiscretion! I am sure he has been simply friendly and charming to my niece. I have no doubt that he only wants to amuse her and give her a good time. That he pities her for all the summer life up here she has missed. I don't think for a minute that he has any conception of the response he may have evoked. Elvira has a wonderful command of her reactions. But I know he would be the last man in the world to want to cause her any pain."

"I can't agree with your low assessment of Elvira's attractions," I forced myself to answer. "But I certainly agree that Gordon would be horrified at the idea of hurting her. And I shall certainly speak to him."

I was so agitated that I had to turn back to the sea. I even took a few steps off the path to stand on a rock and watch the screaming gulls descend on the wake of a fishing boat from which something had been dumped. For how could I speak to Gordon without the danger of driving him to marry the girl out of pity?

I think Miss Mallvern knew just what I was thinking. She took a step towards me. "Of course, I know that your son is a brilliant lawyer and will go far in his profession. And that you in any event will look after his financial future. But it is only fair to my niece, after what I may have said to her disadvantage, to tell you that I intend to make a substantial settlement on her."

In the heat of my exasperation at the weighty problem that she had so serenely lashed to my aching shoulders I was in danger of making the vulgar demand "How substantial?" Instead, I murmured something indistinguishable and hurriedly took my leave.

At home I found Gordon at the breakfast table, working on last week's Sunday *Times* crossword puzzle, which rarely took him more than half an hour. I sat at my end of the table, drinking a second cup of coffee, without answering or even pretending to think about the couple of questions he put to me about clues. And then, all of a sudden, I saw just how to arrange my matter with him. Of course! I shouldn't even have to mention Miss Mallvern. I did not even have to be grave. On the contrary, I could be as jovial as I pleased.

"I was thinking about the Conde de León on my morning stroll."

"Oh?" Gordon did not even look up.

"Does it not occur to you that your visits to Buon Riposo may have given him ideas?"

He looked up now, and with a funny cramped little smile. I could not recall having seen him smile in just that way. "You mean he may be getting down his shotgun?"

"Or whatever it is that grandees get down."

"But surely he doesn't believe that even a Fairfax has enough quarterings to aspire to a daughter of his."

"Perhaps compromise has come with political adversity. After all, he married a Yank himself."

"That's true. And I guess we can match the Mallverns. Though a greater latitude may be permitted a male León than a female. Her *name* would be changed. Unthinkable!"

I was encouraged by his lightness of tone. "Didn't a daughter of Alfonso XIII marry the son of an American woman?"

"Yes, but his father was Prince Torlonia. And, anyway, you know what we Carlists think of Alfonso XIII!"

I thought for a moment that our joint laughter meant safety, but his next question restored the tenseness.

"What sort of a dowry should I demand?"

"Well, that's a tricky point, isn't it? Are there any heirlooms? I suppose that diamond necklace she wore to the ball was her aunt's. I guess we must look to the aunt."

"Is that what you and she were talking about?"

I needed all my control to set down my coffee cup without spilling it. "Oh, did you see us?"

He simply pointed to the big bay window, which commanded a long view of the Shore Path.

"I ran into her on my walk," I explained feebly.

"Dad, one doesn't run into Miss Mallvern. She came after you. I saw it. What did she want?"

"Oh, we just chatted."

"It was about me and Elvira, wasn't it?"

I gave up. "Yes."

"She doesn't like it?"

"It's not that. She likes you very well. It's just that . . ."

"Just that what?" His smile had vanished, and his stare probed me as I hesitated. "Just that *what*, Dad?"

"Well, that Elvira . . ."

"That Elvira *doesn't?!*"

"Oh, no!" I was shocked into the truth. "That Elvira does. Too much. She's afraid Elvira may be hurt."

"Thanks, Dad! I'll see you later." He jumped up from his chair and hurried out to the lawn through a french window. I saw him stride rapidly down the Shore Path towards Buon Riposo. Within the hour he had proposed to the girl and been accepted. I had provided the communication that these two shy souls had lacked.

❧ ❧ ❧

One soon reconciles oneself to romance. Gordon explained to me that they had fallen in love on the night the prince ditched her, but that neither had suspected the other's involvement, and that on their subsequent meetings they had simply discussed their own lives as affected by world events, soberly and contentedly, but never romantically. Neither had been truly in love before, yet neither had the smallest doubt of the depth and durability of this new emotion. "I'd always thought the electric eruption of passion between Romeo and Juliet was stagecraft," Gordon confessed to me. "Now I see why it's a great play."

Fortunately, the lovers were not star-crossed. They were happy then, and they are happy today. I wish I could say that Elvira's looks have improved with marital bliss and two children, but they have not. Still, she has a decided air about her; when she enters a room, people look up. She gets on beautifully with Constance, and her manners with me are perfect. I don't think she has ever quite overcome her initial dislike of me, but as long as it never shows, I can pretend it's not there. Whether or not Gordon is aware of it, I don't know; I suspect she is too wise to have made an issue of it.

She and I did, however, have one bad time towards the end of the first year of her marriage.

Gordon had been hard at work for months on a vast estate plan for the oil magnate Hubert Stairs. He seemed to take an architectural pride in the task; he likened the drafting of its intermeshing network of *inter vivos* and charitable trusts, annual cash gifts, foundations and marital limitations to the construction of a medieval cathedral. He had inherited my love of Henry Adams and would quote him on Chartres: "From the cross in the flèche and the keystone of the vault, down through the ribbed nervures, the columns, the windows, to the foundation of the flying buttresses far beyond the walls, one idea controlled every line."

I decided he had better come down to earth. "And that one idea, I presume, is not the faith that covered Europe with great fanes, but how best to screw the Revenue Service."

Gordon smiled, but ruefully. "You can put it that way, of course. And no doubt that is how Mr. Stairs sees it. But revisionist historians say the cathedrals were built more to satisfy the pride of ambitious prelates than to please the Virgin. Does that make them less beautiful?"

"I suppose not."

"So then to devise a scheme that will embrace and perpetuate a financial empire with maximum immunity from tax — can that not be a thing of beauty?"

"But hardly a joy forever. Only until Uncle Sam closes the gap my clever son has driven his truck through."

"But the truck is through; that's the art. And then I study the revised code to see where to drive my next one."

Gordon was loved by clients for the money he saved them, but I couldn't be unaware that there were those who found him too strict, too rigidly ethical. He would never allow a taxpayer, for example, to claim a questionable deduction on a return in the hope that the return would escape audit. There were clients, I learned, who were happy to pay for Gordon's oral opinion on a question and then instruct their private accountants how differently to implement it. Even Mr. Stairs, who praised my son to the skies and took him on weekend cruises on his sailing yacht, was not above jovially criticizing him. "That young genius of yours," he told me, with a rude poke in the ribs, "should get a commission from Uncle Sam. I verily believe he's killed more deals than he's saved." But I was not really concerned. Gordon's astute predictions of how the tax collector's mind would work in a given situation had made him one of our indispensable associates.

A crisis arose only a few months before the new year in which it had been agreed that he was to be made a partner of the firm. Mr. Stairs, aging, dyspeptic, overweight and increasingly forgetful, had been spending much of his time in Miami, where he had met a man whom he described in a letter to Gordon as "a wizard of an accountant" and with whom he had rashly discussed his personal finances. The man had suggested the retention of a power in a major but amendable trust instrument that would save Stairs, "tax free," several options that Gordon had insisted he renounce. Stairs had instructed the Miami attorney whom he used for minor local matters to draw up such an amendment and telephoned Gordon to announce proudly that he had signed it. His object was to boast to his "know-it-all" New York counsel that he had found someone smarter than he.

Gordon came to my office in a near fit after receiving the call.

"The old man's out of his mind! The mere existence of that power is enough to wreck my whole testamentary scheme! It's like the weight of the central tower in the Beauvais cathedral. The whole thing fell in and was never rebuilt!"

Nothing could have more convinced me of the artist in the

lawyer than such a reference at such a time. I stared at him blankly. "And he's really signed it?"

"Yes! Of course, I told him he must tear it right up. And obviously I must go straight down there."

Mrs. Flax, Stairs's confidential secretary, however, called Gordon back to say that the old man was leaving that afternoon on a cruise and couldn't possibly see him for two weeks, but that she would see that the offending document was destroyed as soon as he came back.

Stairs suffered a severe heart attack while at sea and two more after his return. The third proved fatal. His eldest son, James, who had flown to Miami to be with his father at the end, informed Gordon that the dangerous amendment had been torn up in the presence of witnesses by his father while he was still in full possession of his faculties.

Unfortunately, when Gordon went down to Miami to help with the drafting of the probate papers and called on the officer of the local bank in charge of the Stairs accounts there, he learned something that deeply upset him. The banker was a friendly fellow who naturally hoped to retain the Stairs business, and in the course of a lunch the two fell into a discussion of the destroyed power. Gordon observed how lucky it was that the matter had been taken care of in the nick of time. The banker, who had drunk a couple of cocktails while Gordon sipped his soda water, winked knowingly.

"Between you and me and the proverbial lamppost, it wasn't. Son James told me on the telephone that his father had signed a document revoking the original in our possession and asked me to send it over to be disposed of. Which I did. But that was *after* the old man had kicked off."

"And didn't you ask to *see* the revoking document before giving up the original?"

Again that wink. "I was too tactful to ask an important depositor to show me a document I don't believe ever existed. Old Stairs, from what I heard, was already in a coma when they took him off the boat. I don't think he was doing much revoking of trust instruments in the time he had left."

Fortunately — oh, so fortunately — Gordon did nothing about this discovery until he was back in town and had had a chance to discuss it with me.

"I asked Mrs. Flax to describe for my records just what happened. She told me that Mr. Stairs had revoked the original signed *amendment* by tearing it up in her presence and that of his son. She apparently didn't even know that James Stairs had told the bank that his father had first signed an instrument revoking the amendment. They hadn't even bothered to get their stories straight! And she looked at me, when I pointed out the discrepancy, as if to say: 'What are you poking about for? Doesn't Jason, Fairfax and Richards want to represent a five-hundred-million-dollar estate?'"

"But you didn't answer the implied question?"

"I said nothing. I simply walked out. And here I am."

"Good."

In the pause that followed, Gordon subjected his father and partner — or should I say his partner and father? — to a long, quizzical stare. "I take it we *do* wish to represent the estate?"

"And why should we not?"

"But at what cost? What is our primary duty?"

"To whom?"

"Well, let us say to the law, to begin with. To our profession. Should I sit by silently while a fraud is perpetrated on the Revenue Service?"

"A fraud?"

"Certainly a fraud. Isn't it grossly evident that the existence of an important trust document at the time of the decedent's death will *not* be revealed to the taxing authorities?"

"How do you *know* it existed at the time of his death?"

"Oh, Dad, you heard what I told you."

"It's a possible deduction, yes. It's not proven. *You* don't know that Stairs never came out of his coma. *You* don't know that he never signed a revocation."

"Then why didn't they show it to me?"

"Because they may have regarded the whole matter as nullified. They may have torn up the revocation *and* the original amendment. They may have thought it was none of your business. Which indeed it isn't!"

"Dad! How can you say that?"

"I mean it, my boy! It's not a lawyer's business to go poking through a client's closet and looking under rugs to see if he can find a crime or misdemeanor. What do you think you are? A revenue agent? I wonder if a disclosure of what you suspect to a tax auditor mightn't even be grounds for disbarment."

Gordon got up and walked to the window. After some moments of gazing down at the Trinity Church graveyard, he turned back to me.

"Well, granting your point about blowing the whistle, do you think I can properly serve as counsel to executors who have knowingly concealed the destruction of a vital paper?"

"Executor*s*?"

"James Stairs is an executor."

"One of four. Central Bank is the principal one. You can be sure they have no suspicion of what may or may not have happened."

"Even so."

"Well, if your conscience is so delicate, I can easily arrange to have you not work on the estate. An associate is not responsible for the firm's decisions."

"True. But this estate will be in administration for at least three years. And if I am made a partner on January first, I will be legally and morally responsible for all that happens thereafter, including the preparation of the Stairs estate tax returns, which will include the willful misrepresentation of a material fact."

"And so what do you propose?"

"That I decline the partnership. And, to be totally consistent, that I resign from the firm."

I folded my hands over my waist and leaned forward to bow my head for some moments of profound meditation. When I spoke, it was slowly and gravely. "You mean that, because of private speculations, made in pursuance of your own curiosity and not at your client's instructions, and without having been placed on notice of any wrongdoing, or being obliged to make any statement that you believe to be false, you decline to be a member of a firm, no partner of which had anything to do with the misdeed that you only surmise? And the misdeed itself, if such it even was, being only the rectification of the crazy act of a half-crazy old man?"

Gordon actually smiled at me! "I like the way you put it. Yes, that is just the way it is. If the firm represents the Stairs estate, I will not be a part of it."

I nodded. "Let me ask just one favor of you. Take a week off from the office and devote the time to thinking this decision over. Very, very carefully. I cannot suggest that you consult friends, as that would involve communicating suspicions of your own that might be damaging to a client. But, knowing you, I doubt you will need to consult anyone. You have always made up your own mind for yourself."

"I shall want to talk to Elvira."

"By all means talk to Elvira. She has always been a realist."

"Ah, but there are different ways of being that."

With which he left me, and as I didn't see him when I passed his office the next morning (he was always early at his desk), I assumed he was doing as I suggested. It was a miserable week for me. I wanted to discuss the crisis with Constance, but I was afraid that her naturally contrary nature and small regard for the bar might well induce her to plunk down on Gordon's side, and I didn't want to add a struggle with her to my trials.

On the sixth day of the allotted time I called Gordon's apartment. Elvira answered and told me he was in the library of the Bar Association reading cases on legal ethics. In my despair I asked whether she would walk with me in Central Park, and she politely agreed. An hour later we were circling the reservoir. I asked her if he had come to a decision.

"He hasn't told me, but I think I know what it will be. He will leave the firm."

As in my talk with her aunt the year before, I had water to look at. Water and dozens of gulls along the sandy bar that cut the surface in half. Elvira's voice, always measured and low, was devoid of the least excitement or stress. Whatever Gordon did would be right for her.

"But oh, my dear, think what it will cost him! He'll be giving up not only a partnership, but almost surely the future senior partnership. And of the firm founded by his grandfather! I know he will always do well enough as a tax lawyer, but our firm, after all, *is* something not to sneeze at, and his decision to leave us, for no apparent reason, may add to his reputation for a certain eccentricity. Oh, yes, I'm afraid so, Elvira! Gordon is already known for what some lawyers regard as an excessive scrupulosity, for not being quite 'one of the boys' in the downtown world. You may sneer at that, but these things count. Whereas if he stays with us, he stays with men who deeply appreciate the true worth of his extraordinary character and personality. With the firm behind him, there's no limit to how far he may go!"

"You talk about his true worth, Mr. Fairfax. But his true

worth is precisely what your 'boys' on Wall Street have little use for. Gordon cannot compromise with evil."

"Evil? Aren't you being a bit melodramatic?"

"I call it evil to defraud your government to fill your purse."

"But Gordon wouldn't be doing that!"

"He'd be profiting by those who did."

"He'd be violating no canon of ethics."

"No canon of the *bar.*"

"But my dear child, no one could practice law under such principles. Every time you even suspected a client of keeping something back, you'd have to throw up his case!"

"Gordon might say that was a good thing."

"And do you agree with him?"

"Oh, yes. You will say it's against common sense. But common sense never saved the world from madness." She paused to go to the rail and watch the gulls. "I have seen a world go mad. It destroyed my faith in people. And in God. And in gods."

"I know, my dear, what horrors you must have been through and what . . ."

"No, you don't, Mr. Fairfax," she interrupted me firmly, turning back from the rail. "Excuse me, but you don't. I grew up believing in no one and nothing. Only manners kept me going. I hung on to them because I had to hang on to something. And what was worse, I didn't love anyone. Until your son came and took every ounce of unused love I had in me. I sometimes even wonder if there'll be enough left for children, if we have any. But that can wait. What I tell you now is that Gordon's principles are my principles. That his ethics are my ethics. You don't believe they're practical. But they're practical for me. They're the only practical things I've ever met in my life!"

I saw and accepted my defeat in the sudden glitter of her stare. Without another word we turned our steps homeward.

When Gordon returned to the office the next day, he did not call me, and it wasn't till noon that I walked down the corridor to see whether he was free for lunch. He looked up cheerfully from the open *Law Reporter* before him.

"Good morning, Dad! I was going to call *you* for lunch, but I think I'd better have a sandwich sent in. This brief is due Friday."

"You mean you've got a lot to finish before you quit?"

"Oh, I'm not quitting."

"You mean you'll go on as a clerk, but not a partner?"

"Oh, are they having second thoughts about my partnership?"

I put a hand on the back of the chair before his desk. "They're not. But you?"

"Hardly. I very much look forward to being a partner."

I passed a hand over my eyes. "Gordon, don't play games with me. What was all that about your conscience and the Stairs estate?"

He smiled and shook his head, as if recalling a youthful folly. "I was wrong. You convinced me. I was making an ass of myself."

My mind reeled. "Don't tell me you'll work on the Stairs estate?"

"I'll even prepare the estate tax return. And now, Dad, if you don't mind, I've really *got* to get on with this brief."

I hurried out, even closing the door behind me, as if to close him more surely in.

❧ ❧ ❧

I did not discuss further with Gordon the reasons for his change of mind — I was too scared of tipping the applecart of my good fortune — but on a Sunday lunch at home with guests I did permit myself, after the meal, to approach Elvira, who was momentarily seated alone with her coffee.

"I have to tell you how happy I am at the way things have worked out."

"I'm glad you are, Mr. Fairfax." There was no lightness in her tone, but when had there been? At least with me.

"Aren't you, too? Just the least bit? The practical world isn't such a bad one, is it?"

"I think it is a bad one. But I know I want the world that Gordon wants."

"And he wanted this one."

"He wanted what *you* wanted, sir." And I received once more that steady look of hers. "Gordon couldn't bear to hurt you. Gordon loves you, Mr. Fairfax. I think I rather envy you that love. Or perhaps it would be truer to say that I envy *him* it. I wish I could have felt about either of my parents the way Gordon feels about you."

So there it was. The happiest moment of my life? The sense that a pure, a perfect emotion had been given and received? Not the tumult and competitive love I had with Constance, nor the gratitude I felt for my own father, but a mutual understanding, a mutual faith, a mutual support. Something above any of my friendships. And what had I done with it but use it to persuade him to a compromise below his standards? But his standards were absurd! Surely what I had done for Gordon was the best act of my life. And, equally surely, his wife didn't think so. But she was a fanatic! Wasn't she? Of course she was. Or what was I?

Long may I live, anyway, to think so.

REDUCTIO AD ABSURDUM?

When the young Henry James in 1873 guided his father's old friend Ralph Waldo Emerson through the galleries of the Louvre, he found himself wondering whether life had ever bribed the great seer to look at anything but the soul. James wrote: "I was struck with the anomaly of a man so refined and intelligent being so little spoken to by works of art."

Art in our time has become to many a substitute for religion, but with age I have come to share what I fancy would have been Emerson's misgivings about its new role in our lives. I sometimes tire of what James himself called "the wear and tear of discrimination." It bothers me how often the great art of others is denigrated by the artists who have been my own lifetime favorites. James undervalued the Russian novelists; their works to him were "fluid puddings." Edith Wharton found James's novels of the "major phase" almost unreadable; for her they lacked the juice of humanity. Anatole France thought life too short for a Proust too long; Bernard Berenson disliked Picasso . . . there's no end to it. What is evident, at least to me, is that it is the creation of art, rather than its reception, that saves the artist's soul. What then saves that of the simple viewer or reader, like myself, who does nothing but receive?

Of course, I have had the fun of fancying myself a kind of artist in my study of people. I have always wanted to analyze them, to "write them up," sometimes just in my own mind, sometimes actually on paper, and on occasion I have even seen myself, more boldly, crossing the threshold of their lives and presuming to play in them a supporting role. But I have latterly come to the conclusion that I have placed too great an emphasis on the dramatic aspects of dramatically interesting people. It is all very well to prefer good art to bad, but people are people.

It was Gordon, ten years ago, in 1965, who first pointed this out to me. He and Elvira were living down the road from me and Constance in Mount Kisco, in Westchester County, an hour's commute from the city. My wife had persuaded me, on my retirement from the active practice of law (I remained "of counsel" and went to the office three times a week), to sell our brownstone and buy a country place near our son and daughter-in-law. It had worked out well, and Gordon, who was by now an inured suburbanite, enjoyed filling me in on the characteristics and foibles of our new neighbors.

"It's really high time, Dad, that you mingled with some ordinary folk."

"Is that what your friends are? I thought they considered themselves great successes. I doubt they'd appreciate your term at a dinner party at the Golf and Tennis Club."

"Nor would I be such an ass as to use it there! I'm talking about people who have a large 'greatest common denominator.' You have tended in your life to concentrate on a handful of highly individual characters. Up here my age group — roughly, from thirty-five to forty-five — are a fairly complacent lot. They are launched. The lawyers have made partner; the bankers, vice president. The investment advisers and brokers have steady clients, and a few of the underwriters have even made fortunes. They all belong to a country club, and their children are in private schools. They are mostly Protestants and Republicans, but Democrats and Catholics are considered respectable. Jews less so, but when they're attractive and non-Orthodox, they can even make the club. Of course there are no blacks in the group, but then there *are* no blacks here, except in the village proper. The rules of conformity are not hard, but there are certain minimum standards to be complied with."

"And what are they? No snowmobiles, I suppose, or motorcycles. And you can't keep a pit bull."

"Oh, Lord, no, none of those things. These people are too environmental and neighborly for that. They save the forests by giving up Christmas cards and protest the paving of country lanes. My 'minimum standard' is a financial one. If your children don't go to a prep school or a recognized college, or if you can't afford the club, or if you don't return your social obligations, you gradually fade out of the group. You're not cut or anything like that. You're just someone who hasn't been able to keep up. And that is hell. Henry and Amelia Sigourney, for example. They're the kind of couple who've never attracted your attention."

"Tell me about them. I've only just met them."

"Henry's a perfectly decent guy. Quiet, earnest, sober. Rather dull, actually. Works in a downtown bond law firm and hasn't made partner. Old Knickerbocker family, but on its uppers. That's rare here, where the parents are usually richer. Henry has to help support his old mother. Amelia's origins are less distinguished, one of those dim little families that's managed to stay in the Social Register for ages without ever doing anything, without even having any money to speak of. They stick like barnacles. Her branch, at any rate, finally went under, and Amelia had to teach in a kindergarten until she managed somehow, at age twenty-seven, to snag Henry, supposedly a confirmed bachelor. She thought he'd make the grade as a lawyer, but he hasn't. And now at forty she's desperate at the idea that her two boys may have to stay in public school until they go to college and that Henry may have to resign from the Golf and Tennis Club if his uncle doesn't, as threatened, come through with his annual Christmas present of the dues."

Constance, who was listening, intervened now in disgust. "Well, who could be sorry for as poor a creature as that? She's well fed and well dressed and her sons are being well educated! A woman like Mrs. Sigourney is a sick cat."

"You've got the wrong species, Ma. She's not a cat; she's a suburbanite, responding to the calls of her habitat. With just a little more income she'd be a perfectly amiable person. As it is, she's a desperate nag who makes poor Henry's life hell on earth."

The next morning on the train to town I observed Henry Sigourney more closely. His face was square and placidly expressionless, but his round ruddy cheeks added a touch of seeming innocence or perhaps naïveté to the gravity of his demeanor. His hair was short and thick and stood up from his scalp like quills. His figure was stocky and clad soberly in black. He struck me as self-contained without being in the least self-satisfied. Like myself, he was reading a book rather than a newspaper.

"Good morning, Mr. Fairfax," he greeted me politely when I moved from my seat to take one beside him, and seeing I did not reopen my book, he closed his own.

"Oh, please don't let me interrupt your reading."

"But I'd much rather talk to you, sir." He tipped his volume to show me the title. It was Wordsworth's *Excursion.*

"Do you find it a 'drowsy, frowsy poem,' as Byron did?"

"Not so bad as that. But I love *The Prelude*, and I keep hoping to find some of the same notes. And at times I do. But not often enough."

"Do you always read poetry on the train?" I frowned at my

own question. Why, when we see a person doing something once, must we ask whether he *always* does it?

"Well, actually, yes. Last year I got through all of *Paradise Lost* and *The Ring and the Book*. It makes it the best part of the day for me."

I reflected on what this said for his home life. "But then I really shouldn't be interrupting you now. Even from *The Excursion*."

"I'd much rather talk to you, sir, if you don't mind. I know from Gordon what a great reader you are yourself. I don't think there could be a more wonderful poem in the world than *The Prelude*. Is Wordsworth a favorite of yours, too?"

We discussed the great poet for several stations. The poor man was clearly starved for a bit of literary companionship. Such a thing would not have been impossible for him to find in Westchester, but perhaps he was hindered by a spouse who was hostile to his interests, who may have even attributed to them his failure to get ahead in his firm. I had a sad mental picture of the man toiling in his office over bond indentures, one drearily like another, and coming home to a disillusioned wife and scrappy children. How he must have treasured the daily two hours of independence on the train and the oasis of Wordsworth!

> . . . for I would walk alone,
> Under the quiet stars, and at that time
> Have felt whate'er there is of power in sound
> To breathe an elevated mood, by form
> Or image unprofaned; and I would stand,
> In the night blackened with a coming storm,
> Beneath some rock, listening to notes that are
> The ghostly language of the ancient earth,
> Or make their dim abode in distant winds.

Perhaps it really was enough for happiness, if his appreciation was intense enough!

"Do you ever try your own hand at verse?" I asked him.

He was silent for a moment. We had stopped at another station, and he watched the crowd on the platform move forward. He was probably debating whether my interest was merely perfunctory.

"I do, actually."

"Have you ever published any of it?"

"Oh, no!" he exclaimed, with an emphasis that seemed designed to allay the anger of gods at such suggested hubris. "Only in school journals. And once or twice at Yale, in the *Lit.*"

I smiled. "Once *or* twice? Don't poets always remember?"

He nodded. "Three times, then, to be exact. Two sonnets and an ode."

"Would you let me see some of your things?"

"Oh, Mr. Fairfax, they're terrible! Really and truly."

"Can't you let me be the judge of that?"

"You're too kind." He hesitated. "But I admit I'd love to have your opinion of them. Will you be quite frank?"

He mailed them to my office that same day, and I read them over the following weekend. Most of them were dramatic monologues in blank verse *à la* Browning. They were certainly not very good, but one of them was not at all bad. It was the lament of Ariadne on Naxos that she had allowed herself to be consoled by Bacchus for her abandonment by Theseus. She would have preferred to be the tragic discard of a hero, sustained by a noble and picturesque self-pity, than the rollicking companion of a beguiling clown in a vulgar "slap and tickle."

I told Henry on our next train ride how much his Ariadne had diverted me, and he was almost pathetically pleased. Evidently I was his very first reader! We now sat regularly together on the train, sometimes reading, sometimes discussing poetry. His opinions varied from the banal (he had not talked enough with other readers to know they were that) to the acute and even penetrating. He showed considerable insight into the early Wordsworth of the *Lyrical Ballads* and the "eternity poems" of Emily Dickinson. He had trouble with the obscurity of twentieth-century verse, but he had dutifully studied Jessie Weston's *From Ritual to Romance* in his effort to fathom *The Waste Land.*

I was naturally curious about his wife, whom he rarely mentioned, and the role she played in his life. One Sunday at noon at the buffet lunch at the Golf and Tennis Club, when I had taken a table apart to wait for Constance, who was to join me there after her game, I had the occasion to examine Amelia, chatting with a friend by the serving table. Thinking back on this, I can now see that, born in 1925 or thereabouts, she belonged to the last generation of women to whom careers were not important. I do not say she was typical of her age group (the feminists would have my heart for that!), but she was certainly a type that would have made one welcome the coming change. I would have wagered she spent her mornings chatting on the telephone and her afternoons at the bridge table. She might have once passed for pretty, but at forty her skin had hardened, her touched-up blond hair looked stale and her hips had widened. And I could see she had a bad habit of nervous gesticulation: wriggling her shoulders, twisting her torso to adjust her girdle, opening her compact to dab her nose with powder.

She must have noted my observation of her, for she suddenly turned and brought her lunch plate over to my table.

"Do you mind if I join you, Mr. Fairfax? Henry has been singing your praises to me, and I'm dying to know you better."

"Please don't die, Mrs. Sigourney. And do sit down."

"It's wonderful, your taking such an interest in him. He tells me you've even read his poems. Of course, he won't show them to *me.* I'm not literary enough for that. But anyway I want you to know that I appreciate your being so kind to him."

"I'm not being kind to him, Mrs. Sigourney. I . . ."

"Oh, please call me Amelia!"

"Amelia. I think your husband has written some nice things. I hope he goes on with it."

"Oh, yes. So long as it doesn't interfere with his real work. Though even that doesn't seem to matter too much. Has he told you, Mr. Fairfax, that he works for the meanest, stingiest law firm in town? Scrooge and Marley, I call them!"

"Dear me, I hope you don't tell everyone that. It might get back to them."

"Let it! Except no, I don't really mean that. But you see, Mr. Fairfax, how I trust you!"

"I don't really see why you should."

"Because you're so fond of Henry!"

I nodded. It *was* a reason. I wouldn't have thought it had occurred to her. "Is it because they haven't made him a partner that you feel that way about them?"

"Yes! Of course they *ought* to make him one, for their own good as well as ours. He does enough of their work, God knows. I tell him he ought to march right into the managing partner's office and demand it. Put his foot down. Don't you agree?"

"Well, really, that's not for me to say. I don't know his situation. Besides, being a partner isn't the be-all and end-all of life."

"You can say that because you *are* one. And have probably been one forever. But you must know that being an associate, or clerk — to use the right word — in your mid-forties is a kind of social death. At least it is here in Westchester. How would *you* feel if your son Gordon weren't a partner? But of course with your rank in the firm that wouldn't be conceivable, would it?"

Proust wrote somewhere that there are people who will sacrifice a life's ambition for the pleasure of making one disagreeable remark. I suppose the poor woman got a jag from implying that Gordon's success was based on nepotism.

"I can't go along with you there, Mrs. Sigourney — Amelia, I mean. There are senior associates in some of the big firms who are well-paid and well-respected specialists who don't even think of becoming partners. Who may not even want to be!"

"You mean they've given up. I'm glad to hear, anyway, they're well paid. That's more than I can say for poor Henry."

"Oh, come now, you live pretty well. That's a lovely little house you have — I always look at it when I drive by. And here you are at the club, and I gather your boys are at a good private school."

"Oh, Mr. Fairfax, you don't *know* about these things!" Her voice rose to a near wail. "If my boys don't go away to Andover or Saint Paul's or Choate, what sort of friends will they have if they get into an Ivy League college?"

"I may not know about these things," I retorted stiffly, "but I know false values when I see them." After all, in age, she could have been my daughter. "And I certainly see the danger of regarding educational institutions solely in the light of their social advantages."

She looked at me hopelessly. Obviously, her attitude was "So he's one of *those*." She not only took the simple view I had just stated; she regarded any other as that of a frenzied idealist. "Well, I suppose you've always had the pick of the best."

"Enough so, perhaps, to wonder whether it always *is* the best."

"Well, try second best sometime. Or even third. You mustn't think I'm greedy. I simply want what everyone in this room wants."

"And what's that? To have two cars, one a station wagon and one for the train? A country club, two Labradors, a trip to the seashore in summer and Saturday night dinner parties preceded by a two-hour cocktail hour? Don't you have it already?"

"Oh, well, if you're just going to laugh at me." She looked away from me; I had gone too far. But one thing on my sarcastic list caused a belated reaction. "And I'm not even sure of this club! Henry says we may have to give it up to pay for his mother's companion. And really, I don't see why! Mrs. Sigourney lives better than we do, and I happen to know she helps out her daughter May. If I do say so, she's a selfish old bag who's always had it in for me. She never thought I was good enough for her darling Henry!"

I had begun to repent of my goading the poor woman. As Gordon had said, she was only being true to her species.

"My dear lady, is there something you think I can do for you?"

I had quite faced the fact that I was opening myself up to a plea for a loan.

"Oh, can I really tell you?" She clasped her hands with renewed eagerness. "If you could only offer Henry a job in your firm! You wouldn't have to promise him a partnership or anything like that. But I'm sure any associate his age there would make more than he's making now!"

I stared at her. Had I detected a true note of marital affection in her tone? "But he'd still be an associate, and you say that's social death here."

"Oh, but I've got that figured out! You've just helped me! In your firm he wouldn't be a clerk. He'd be a *specialist!* You would have taken him on for his particular expertise. The dreadful words 'passed over' wouldn't even be mentioned in his case."

Across the room I now saw Constance approaching our table.

"I'll think about it," I said gruffly, and Amelia, realizing, with unexpected sensitivity, that she had said enough for the moment, took her quick departure.

Early at the office the next morning, a Monday, I asked Gordon to come to my office, and told him of her plea.

"She really is desperate, poor girl," he commented. "Of course, you told her it wouldn't do."

"You don't think it would? I have a feeling he's quite a good lawyer."

"I daresay he is. But what would come of your policy of making partners only from the ranks of those who have started here? Uncle Grant having been the sole and sacred exception?"

"But he'd never be a partner. That would be the deal. We can always use an extra hand in the municipal bond department."

"It's not that, Dad. It's that our associates wouldn't understand it. We've never hired a 'specialist' before, and there's no reason to think he *is* one. If he did well, why shouldn't he make partner? It would throw your whole system out of whack."

"We couldn't make just one exception?"

"Dad! What has this woman done to you?"

I thought Gordon was being rigid. Gordon was inclined to be rigid. But he was, at my urging, taking on more and more of the running of the business side of the firm, and I was certainly not going to interfere with his administration of a policy devised by myself.

When he left, however, my secretary, Mrs. Anderson, had an interesting comment to make. She had been with me for thirty years and knew everything — too much — about me and about the firm. She was a "character" — buxom, stout, energetic, with flaming dyed red hair, outspoken to a fault, loud, efficient, infinitely practical and utterly loyal. She had been in and out of my office during my talk with Gordon, ostensibly to file last week's correspondence in my personal cabinet, but actually to listen to us. She never made the smallest effort to disguise her eavesdropping, which was always, she claimed, in my interest.

"I know something about that Henry Sigourney," she announced. "He works at Abbott and Grimes. My friend Miss Larkin is the controller there. Has been for twenty years or more. It's a mean little firm, not more than twenty lawyers in all, and she has to keep the books herself, without any assistance, but she says they pay her well. At least they know a bargain when they see one. And she says Sigourney does half the work of the firm. They take cruel advantage of him."

Needless to say, I was all attention. "Then why doesn't he do something about it?"

"He's too innocent, I guess. A lamb led to the slaughter. It's amazing what men like that will put up with. I guess they ask for it."

I thought intently for a few minutes as she continued her filing. "Do you suppose you could glean a few facts about Abbott and Grimes from your friend? Even confidential ones?"

Nothing could have more interested Mrs. Anderson. She came over and took a stand before my desk. "Such as?"

"Well, could you get out of her how much of the firm's gross is attributable to Sigourney's time sheets? Of course the fees are credited to the different partners, but the hours show who does the actual work."

"Very easily. Miss Larkin has all that kind of thing in her head. But she'll want to know why *I* want to know. What's there in it for her?"

"Just this. That when I've used the dope she supplies to make poor blind Sigourney a partner, she'll get an assistant bookkeeper. And when he's senior partner there'll be raises and bonuses for all!"

"I'll call right away and see if she's free for lunch. Would you care to join us, Mr. F?"

"No, that might put her off. You'll handle it better alone."

Mrs. Anderson winked. "Leave it to me! But tell me one more thing. What's there in it for *me?*"

"A champagne dinner with me at the '21' Club."

"You're on!"

❧ ❧ ❧

I had a rough time with Sigourney, even though the figures were indisputable. Thirty-five percent of the firm's gross was directly attributable to his hours, and, according to the enthusiastically cooperative Miss Larkin, the two most important municipal clients would certainly follow him if he left the firm for another. He had only to state his terms. I suggested that he demand not only a partnership but one on an equal basis with Messrs. Abbott and Grimes. At this he went into something like panic.

"But supposing they kick me out altogether?"

"They won't."

"But if they *do?*"

"Then set up your own firm. I'll bet half the associates would follow you out the door."

"But I've never done anything like that before! Honestly, Mr. Fairfax, I can't handle this sort of thing!"

I had to agree that maybe he couldn't. Maybe he was even clinging to his old serfdom. After years of subjection, that sometimes happens. I recalled reading of an inmate of Auschwitz who, reduced to bestiality by long starvation and torture, had picked up, like a beaten hound, the discarded tissue paper of a nose-wiping guard and pressed it reverently to his lips. Perhaps Sigourney actually preferred his somnambulistic existence, with its daily two hours of awakened reality reading Wordsworth on the train.

"Then you must gamble on their caving in," I continued remorselessly. "You know the old hymn: 'Once to every man and nation comes the moment to decide.'"

Henry wiped his moist brow. "'And the choice goes by forever, 'twixt that darkness and that light.' Yes, I know the hymn. Well, I'll promise to think it over."

"No, if you think it over, you'll never do it. You must make the demand today. This very morning." We were on the train headed for town. "And tell me on the five-forty-five tonight what happened. We'll celebrate with a drink in the bar car."

"Oh, Mr. Fairfax, please!"

"And if you don't," I pursued grimly, "I'll tell your wife."

Well, of course, that did it, but when we parted company at the station, he looked so wretched that I felt almost sorry for my intrusion into his static life. The face, however, that greeted me on the 5:45 was radiant. No, he had not asked for an equal partnership with the two seniors, nor had he demanded a specific percentage of the net profits. But he had suggested that he be considered for a partnership at the end of the year, and Messrs. Abbott and Grimes had graciously agreed to consider it.

Of course they made him a partner; they had no option, and today, ten years later, he is running a larger and more prosperous firm under the new name of Sigourney, Abbott & Grimes. His two boys went to Andover; one graduated from Princeton and the other is still at Brown. Amelia is now on the board of the Golf and Tennis Club and president of the local chapter of Cancer Care; she has smiles for all. And Henry has had a slim volume of dramatic monologues published by a small but respected press; it received a pleasant notice in the *New York Times* Book Review under "Briefly Noted."

Gordon says that I have found my milieu at last, that I was always meant to be a "private investigator"; he likens me laughingly to the psychiatrist in *The Cocktail Party.* And it is true that in the last several years, by keeping my eyes open, I have spotted cases where a little subterranean work may change a serf's life for the better. Henry Sigourney, however, remains my most significant success.

Do I do it to flatter myself that I am in the least a good man? T. S. Eliot's Becket, in *Murder in the Cathedral,* finds that the ego is always, whether crudely or subtly, at work behind every seeming act of charity, and he despairs of being virtuous until he is willing to merge his identity altogether with God. But there is too much of my mitred grandfather in me to find much satisfaction in anything as spectral as that. The bishop had no use for an afterlife that did not contain a reasonable facsimile of the Right Reverend Oscar Fish. So I hang on to my ego and simply hope that so long as we *do* a good deed, we can pretty well skip our motive. That is my bible or at least my new testament, and, in the long run, perhaps all that I have gleaned from my education. Henry Adams didn't even admit he'd had that much, but then he was a bit of a poseur. He didn't have a Constance to knock it out of him.